Dim Fairy Tales

Justin Alcala

`

Prologue

Long ago, during the dreaming dawn of history, there lived a young maiden within the hollow of the *Harvest Woods*. Born on a day when the sun and moon rose as one, it was said that she was destined for greatness, if only she could survive her early hardships. For the girl's mother passed shortly after giving birth, and soon after, her father was lost to war. Alone amongst the trees and stags, the girl grew up unaided, pitied by the villagers whose fate was far too meager to offer charity. There, within a cottage made of stone and thatch, she cared for herself, surviving through the seasons with little more than resolve.

Yet the maiden never despised her circumstances. Because for her, everything she thought she'd needed was bequeathed to her by the Harvest Woods. It fed her when she hungered, bathed her when she was filthy, and hummed her to sleep under the twinkle of the stars. It gave her friendship in the wildlife, family in the trees, and wisdom in seasons. How she adorned her forest, and in return, the forest adored her.

Soon, though, the young maiden came to understand that although the woods were very dear to her, they could not always offer what she required. For curatives, tools and proper clothing, she was forced to travel to the markets where she traded the forest's bounty in exchange for the necessities she so desperately needed. And though her fire licked hair and grass colored eyes drew the heads of the young boys, the maiden always returned home to her true love, *the forest*.

But time has a way of changing what doesn't wish to do so. Soon the young maiden grew to be even more beautiful, and although she only desired the woods for the rest of her days, rumors in the village whispered that she would make a fine wife for anyone cunning enough to tame her. So, it was no surprise that once summer began, all the young villagers trudged through the woodlands in search of their bride. Day after day they arrived with offerings of coin, cattle and jewelry, and day after day the maiden declined.

"I owe my hand to the autumn harvest that feeds me," she'd reply, "and the harboring oaks that keep me safe."

But the will of men is strong, and their yearnings even stronger. Soon affluent suitors from faraway lands received the maiden's reputation as a challenge and came crooning with great promises. They offered feasts fit for kings, castles built for armies, and riches suited for cities. Yet no matter how musical the musician or noble the nobleman, her answer always remained the same. With a gracious smile she'd reply, "I owe my hand to the autumn harvest that feeds me, and the harboring oaks that keep me safe."

Then, one crisp autumn night, on a week that had three Sundays, fate stepped in. The young maiden had just snuggled into her blanket by the hearth when a wrapping came at her cottage door. It was near the witching hour, and the young maiden answered with warranted trepidation. To her surprise, waiting at her entrance was not some monstrous monster, nor another suitor in silks or admiral in armors. Instead, stood a stranger like she'd never seen before. He was tall and regal, stitched together by arcadian beauty. His hair flowed like wheat and his skin colored like honey. He wore a cloak weaved from the fall brush and a tunic of blood red. The stranger bowed when his eyes met the maiden.

"Good evening my Lady," he greeted.

"Apologies young sir," replied the maiden as she clung to her cottage's door, "but I'm afraid that I'll be hearing no more offers this evening."

The young man lingered as a simple smile spread across his sharp face. The maiden had seen such persistence before. It would not be long now before the stranger proposed his dowry. She gave a short curtsy and then wished a good night. But as she thrust her arm to secure the cottage door, a fierce breeze whistled from the forest, disputing her intentions.

"My lady," said the stranger over the dying wind, "I apologize for my daftness, but allow me to make amends. I am in search of my bride and have finally come to claim you. I adore you and wish to be yours forever." But to this, the maiden only answered as she had done so many times before.

"Your words are sweet like plum wine and promising like the morning sun, but I must insist that you go. For I owe my hand to the autumn harvest that feeds me, and the harboring oaks that keep me safe. My loyalty is in the flowers and grass I walk on. I love that only for the rest of my days."

Contrary to the maiden's anticipation, the stranger did not grow crestfallen. Instead, he beamed with delight, placing his hand over his heart. With a bold step forward he moved to one knee, digging into his cloak and removing a crown made of branches. The young maiden watched as the bachelor offered a diadem of wood and vine. As the young maiden studied the offering, her own heart began to flutter. Gazing into the young man's eyes, she felt her very soul stirring and drawing open. For the feeling she had was the same she felt when she stroked a doe or drank from the brook.

Reaching her arms out, she removed the wood crown from the young man's hands and placed it over her fiery head of hair. The stranger arose, striding backwards into the trees. As he did, his boots rooted into the soils and his cloak faded into leaves. And as the winds took him up and the earth brought him down, with a whisper and tender smile he bid her farewell.

"And I will always love you," he confessed.

So it went, her and her love together. He fed her when she hungered, bathed her when she was filthy, and hummed her to sleep under the twinkle of the stars. He gave her friendship in the wildlife, family in the trees, and wisdom in seasons. How she adorned her husband, and in return, he adored her.

Chapter 1

"Uncle wait," I pleaded as I sprinted through the wood line, a furious troll trampling behind me. It always ended like this when gallivanting through the Autumn Lands with Uncle. It was in his nature to be mischievous, and every *sídhe* in the realm knew he was more than just your common lark. Yet, no matter how infamous he became, the free folk were always quick to anger when the joke was on them. Worse yet, I was starting to earn his dodgy reputation.

"Damn you Uncle," I hollered while evading a handful of yellow claws. The hulking beast, who had swamp moss for clothes and fungus growing from its face, swung wildly, smashing into a fire-oak. The tree wept embers from its branches into the troll's eyes. "You're going to get me killed," I shouted over the beast's groans. Uncle, who was at least ten gallops ahead, looked over his shoulder with a grin. He took a second to admire his work, watching the troll scratch at her scorched eyes with her newfound braids of flamingo pink hair.

"Rule number one Adair," he croaked with a gruff voice made for the grave. I watched as he removed the top of the drinking bladder that hung from his shoulder, "Never play a trick that you can't get out of."

He steamed forward towards a large ivy covered spriggan tree and extended the bladder. He stopped at the base, offering gold liquor onto the roots before directing me to climb up. "Come now," he said calmly as the troll stampeded forward with tears running down her eyes. "Up you go."

While I'd never trusted Uncle's good will, I was confident in his escape plan. I grabbed onto a few loose branches and clambered up. The troll took one last desperate swing at my leg before watching me ascend. Step by step I crawled my way to the top of the tree where Uncle was already waiting, his hands resting behind his head. I took a moment to catch my breath. Uncle studied me as I gasped for air.

"Show off," I said between breaths. Uncle smiled. He was a funny looking fairy, even for sídhe standards. His beady eyes, beaklike nose, and deep dimples separated him from the rest of the highborn, who were above all else, exquisite. His even stranger hair, russet with stripes of white, spread atop of his head like bird wings. His fashion sense wasn't any better. He wore a woolen greatcoat, olive in color, with a patchy orange waistcoat and a lace neck cravat.

"Uh oh," he mocked as the pink haired troll growled below, "it looks like Rundura isn't in a forgiving mood."

Rundura the troll, with hands as large as gourd baskets, wrapped her fingers around the tree base and began shaking it. I grabbed at a thick branch, holding on for dear life. I looked to Uncle for our next plan of action, but as usual, he remained impishly quiet and unruffled.

"Um, Uncle," I gulped. "Pardon me for saying, but this isn't one of your better escape plans. In fact," I said between breaths, "it's pretty sucky."

Uncle gave a snort. "Look at you boy, stiffer than cat whiskers." He clasped his free hand onto his lapel. "Have no fear. This is a spriggan tree. We'll be just fine."

As if on cue, several of the branches around the crown of the tree began to crack and sway. The limbs rose, taking the form of a lean woman covered in bark. Wood casing masked most of her features, though her emerald lightning bug eyes grew in alarm.

"Evening Mairéad," greeted Uncle in his gruff voice. The dryad gazed at him, clicking noises reverberating from her throat. I tried not to look creeped out as her glare shifted to me. *Boom!* The tree shook from the troll's fists below. Mairéad's head spun like an owl, pausing and focusing on Rundura. "Tisk,-tisk," Uncle said with a shake of his head. "It appears that not everyone in the forest respects your ward."

Mairéad narrowed her pupils at Rundura, the clicks in her throat becoming louder. She stood and balanced herself on a nearby vine as if it were a tightrope. After scrutinizing the troll for another moment, Mairéad opened her arms and with a leap forward, swooped down onto the troll. Rundura roared as she tried to swipe at the dryad, but Mairéad was far too quick for the beast. Mairéad leapt from the monster's shoulders, placing herself between the troll and her spriggan tree. The pair began their ballet, sidestepping in half circles before lunging at one another.

"Well," Uncle smiled while taking a swig from his whiskey bladder, "that's our cue to go. Let's leave these two alone."

I opened my mouth, ready to spit out the first curse word that came to mind, but before I could, Uncle blinked out of existence, leaving a cloud of dirt, acorns and twigs. *Cool, I'm sure I'll manage by myself Uncle. Oh wait, I don't have freaking superpowers.* I searched the forest's horizon as the cacophony of growls and hammering grew below. Finally, I spotted Uncle. He was at least ten hurtles away, waiting patiently by a cranberry brook. With no other options, I coiled up on the branch and jumped forward, trying to hop over the skirmish.

Perhaps it was out of panic, but as I fell, my arms waived like a bird before I crashed hard onto the ground. The air in my lungs escaped, leaving me gasping. *Brilliant Adair.* The scarlet leaves decorating the forest floor smelled sweet, and their feathered edges tickled my cheeks, which were now firmly pressed against them. I could feel Rundara stomping nearby. I barrel rolled to my feet and sprinted away from the clash towards Uncle. He held his hand over his head, wiggling his spidery fingers.

"High-five?" he asked. I closed my eyes and tried not to punch him. "Oh come now," he persisted, "it's not fun unless it's dangerous."

I pried my eyes back open. It *had* been fun, even if I'd almost died. And that's why I loved Uncle. Not only did he tolerate my sarcasm, but we shared an interest in mischief and stupidity—A winning combo. I raised my hand and slapped it against his.

"That a boy," he snickered as we walked together, the sounds of the scuffling troll and dryad slowly being muffled by the chirping of birds.

"For the record, though," I said while limping next to him, "I hate you."

"Ah yes, I care for you too Nephew."

"No seriously," I insisted, "you keep forgetting that I'm not a full blood. I *can* die. Remember that next time you want to pull a prank with any trolls."

"Yes, you're right. Trolls are quite boring. It's far more entertaining with humans. They're much more gullible."

I could hardly remember my brief time in the Firbolg lands, though the image of Mother was something that I'd never forgotten. Her fiery hair and warm smile were branded in my mind. While none of the sídhe ever let me forget that she was Firbolg, Uncle always insisted that she was every bit sídhe at heart.

"Granted," continued Uncle, "you do have to be careful with them. Their minds are far too feeble for most enchantments."

Uncle was one of the few sídhe who was still allowed to visit the Firbolg lands. Though his trips were becoming less frequent, he always brought me back the most interesting keepsakes. I kept my vast collection of horseshoes, flintlock pistols, bellbottoms and CD players carefully hidden in my room so that no one, even Father, could find them. I got a kick out of keeping up with the humans, and it helped me feel somewhat connected. Yet, it was only during Uncle's latest trips that I truly became obsessed.

The humans gave rise to all sorts of clever folklore and fables over the years. Somewhere in the last century, they created my slavish addiction, *comic books*. From the moment I laid eyes on them, I was hooked. There were heroes and villains, civil wars and zombie apocalypses. They had radioactive bugs, mutant vigilantes, and aliens from other worlds. *I pined over every page.* And since I couldn't tell anyone about my contraband, I was technically *the* ultimate closet nerd in my realm.

"Uncle, what's new on Earth? Anything cool happening?" I asked while hopping over a patch of humming mushrooms that had grown from the corpse of a wild cat. Uncle had just returned from another trip to the Firbolg lands, working on a top-secret mission for Queen Aveline.

"*Cool?*" Uncle questioned. "Nephew, if the courts hear you speaking like that, they'll cut out your tongue. I may need to confiscate those comic books from you. They're starting to become a bad influence."

I blinked several times. "Uncle, *you're* the bad influence. Now, stop trying to change the subject."

"Oh, here we go," he moaned while picking at his ear. "Adair, if I ever doubted that you were autumn blood, allow me to apologize."

"Spit it out. What's new with Earth?"

"Come now. You're sídhe boy," Uncle slapped me on the shoulder with his free hand. "Stop doddering on about that other half."

"Easy for you to say. You're not treated like an outcast here."

"Oh no?" he challenged while sniffing some earwax on his finger. It must have been a healthy gob, because he smiled before flinging it.

"Okay," I admitted, knowing full well that Uncle was as wanted as warts. "But you did that to yourself."

"Please," he uttered. "I did it all on purpose." I belted out a laugh that sounded something like a grunting mule. "No, really I did," he insisted. "I want to be excluded from court affairs. The more you wag your tail with those monsters, the more they tell you to roll over. All I have to do is report to the wretched Queen, and I'm left alone. Plus," he said while pretending to box with me, swinging a wild haymaker that stopped just before striking my chin, "it gives me more time to bother the likes of you. Now, what would you like to do next? Shall we spike the rivers with brandy again?"

Uncle's strange and playful nature was mostly a treat, but at times like this, it also made him quite trying. He was the definition of aloof to be sure, even for sídhe standards, but it didn't mean you couldn't get answers out of him. You just needed to know how to go about it. Besides Father, I was one of the only real people Uncle cared for, giving me access to his heartstrings. I stared at my boots and conjured a sigh and frown. Uncle tried to counter by twisting my nipple, but I didn't budge. After a moment, he dropped his shoulders in surrender.

"My word, you're as stubborn as Oran," he said while poking my nose. "Fine, answer me this riddle and I'll give you what you want." I motioned with my hand for him to go on. He pulled up his puffy sleeves, and then, as if aiming the riddle, pointed his sharp clawed index finger at my head. "The cuckoo and the gowk, the laverock and the lark, the twire-snipe, the weather-bleak, how many birds is it that I seek?" I mulled it over for a second, thanking fate that Uncle wasn't as astute as he was mischievous.

"Three," I answered with a smirk, "because the second name in each line is simply a synonym for the same bird."

"Very well then, I'll answer your question." He rubbed his chin and gave a raspy hum that sounded like stones grinding together. "As I've said before, it's a lot duller than you think. Those comic books are starting to give you false pretenses. The Firbolg are more morose than the Winter Court nowadays, and twice as serious." I tilted my head at him. "All those toys and gadgets I bring you are the only ways humans keep their sanity. It's all work. Every beggar wants to be king. There's no adventure anymore." Long ago, Uncle was a legend amongst humans, and rubbed elbows with some of the most influential mortals Earth had to offer. As he likes to explain it, once Firbolg become disinterested with sídhe, so did he become bored with them. "It's all corporations and media companies now. And all they want to do is acquire."

"Acquire what?"

"Money," he frowned.

"Money?"

"Yes, think of it as we do secrets and favors. It's their currency."

"I know what money is thank you," I hissed. "It just seems like such a waste."

"Hmm, yes."

"But you're avoiding my question. What's going on over there these days?"

"It depends where on the map you go. But it's mostly squabbling about who is in charge of their sinking ship."

"Where on the map do you mostly go?"

Uncle rolled his eyes while swatting at a sprite that had flown down strumming its off-tune harp. "All right *Adair*," he said slowly over the sprite's music, pronouncing my name with clarity—first the *Uh* and then pausing before adding the *Dare*. "You want a story don't you?" I nodded while flicking the bothersome sprite from the air. The little guy landed on the forest path, but quickly stood back up and flashed a rude gesture. "Luckily for you, your uncle is the best storyteller in the Autumn lands. Did I ever tell you the time that I met Lady Gaga?"

"Who?"

"I have a lot of explaining to do," Uncle snickered.

***

For nearly the rest of the walk home, Uncle explained to me the latest in Firbolg affairs. While I was trying to use his tales about celebrities and microwaves to build a better picture of Mother, the times had clearly changed too much. Such is why Uncle reiterated, sídhe are prohibited from fraternizing with humans any longer. Our presence has always driven great passion in their hearts—a passion that could lead to a war nowadays that would make the campaign against the Gaels seem like child's play. Only select sídhe like Uncle, who had been given permission by the courts, are able to visit any longer.

It was nearly nightfall, and we were but a few songs away from home when Uncle stopped to finish explaining the applied science humans used to make light bulbs work. He used the Will-o'-the-wisps floating over the pumpkin patch as an example. But before he could finish his description, a sudden clamor came from the nearby briars. Jutting from the leaves was my Father's humble servant Fergal, a miniature sídhe who road on his beige bat Tess. Fergal was wiry with long bushy hair that would make members of *Twisted Sister* jealous. He had sharp features, tangerine skin and was all but naked except for his fishnet stockings and phallic gourd that covered his manhood.

"Where have you two been?" Fergal challenged while pulling on the reigns of Tess. Tess squealed. We couldn't exactly tell him the truth, as teasing free folk was not to be taken lightly.

"None of your business," Uncle bit back. Fergal and Uncle were as friendly as fire and ice. Their eyes locked and furrowed.

"Don't test me," Fergal threatened. "I'm in no mood today."

"Go bite some cold iron," Uncle spat back. Fergal squinted. "Fine, if you must know," Uncle said through a grin, "we've been scouting the lands in order to find a new servant for brother. His current one may turn up dead tonight." Fergal slapped on Tess's reigns again, swooping past our shoulders.

"Please, don't make me report your insolence to Oran," he said sternly. "Now, I'll ask you again, where have the two of you been?"

Unlike Uncle, my father Oran, was one of the noblest princes in *The Lands of Change*. The pure blood son of the King and Queen of Autumn, he was the male heir if Grandfather ever stepped down. Unfortunately, during his search for a bride, he'd fallen in love with my mother. Although he was warned many times that marrying her would cost him the kingdom, Father insisted. Before long, he was declared unfit to inherit the throne. Still, king or not, it was still very dangerous to upset him. There were goblin heads mounted in his chambers to prove it.

I chose my words carefully as they'd definitely be reaching Father's ears. "Fergal, is something the matter?"

Fergal raised his foot onto Tess's head and puffed out his chest. The bat slowed down to a lazy glide. "Stop trying to avoid the question."

"I'm not," I lied.

"Fine," Fergal frowned. "I will invoke *The Rule of Three*. Where have the two of you been?"

And with that Uncle and I both belched out the truth.

"We were teasing wild folk," I confessed. Uncle's answer was something a bit more perturbing.

"We were trying to do something fun for Adair in this ever-oppressive realm."

Fergal grimaced."It was my hope that you would not force me to coerce answers out of you, but if I must I must."

"Yes, yes," Uncle groveled. "Next time Adair and I will report before we use the bathroom so you can help us wipe. Now, why are you so concerned?"

Fergal landed Tess onto my shoulder. "There has been an incident." My teeth clenched. "And because of it, the four courts are being called together immediately. Your father's presence has been demanded." Fergal paused. "As well as yours Adair."

"Me?" I cried. "Why me?"

Father was an important figurehead, even if he weren't going to be King of Autumn. But me, I was just a half child. There were dozens of changelings and half-bloods littered across the realm. The courts looked at me as nothing more than a privileged waste of space. While they couldn't question Father's ward over me since he married under contract, they weren't looking to do me favors anytime soon. It bothered me to think that I was needed for something courtly.

Fergal leaned into my ear, sticking his head in it as if it were a cave. In a hushed voice he added, "I'm not sure Adair, but he's acting quite peculiar. I worry that there is something dark afoot."

Fergal was rarely this frank to me, especially with Father's affairs. If he were nervous enough to confide, then it warranted good reason for me to be worried. I gave a quick glance to Uncle. He was keeping himself entertained by splitting his vision in two, one eye starting up at an insect traveling across his bushel of hair, and his other eye blinking in my direction.

"Well then," said Uncle with a shrug. "This sounds serious. Lead the way Fergal."

With that, Fergal slapped at Tess's straps and flew towards home. My stomach began to churn as if I'd had too much cinnamon milk, and my instincts were on high alert. Nothing good ever comes from the courts. I had a feeling that Fergal's warning was a terrible omen of things to come.

Chapter 2

In a land that never was, in time that could never be, there lived a sídhe like none other, and his name was Oran. His mother, who was Queen, was made of spiders and his father, who'd been the King, was shallower than a road puddle. So wretched were they, that Oran swore in his cradle to contradict them for the rest of his days. At first, this proved difficult, as Oran depended on their generosity. As time changed, however, so did Oran. He turned away from the highborn, favoring the wild fairies of the forest. When riches could help them, he willed it. When decisions could make their lives better, he plotted its course. And it went this way until his very presence was despised by the Queen and King.

Time moved strangely, as it always does in The Lands of Change, and one day when Oran was ripe enough, he planned a journey that would take him past the fairy wilds. A great many tales were told about him during his trip. He was known as the only Autumn noble with a true heart, and even truer blade. He saved villages from hobgoblins, negotiated treaties with dragons, and fixed that in the realm which was deemed unfixable. Yet for as much success as Oran had, there was an emptiness inside him. It was the kind of emptiness that woke him every dawn and fed on him every evening. So, he set forth into the Firbolg lands with his trusted half-brother for a year and a day, searching to fill that hollow hole within him. And fill it he would on that day when Oran entered the Harvest Woods.

It was a time of swords for the Firbolg, when the country was still untamed. There in the woodlands he begged the Earth oaks for answers, but they gave him only one. The trees guided him to a young maiden with hair like the sun and a smile made from ocean sparkles. Oran watched the orphan girl day and night in hopes to solve the Earth oaks' riddle. He watched her until she was no longer a girl, and before long, Oran began to care for her through the shadows of the wilds. He fed her when she hungered, bathed her when she was filthy, and hummed her to sleep under the twinkle of the stars. Care became affection, affection became love, and soon Oran only lived for the maiden.

But he wouldn't be alone in his affection. Every morning, Firbolg suitors of gold and silver came the maiden's door, requesting her hand in marriage. Oran pondered his predicament until he pondered a hole in the ground. So hated was he by his parents the Queen and King, that they'd surely not allow a human bride in their lands. And so human was the maiden, that Oran would have to give up everything. And so, with no thoughts left in him, on the last hour of Autumn, Oran made his decision. He requested the hand of the woman who'd never met him, and in return was given a hand that he'd never let go. With the help of his half-brother, Oran and the maiden bound themselves by a contract deemed indisputable from free folk.

Time passed, and soon Oran and the maiden were expecting. On the eve of Samhain, the pair bore a son. The boy's hair was as bright as a bonfire, but the rest of him was as highborn as it comes. For seven years, seven months, seven weeks, and seven days the family of the Harvest Woods lived happily. They fed together when they hungered, bathed together when they were filthy, and hummed themselves to sleep under the twinkle of the stars.

But ill fortune spoils all, and shortly after summer, Oran's son became ill. Oran begged his half-brother to help, but the illness was beyond any care. There was only one cure. The boy would have to be taken to *The Lands of Change* by a parent, where his health would be restored through a great many moons. Oran and the maiden were crushed. The maiden would surely not be welcomed in the fairylands, but the boy would surely die if Oran did not present him. So, after a great many tears and *I love you's*, the boy was brought where few humans ever go, and even fewer return. And although Oran drank to his son's health, his heart split in two. For *The Lands of Change* are anything but changing, and a single drop of sand within a fairy's hourglass can be a century of time on Earth.

Chapter 3

The four courts of the fairy kingdom were formed after the sídhe abandon the Firbolg. Each court has a King and Queen who reign over their dominion. Though the seasons often rival each other for control, it's no secret that the balance has always equaled itself out. Each season merely takes its turn ruling. At the moment, the most influential power was the Summer Court, which meant that we'd have a long march to the Crystal Spire in order to fulfill our summons.

Uncle and I arrived home shortly after meeting with Fergal. Havgan was already bustling with activity. The warriors were forming across the glen in full regalia, adorned in their gilded armor shaped like overlapping leaves, and covered in cloaks of scarlet, yellow and orange foliage. A smattering of spirits formed behind the troops, swelling the ranks to boast prowess. It was all for show. Somewhere out there, three other armies were preparing in the same way.

Uncle and I hurried past the army towards Havgan's Redwood Tower. There'd always been an agrarian regolness to the keep, even in down-season. The throne room was decorated with furniture made of twisted wood, squash-lanterns, and our flag, wine red with a single gold leaf. A small troupe of servants packed trunks for the last-minute trip. I watched as the tower's gnomes and henner hurried to load crates with baskets of fruit and casks of cider. It baffled me that the servants, creatures of the wild, were so willing to surrender their freedom for a chance to work in Havgan, while I was trying to do the opposite.

"Well, well," said Uncle in a monotone voice while watching the scurrying help, "it seems that your grandparents are in quite the hurry to meet with the courts."

"I do not expect you to understand," called out a steely woman's voice. Grandmother, who we'd failed to spot upon entering the throe room amidst the chaos, perched upon her straw throne, a plume and crimson envelope in her hands. Her chair was decorated with exotic feathers and bright flowers, making her seem as if she were sitting on the eggs of some elegant bird's nest. Next to her was her royal guard, General Stroxson. He had milky eyes with no pupils and a sharp chin covered by a curling beard like a goat's. His helmet was marked with two bronze horns over his forehead, but otherwise, he was suited like every other Autumn soldier.

Uncle smacked his lips together. "Damn my tongue," he said with no real change in tone or emotion before bowing three times. "Forgive me your majesty." Queen Aveline studied Uncle with a flat expression. "Might I add that you look striking as usual?"

Though all highborn were lovely in one-way or another, my grandmother was exceptionally so. Her face was narrow with copper eyes that flickered in the firelight. She had long brown cords of hair that she wore up in a braids and sun kissed skin with a splash of freckles that made her appear eternally youthful, which she was. She wore a formfitting ginger gown, laced with vermillion silk and elaborate jewelry that matched the gilt crown wrought like pumpkin vines.

"No you may not," she responded.

"Well then," Uncle said while rubbing the back of his neck, "this is awkward. I guess," he gave a crooked frown, "I take it back."

Queen Aveline blinked several times before turning her gaze to me. She parted her puce lips to speak and as she did, I could see ink stains on her tongue. Her eyes alone could conjure both fear and lust in any creature, though her disdain for me over the years taught me which of the two instincts one should trust.

"I suppose you're looking for Oran?" she asked pleasantly, which frightened me even more. *Oran* was not Father's true name. Only those above him knew that. I bowed graciously, though in truth I wanted to run back to the wilds.

"I am *Grand* ...," her eyes went wide, "um, my Queen."

"He's just finished conversing with King Ruari," she said politely, though her face remained stern. "He's in his chamber. Go to him." I narrowed my eyes in suspicion, as the highborn chambers were off limits to me. The Queen studied my expression. She nodded. "I grant you permission Adair," she insisted, "go to him." I turned to Uncle. He shrugged. The Queen gave a single clap of her hands, and her leading lady, Liadan, floated through the walls.

Liadan the banshee, also known as Liadan the baby eater and Liadan Red-Palms, was the scariest specter I'd ever laid eyes on. Her ghostly grey outline drifted in like mist, and the red globes that made up her bleeding eyes flashed when they saw me. She had a main of dry ivory hair, taut skin, and a silver dagger that pierced through one cheek and protruded out of the other. A cloth ribbon, blood colored, wrapped around her head as if to keep her jaw tied shut.

If Queen Aveline was the Wicked Witch of the West, then Liadan was her nasty winged monkey. The banshee is said to have murdered the Spring Court warrior Tam Lin with a single hum of her song and feasted upon his gizzard in order to gain his power. Unlike Grandmother, who schemed and plotted to gain influence within the courts, Liadan took pleasure in her foulness. The loathsome specter had tried to kill me several times as a child, and I was certain that she'd try again had Father not stepped in.

I could still see Queen Aveline through the banshee's transparent figure. She gave an approving nod as she crossed her legs.

"Lady Liadan, I want you to escort Adair to his father," she ordered. "He is family after all."

Grandmother admitting that we were related was about as promising as vultures circling you in the desert. In all my time amongst the sidhe, she'd never confessed more than intolerance for me. Liadan bowed her head, allowing her raggedy hair to fall to the steppingstones. Queen Aveline turned back to me, her hands now balled into a fist.

"Go to him," she commanded. And with it three times spoken, I had no choice. My legs kicked from under me and began to walk towards the unlit halls, Liadan at my side. Uncle clanked his heels and began to follow, but he was stopped by the Queen.

"Not you," she said in her usual overbearing tone. Uncle halted. "I must speak with you alone," she paused, mulling over what to call him, "Child of Ruari."

Uncle stared at me reluctantly. "I guess I'll have to find you later Adair." He glanced at the Queen once more before saying from the side of his mouth. "It appears that I have other matters to attend to."

There wasn't a bone in my body that trusted what was going on, but I had little choice in the matter. I'd heard that on Earth, highborn couldn't use enchantments over those sidhe beneath them, but that was Earth. My feet continued to kick forward. One after another into the pitch-black hallway, the banshee's red eyes my only source of light. Though I could hardly see her, Liadan's presence could be felt. A thickness of gloom, despair, and hatred filled the air. Finally, we reached Father's chamber door, which was lit by a single flickering torch in a bronze sconce. Liadan pointed with her willowy hand towards the entrance. I gave her a fleeting glance and noticed that for some unwarranted reason, she was beaming.

"You should smile more often," I said while pushing open Father's chamber door. "It suits you." *Remember kids, sarcasm helps keep you from telling people what you really think of them.*

The spiced aroma of blaze-root burned my nostrils. Father sat at his table, flipping through the pages of a ragged tome while balancing a goblet of steaming froth in his offhand. There were several items placed neatly across his table, including Mother's diadem, a pair of acorns and his legendary Dragon Tear. Since dragons were one of the only creatures that could slay sidhe without cold-iron, they were feared more than anything. And since Father had nurtured a relationship with one by the name of Faro, he was also feared. Legend has it that if Father were ever in trouble, he could cast the jewel upon any living creature, be they flea or steed, and it would take the form of the great dragon.

Father appeared to be in a grim mood. A fork had been forcefully pierced into one of the maps spread across his counter and a pane of stained glass from a window behind him had been shattered. I closed the door behind me, waking him from his trance. He drew his gaze from the tome to me, a sudden jolt of life taking over him. He placed his goblet on the table and pushed out from the chair.

"Adair," he said in a shaky voice while making it to his feet. My legs had finally been given back to me, and as I went to embrace him, I could make out strain in his face. Though he was striking and youthful with his mountain brown hair and copper eyes, all other color had been drawn from him. His now pallid skin clashed with his gold shoulder pads, autumn cloak, and goose plume crown. Some of the kinder sidhe said that we could be twins if not for my shorter orange mane, but I knew that they were only being polite. I had Firbolg blood in me and would always seem alien.

"Father," I said with a dab of playfulness in my voice, "I thought fairies were supposed to be beautiful?"

He looked into his cup, staring at his own reflection. He patted his hair down before slapping his cheek. "That bad, huh?"

"I don't even think you try anymore."

He laughed. "It's been a long time since you've been in here. I'm glad the Queen allowed it."

"Yeah, about that. Father, why is the Queen being kind to me?" I said frankly, cutting straight to the chase. "What's going on?"

Father drew back, staring at me with trepidation. He remained silent as he leaned on the back of his chair. He took a deep breath.

"I can't tell you," he said brusquely. His answer lashed like a whip.

"Uh," I hummed. "What?"

"As in," he paused, apparently digesting his own thoughts, "I can't."

"Father," I begged, "come on. What's happening?"

Father stared down at the floor. Then, after a moment he raised his chin and tried to speak. A choking sound croaked from his throat as he grabbed at it, and foam spit from his mouth. That's when it hit me. Father couldn't tell me because he was ordered not to. And since Father was the Prince, it meant that the only ones who could give such pitiless orders were the Queen and King. My heart dropped. He was powerless, and undoubtedly, his instructions were seamless. There'd be no exposing the terms.

"The rule of three?" I asked. Father didn't speak. He just continued to twitch. "Father, I'm sorry," I apologized, knowing full well that his circumstances were tormenting him. "Does it have to do with me?" The veins in his head creased and his eyes bulged. The orders were working against him, and I was torturing him just by asking. "No, never mind," I cut in, "don't answer that."

Father clasped one of his hands on my shoulders, propping his weight on me. "Don't worry," he coughed. "I've been working on something." I padded him on the back, letting him catch his breath. "I won't let her get away with this."

Grandmother was up to something as usual. I'd grown accustomed her getting her enemies beheaded, but I'd always thought Father and I were off limits. Clearly, I was wrong. I needed to do something. Then again, what was I going to do? I'd learned at an early age that with highborn, you usually had no choice. If they willed it, such was so.

"In the meantime," Father continued, fighting for air, "I want you to do me a favor?"

"Yes," I said quietly, squeezing his hand. "Of course. What can I help with?"

"I apologize for being mysterious, but I must say it."

"Please, just spit it out."

"A lot is about to happen and I'm not sure exactly how it will end. When the time comes, though," he said while staring me in the eyes, "you must listen to only me. Do you understand?"

"Uh, not really," I stuttered.

Father grabbed me by my shoulders and slowly said the words again. "Adair, hear me again. You must *listen* to only me. Let your ears grow deaf to all others."

Father was trying to give a clue, but what this riddle meant was wasted upon me. I needed more.

"Yeah," I belted out. "sure. I'll grow deaf to all others."

"Good," Father said with a weak smile. "Now, we'll be going to court on the morrow, so you'll have to dress appropriately." His eyes went wide as he held out his hand. "Please don't ask what it is about."

"I won't," I agreed, terrified that I'd hurt him again. "Don't worry."

He took a step back and studied me. "You've grown since your coronation. I fear there is little chance that you'll be able to fit in your robes any longer." He rubbed my shoulder gently before letting go. "The Queen, your grandmother ,whether she likes to admit it or not, has prepared garments for you. They'll be in your room by sunrise."

"Do they involve manacles and iron spikes?"

Father grunted. "Maybe," he said with a weak smile. "And if you're lucky, shoes made out of broken glass."

I smirked. There was a long pause between us. After a short while, I finally gathered the nerve to speak again. "I know this is bad."

"It's not all bad," Father said calmly. "She's lovely."

"Who?" I challenged.

"All in due time," he said with a laugh. "But let it be known, she's as sweet as sugar. She'll make you very happy."

"Who? Grandmother?"

"Oh, heavens no," he said with a scrunched face. "Please, are you kidding?"

"I'm so confused."

Father smiled again. "All in due time. Now," he paused to kiss me on the cheek, "get some rest. Tomorrow's march will be long."

"Okay," I said before bowing. I had hundreds of questions, but they'd all end the same. Father would convulse or scream in pain from the Rule of Three. I needed to try and figure this one out myself. I headed to the exit and paused. "Father," I called out. He looked up, his hand gripping his side as his face winced in discomfort.

"Yes?"

"I'm not going to let her get away with this either."

"I understand that you want that Adair," Father said with a nod, his eyes squeezed together in agony. "But it's not worth it. Please, just follow the string." I nodded before shutting the door.

There's not a sidhe in The Land of Change that I trusted more than Father. Even the kinder fairies were marked by their capricious nature. Father, though, was the exception. His love for both my mother and I was his most admirable quality, especially in a realm where love isn't easily comprehended. So, while I understood that my grandparents might have a terrible plot in store for me, if Father said that he was working on something to end it, I believed him. By no means would it stop me from trying to thwart it on my own, but I believed him, nonetheless. Tonight, I'd muse over it all, preparing myself. Come tomorrow, I'd need to be on my toes. Whatever Father's plan was, I'd follow it to the end.

Chapter 4

There's a moment in every comic book when the burdened superhero stares down onto their home city from a skyscraper, vowing to stop their arch nemesis. You could say that I was kind of doing that. Only instead of a towering building, I was gazing out from my tree-lodge window. And instead of clenching my fists and swearing an oath to the skies, I was sipping butterscotch and praying for Grandmother's mercy. My thoughts were twisted around Father's predicament, and I was drawing a blank as to any sort of plan that could help. I sat on my favorite chair listening to the winds while rereading my favorite illegal comics and listening to my contraband headphones. They had a way of calming me when I was troubled. The King and Queen were cruel, as all kings and queens are, but their schemes frightened me. It frightened the life out of me to think about what they were up to. Perhaps they'd found a breach in my parent's contract? But if that were the case, why present it to the courts. Plus, Fergal said that there'd been an incident. What would my expulsion have to do with that?

Dawn chased the moon away, and although I'd only just fallen asleep, a knocking came at my door. My lodge, a simple wood hut, had been placed on the shoulders of an oak just outside of Havgan. I jetted up from my bed and collected my banned comics, hiding them in a false panel that had been enchanted along my wall. After a final scan of the room, I answered the door.

"Still asleep?" greeted Fergal with a mouthful of fruit as he balanced himself on Tess. The pair had cleaned up for the day. Fergal wore a carrot colored ribbon in his hair and a black cloak that nearly hid his gold-plated penis gourd. *Yes, penis gourds can be classy.* As for Tess, her fur had been painted with spiral designs of yellow, along with orange streaks across her wings and back. Gripped between her feet was a red handkerchief. "Have you received your attire?" Fergal continued before taking another generous bite from his juicy berry.

I looked over my small home for any signs of new clothing. Across my dining table, just next to the stein of half drunken butterscotch, was a neatly folded stack of autumn colored clothes.

"Yup," I said while scratching at my mane of stubborn hair, "looks like the Queen's enchantments are still in working order. Yay," I said with a dry tone and slow fist pump. Fergal swooped into the threshold of my doorway, directing Tess to fly closer to my ear.

"Your Father asked me to give you this," he said while patting Tess so that the bat dropped the tightly packed handkerchief in her claws. As the cloth fell, it unfolded, growing in size by tenfold. Soon, a seasonal cloak made of fall foliage was on the ground. There was a parchment of paper clipped to the collar. I removed the note, unrolling it from its curl before reading it.

Dear Adair,

I wore this the day I married your mother. Please do me the honor of dressing in it this day.

Your Loving Father,

Oran

Fergal gave me a smile. "He cares about you more than anything Adair. I sometimes don't think you deserve it."

"Jeez Fergal," I winced. "You really have a way with words."

"I meant no offense."

Fergal wasn't very good with sentiment, but I gave him credit for trying. The little guy would do anything for Father and had proven it on more than one occasion by risking his life.

"Well," I said hesitantly, "I guess I should get ready then."

Fergal nodded, drawing Tess out of the door. "Yes, you should," he agreed. "It's bad manners to be late." I bit my tongue. Fergal took one last glimpse at me before adding, "The convoy will be leaving shortly. I'll see you there." Then with a swoop from Tess, the pixie and the bat flew out from my entrance area and disappeared into the trees.

It had been sometime since I dressed up, and I was curious to see what Queen Aveline's servants had chosen. Resting on top of the pile was another autumn cloak. I tossed it aside and moved on. Next was a pair of black leather trousers. I slipped inside the leggings, hearing an uncomfortable squeal as the rubbery surface rode up my backside. I shuttered before continuing. After the pants were a sleeveless crimson tunic with pointed shoulders. Sewn over the chest was Autumn Court's gold leaf. I navigated through the neck hole and straightened out its front. Finally, I reached the bottom of the clothing pile. Along with the fine calfskin belt were a pair of leather bracers and matching knee-high boots cuffed at their tops, stolen directly from a pirate's wardrobe.

After trying everything on, I decided that I wanted to have a quick look at myself. Since mirrors were outlawed after the doppelganger scare, I decided to use the nearby riverbed's reflection. I climbed down my tree and made it to the falls where some of the fountain elves were bathing. Their sparkling skin was like an ocean's surface at sunrise. The shine blinded me.

"Do you mind?" I asked as I shielded my face. "I'd like to have a look at myself?" The silent sisters didn't answer. Instead they patted out of the pool with their wet feet, heads shaking at the indecency of my request. I looked myself over in the pool's surface. My wild hair rose up like a flame. I tried to pat it down, splashing a little water on it, but I knew that it wouldn't do any good.

"Well, at least the clothes fit me," I said to myself. The fine clothing didn't look half bad, and for once, I felt a bit important. Then again, going to church doesn't make you holy, and standing in a stable doesn't make you a horse. I needed to remind myself that I was likely dressing up for my own execution.

Bah, buh, buh, bappa, buh, bah! trumpeted a horn.

The distant call of a brassy instrument echoed through the lands, triggering a harmony of heavy drums, flutes, lyres and chanting after. It was the marching song, "A Fall of Tears," and it indicated that our procession was leaving. *Damn.* I hurried to the clearing where Uncle and I had first seen the gathering of warriors and watched as the columns made their way into the woods. *Double damn.* I sprinted towards the procession, my Father's cloak flapping behind me. Mortal or not, I wasn't going to let fatigue slow me down.

I suffered through my burning lungs until I was at the back ranks near the King and Queen. The pair was each mounted on a throne carried by specters. King Ruari, whose distinguishable hay colored skin gleamed in the sunlight, gave a glazed look. A black oil dripped off his lips from the moon-tar he chewed. He wore a crown made of elderberry and dressed in a grand robe, similar to Queen Aveline's, marigold with walnut embroidery. The Queen, who held her head high, wore a circlet made from black nightshade. Her eyes, which were highlighted in bronze, stared callously ahead, glaring at the wood line.

"Adair," called out a familiar voice. I turned to see Uncle in the ranks. He was wearing a skintight rose outfit and matching fool's hat. "Adair, come over here my boy."

I did my best to not draw attention as I slipped through the ranks to Uncle.

"You look ridiculous," I jabbed. Uncle lifted his chin and straightened out his floppy collar.

"Thank you," he said wit drunkard's grin while shining his dirty fingernails across his chest. An irrepressible laugh came out of me. Uncle studied my clothing. "It appears you've had an upgrade yourself young nephew. Gifts from your beloved Queen?"

I lifted my head to get a glance at Grandmother before speaking. Her scowl and glare remained as it was.

"Yeah," I whispered.

"Any idea what this is all about then?"

"I have a guess," I said while keeping an eye on Grandmother. "Father tried to give me clues, but he can't talk about it. He's definitely under the *Rule of Three*. However, he hinted that my grandparents are up to no good. My best guess is that the courts plan on casting half children out from the realm?"

"Ha," hooted Uncle. "Not likely, especially with the Summer Court in charge." He shook his head. "Queen Orla loves her half daughters."

"Well then, Grandmother will just have to do away with Queen Orla as well," I said in jest. The words seem to strike a chord with Uncle. He chewed on his lip, letting the mournful marching music take my ear. I nudged him with my elbow, trying to lighten the mood. "Oh come now. I'll be fine."

"Adair," he said seriously, which was rare, "if you do go, you know, back to Earth, I want you to promise me something."

"What is with everyone and all these promises?" I said flippantly.

He ignored me. "If you're ever lost, find the Bleeding Wolf. There's a man of mine, Eamon. He owes me a boon. Tell him it's time to collect on that favor he owes me."

"Any injured wolf or do you know one with a nose bleed?"

"Find the Bleeding Wolf," he said louder.

"Okay, okay. Find a bleeding wolf," I repeated. "Sure, no problem." I had hoped that Uncle was going to put my mind at ease as he typically did, but clearly, I was in as much trouble as I'd thought I was. Not much moved him usually.

"Secondly," he said with a bit more mirth in his words, "you have to promise me at least one trick a day."

"Come again?"

"A trick," he groaned. "You know, a joke, a prank, something funny."

"Why?" I asked hesitantly, my sights still on Grandmother.

"It would do you some good for once to just humor me," he grumbled.

"Fine," I surrendered, "A trick a day."

"Good. Thank you." There was a pause. I studied Uncle and saw that his hands were fidgeting. He knew something. "Now, let's play a game," he said hastily. He snapped his fingers. "Oh, I know. How about we think of different outlandish ways the Queen might torture you." And with that, we plodded through the Autumn lands, coming up with different disturbing ways that I'd be hung or flayed. It wasn't that I didn't want to learn what Uncle knew, but when you get close enough to some people, you learn that even your best frown or guilt trip won't work. Maybe it's because I'd hoped Father's plan was going to fix everything, or maybe it was the shock of being helpless, but at the moment, I'd decided there was nothing I could do besides flow with the current.

The march to the Summer lands wasn't so much arduous as it was repetitive. All the trees began to look alike and even the most exotic creatures became uninteresting. To add injury to insult, the same songs we'd been marching to played over and over again, forcing me to contemplate stabbing my ears out with a twig. As the day went on, we made it to the center of the realms where the famous Cold-Iron Pillar awaited. The metal pylon was forged in cold-iron so that no sidhe could tamper with it. Engraved in its center were directional arrows along with description.

See the northern flames of Summer.
Taste the southern waters of Winter.
Hear the eastern winds of Autumn.
Smell the western flowers of Spring.

We rested at the site for a short time before making our way north for what seemed like forever, and then add a moment or two. By sundown we'd reached the solstice borders. Summer had gone through great measures to impress us. Their lands, green and lush, were adorned with weeping willows that draped sparkled branches along our path. Paper lanterns, thousands of them, hovered through the sky above, and as we gazed upon the Crystal Tower in the distance, we could hear a choir of sirens.

It took us a moment to settle our ranks once we reached the doors of the fortress. The surrounding walls were decorated with the banners of the Summer Court, green with an aureolin sun. The large crystal doors were taller than any height in Havgan. A great thunder rumbled from the gate seam, and soon the doors opened. Light poured out from the castle, bathing the autumn army in white. Queen Aveline, unimpressed, thrust her hand forward, ordering the columns of autumn warriors to enter the gates.

The immense courtyard was a forest in itself, with wild juniper bushes and emerald beech trees placed neatly as far as the eye could see. Hundreds of summer guards and highborn littered the grounds around a pool of water known as the Weeping Pond. The courtyard, the largest in the entire realm, had hosted several battles in its time, and although the sidhe were currently at peace, it would take little more than a misunderstanding to get the courtyard to host another. As we continued to pour in, Uncle made note that the Spring Court had already arrived.

"Look at them," he said while giving me a nudge. "The lazy dolts are finally on time to something."

Spring had been stereotyped as absentminded by others. Though they were technically our rivals, I'd admired their carefree approach to the many trivial matters of the realm. The majority of their ranks wore light coats and sashes with their season's colors, turquoise and vibrant green. The highborn had pallid skin and bleached hair that they wore up in elegant braids. Their forces were far less numbered than ours, and not as sturdily armed, though their massive wild fairies of thick fur and deadly horns more than made up for it.

Once our warriors had fully filed in, King Ruari and Queen Aveline descended from their thrones and moved to a platform stationed between armies, where they greeted the other seasonal kings and queens. Watching Queen Aveline's attempts to be pleasant was like watching a viper trying to smile. Though the King and Queen of the Spring Court stood proudly, most of Aveline's attention had been drawn to the Summer Court. Queen Orla of Summer was equally as beautiful as Queen Aveline, though it was more ostentatious. She had tresses of blonde hair weaved with sweet grass and glittery green eyes. She wore a pear gown that left little to the imagination, a gold diadem, and bore canary colored ruins, which were masterfully painted onto her flesh. Her counterpart, King Branwen, carried himself like a general, with a stiff back and imposing posture. He had beautiful ropes of brown hair, bronze skin, and a lion's scowl. His green cape draped around him, concealing the rest of his garments. Most distinguishing, though, was his pointed crown, wrought like sun rays and adorned with various animal eyes that blinked and moved on their own.

We waited. As I continued to study the crowd, I spotted my old Summer friend Kalen. His skinny frame, wavy cyan hair and braided chin beard hadn't changed in ages. He and I were once thick as thieves until I'd mucked it all up. I waited for our eyes to meet, but when they did, he shot me a dirty look before turning away. *I deserved it.* With nothing left to do, Uncle and I whispered nervous jokes to entertain ourselves when the clang of gongs called from outside the crystal walls. *Winter Court had arrived.* The great crystal doors once again parted, and soon the brooding forces of the ice sidhe filed into the courtyard. Though the air was warm, a bitter cloud permeated inside. The winter soldiers, swathed in black cloaks frosted in rime, kept their heads down as if part of funeral procession. Their masters, King Wynnfrith, and his latest wife, Queen Jessa, were carried in on rocks of ice, their silken black hair and smooth sallow skin eerily alluring. Winter was renowned for their intelligence, and the orderly ranks weren't to be ignored. I watched as Queen Orla, whose glare bore into the Winter Court, muttered something in Grandmother's direction.

King Branwen wasted no time. He took to the front of the platform before King Wynnfrith and Queen Jessa could fully settle. "Now that the four courts have arrived," called out King Branwen in his deep voice, "let us call for order." The servants of each royal leader scurried to bring their master's thrones to the center platform. Spring's chairs, made of clay and moss, paled in comparison to Summer's, which was constructed entirely of fairy-fire. All eight leaders sat themselves, their bloodline and retainers closely behind them. I noticed Father positioned himself between Grandfather and Grandmother. Liadan took to Grandmother's side, her gaze locked on Father.

"We shall not waste time honoring our ceremonies today," called out King Branwen to the crowd. "There is far too much to discuss. Loyal subjects of the Seasonal Court, settle yourselves." King Branwen waited for the assembly to quiet. Many of Summer's sidhe went hush, while several Spring and Autumn fairies continued to murmur. The Winter folk were as mute as when they'd entered. "We have assembled the courts in order to bring light to a pressing matter." The courtyard remained still and silent.

"It has come to our attention," the Summer Queen broke the settling white noise of those gathering, "that an unsanctioned individual has breached the veil between our world and that of men." Many in the room began to whisper. There was an abundance of *who's* and *what's* muttered around me. I glanced at Uncle. He was ogling the Autumn Court, his lower lip stiffening. "As you know," Queen Orla continued, "this act is illegal to all sidhe, unless given special permission."

"And how is it," Queen Jessa of the Winter Court cut in, "that you have come across such knowledge?" Queen Jessa's solid dark eyes and coal eyeliner made it appear as if her sockets were black holes trying to suck the Summer Queen in. The Summer Queen turned her cheek as if slapped. She took a moment to exchange spiteful stares with her rival before answering.

"Queen Jessa," proclaimed Queen Orla with a smile, "I forget that you are new here, being King Wynnfrit's *latest* wife. Allow me to elaborate. We know," she said as if it were obvious, "because it has happened across Summer's lands." A young maiden to Orla's right, a thin sidhe of flaxen hair and bronze skin, gave Queen Orla a nod of approval. There were rows of white diamonds pinned into the girl's face. This must have been the Orla's favorite half child, Ailsa, whom Father would have married had he not met Mother. She was notorious for her cruelty, partaking in the burning of free folk for entertainment sake.

"Yes," the Summer King supported, "as it is known to all Kings and Queens when the veil has been breached on their lands."

"Forgive me for saying," challenged the gravelly voice of the Winter King, "but how are we to believe you?" The crowd began to speak in hushed tones as the verbal battle continued. "I am quite knowledgeable of our people's history. Many nobles have accused rivals of doing the same before. Hence why contracts were arranged to force a second court to verify such offenses." The assembly's volume increased. I nudged Uncle, but he seemed to be in some sort of trance. "I know that the Winter Court has not been reached out to," continued King Wynnfrith, the black stitches on the sides of his mouth making his frown even grimmer. "Is there perhaps another court who can verify?"

"Not ours," said King Ryland from the Spring Court. His pale hair, drawn tightly in a braid over the top of his head, made his long hook nose and pointed face appear even larger. His son and champion, Carrick, known as *The Knight of the Swan*, stood beside his father, donned in silvery armor. He had a black stripe of paint over his eyes and an orange line down his nose. Carrick placed his gauntlet on his father's shoulder in support. "So," King Ryland continued, "what say you?"

"But the accusations *have* been verified by another court," called out Grandmother. My heart began to fluster as I heard her familiar flat voice. It was the pitch she used when she was up to something underhanded, calm and rational. I tried to swallow the lump in my throat. "Both King Ruari and I have verified such." The sidhe of the courtyard were now in a state of uproar. The King of Summer clapped his hands several times.

"Settle yourselves," he roared, his enchanted voice echoing through the courtyard. "I demand it at once." The crowd's volume lowered but was far from silent.

The Winter King stood up from his throne, tapping his soft souled boots across the platform as he picked at a loose stitch on the edge of his lips. He bobbed his head several times in consideration. "You *do* know Queen Aveline," he said in a voice laced with venom, "that a treaty between any season is considered treason? How come you did not notify any of the other courts that you would be supporting Summer's claim today?"

The Autumn Queen remained completely still; her copper eyes steady like a stalking crocodile. "Because," she said calmly, "we had to conceal our information from everyone, even our own kind." Disbelief bellowed through the courtyard. *Lies* and *nonsense* were said under the breath of several Spring sidhe. Numerous Autumn warriors in front of me traded speculative stares.

"And why," asked King Wynnfrith, "would you need to do that?"

"Because," Grandmother answered, "the sidhe who committed the crime is of Havgan stock."

A fairy from the Summer Court screamed before fainting. Everyone within the courtyard was now amidst conversation—that is, everyone except me. The blood drew out of my limbs and my fingers felt cold. This is what Grandmother had been planning all along. Together with the help of the Summer Court, she would finally rid herself of her cursed grandson. I'd been framed as a border crosser and would put to a cold-iron sword. I squinted my eyes and bit my tongue hard to get a hold of myself.

"Queen Aveline, if you would," called out Queen Yoratha of the Spring Court in a weak voice, speaking for the first time. She was lovely as a doe, but fragile as glass with her slender physique and pale features. It is rumored that she starved herself, consuming sugar dew alone to keep her pristine beauty. "Please enlighten us as to who this criminal of Havgan is?"

"Of course," Queen Aveline replied, tranquility still in her voice, "but before I do, I must first call upon the sidhe who witnessed the crime." And with those words, Uncle pushed me aside, navigating between the masses onto the platform.

I was in complete shock. *There's no way Uncle would betray me, would he?* We'd been partners in crime since I was a child. He was my only true friend besides Father. He'd taught me the ways of the fairy. There must have been a misunderstanding. Then again, who else would be so believable to attesting for my whereabouts? I took a few steps backwards, trying to swim against the mob, who was constricting the platform. Uncle stood in front of Grandmother with his head down. The whispers from the crowd grew into a keen collection of sharp hisses and low grumbles.

"Also," Grandmother added, "allow me to remind the courts the consequence for such actions. Any sidhe who does not honor the contracts set about by the courts shall be put to their final death."

"Yes," said the Winter Queen impatiently, her legs tightly crossed together. "We all know how it works Queen Aveline. Now, who is it that breached the barrier?" Queen Jessa glowered at Uncle. "Speak you fool."

Finally, the crowd had gone quiet, as if a void entered the gardens. All eyes shifted back and forth between Queen Jessa, Grandmother and Uncle. Only the cackling of fire from the Summer Court's thrones could be heard. I clenched my fists and readied for my name to be called. But before it could, a voice shattered the silence.

"I am," announced Father as he stepped forward.

"No," I blurted out, though no one seemed to notice. Everyone was too busy gasping and cursing again. I began to push forward in panic, trying to get nearer to the platform. After squeezing between several autumn warriors, I reached the front. Father was now defiantly facing all eight leaders and their gentry, his back partially facing the jeering crowd.

"Settle yourselves," growled the Summer King. The eyes of his crown narrowed along with his own.

"Prince Oran," said the Summer Queen in a falsely concerned tone, "while your honesty is admirable, you do realize the severity of your actions? You will forfeit your life." I tried moving onto the stage, but several summer guards pushed me back into the masses. *Why was this happening?*

"I do," he said, his stare locked on Queen Aveline. General Stroxson, who'd been at Grandmother's side, readied his spear. "And I *shall* forfeit my life."

"And why would you commit such a crime?" demanded the Winter Queen. "You are the Prince of Autumn. You could have easily been granted permission."

"Why I did it," he bit back, "is none of your concern. What *is* important however is my life." There was a pause. "As the courts have discussed, breaking court contracts is punishable by death. However, I refuse to surrender to any king or queen." Grandmother tilted her head curiously like a hound listening to a whistle. "I will surrender it only to my son." Father turned to the crowd, scanning it. After a moment his eyes fell upon me, and as they did, he mouthed a mixture of words. *"Listen only to me."* Behind him, the champions of the courts had now created a protective wall between Father and the gentry. Liadan floated in front of Queen Aveline, her hair swimming in curved strands as if each of was a coiled snake. I watched through the banshee's body as the seeds of what almost resembled a smile curled up Grandmother's lips.

"Sidhe of the realm," Father called out. "The courts are no longer balanced. Let not the old ways return. There will be a day when my words are wisdom," he shouted. "When the time comes, use what I've given you." Father returned his gaze to me. "When the time comes," he repeated, "use what I've given you." A current of heat ran through my veins. Several of the guards went to apprehend Father, but a flurry of air rained from the heavens and pulled him up into the air before bringing him down into the crowd.

He scoured the area for me once more, and as he did, I called out, "Father." He reached out his arm towards me, bridging it over a few of the confused autumn warriors. Grasping my hand, he repeated once more.

"When the time comes, use what I've given you."

Another heavy gust of wind drew through the courtyard. Upon blowing on Father, the wind began to make him come apart. Every piece of Father broke into colored leaves. For a moment they remained still, keeping Father's form, but then the foliage twisted into a cyclone, and without warning, rushed into my chest. I could feel a surge of electric coursing through my body as I lifted off the ground. My fingers curled and my eyes opened wide as energy continued to flow. A number of warriors nearest me began to withdraw as gales of wind blew out of my gaping mouth. Everyone with the courtyard seemed uncertain as to what to do.

In this moment, I was lost in time. My mind drew blank, and any hurt inside me hide from my heart. I stared above the masses, unmoved by their horrified faces. I could taste sweet grass in my mouth, and a heavy popping in my ears. But as quickly as it came did the surge unexpectedly cease, and I was dropped to the ground. Shocked, I sprang up from off my back, pushing up into a sitting position. My eyes watered, and as I wiped the tears from them, I noticed several blurry figures approaching. A squad of summer guards had hurried over to me, pointing their spears in my direction. As my vision cleared, I could see both Grandmother and the Summer Queen standing at the edge of the platform. Raising her hand, Queen Orla pointed at me.

"Seize him," she hollered, and the guards stretched out their gauntlets to grab me.

Chapter 5

Whatever Father did to me put my senses into overdrive. Time slowed down a snail's pace. The muttering of the crowd transformed into a thunderstorm so loud and strong that I cupped my ears. Without consent, my hands drew away from my head, digging into my cloak. I watched as my fingers scratched at something sewn into the lining of my cloak and dug it out. In my palm were two tiny acorns. I tried to will my body to stop so that I could make sense of everything, but my hands continued to plug the acorns into my earlobes. Though the voices of those around me had gone mute, it would only be a temporary relief. An approaching guard clamped down on my neck, capturing my wits.

"Come with us," mouthed the guard as he tugged at my cloak's lapel. But no sooner than he'd spoke, did my body decide to burst outward short of my consent. My chin lifted, my arms extended, and my legs spread wide. An eruption of wind poured from me like a hurricane, knocking over everyone within line of sight. I read the lips of one of the warriors as she mouthed a few words.

"Look at his eyes," she seemed to say before being lifted off the ground and hurled into a pack of soldiers behind her.

Father commanded three times to use what he'd given me, and my body was now enchanted to see his intentions through to the end. It was the rule of three. I was a prisoner within my own form. My eyes studied the gardens. Sometime during my possession, the eight leaders had been encased in a semitransparent dome of ice. While some of the highborn were now squabbling inside the frost fortress, Grandmother leaned across its surface, her hands pressed on the frost as she watched me. It didn't take long for some of the guards to get back to their feet. I was battling for ownership of my body, and as I turned my head to see the warriors rearming themselves, my mouth allowed me to speak.

"Gah, this sucks." *I know. It wasn't the most elegant war cry.*

My legs kicked forward and began running towards the closed gates of the crystal tower. From the corner of my eye, I could see Liadan slithering through the ice. She was untying the ribbon wrapped around her mouth with one hand while plucking out the dagger in her cheek with the other. Along with several guards, the banshee pursued me. As I neared the gates, my hands thrust frontward and began waiving as if I were trying to catch a falling ball. Another cold blast of air surged from my palms, and shortly after a gray whirlwind jutted in the direction of the enormous crystal entrance. While the slabs didn't move much, I could see that the current of air had pushed open a small sliver of space between the door seams large enough for a person to fit through. I slipped between the opening, and as the winds died down, I could feel the impact of the doors slam at once behind me.

The Rule of Three ordered my feet to continue. I tried to look behind me to see if anyone was on my tail. As greedy as the enchantment was, it allowed me to peak over my shoulder. The good news is that there was only one person still trailing me. The bad news is that it was Liadan, and she appeared to be gaining ground fast. Her body levitated inches over the fields, and her gaping mouth screamed with fury. *Listen only to me*, Father had told me. I could feel the acorns jammed in my ears reverberating. His enchantment had once again saved my life.

I looked ahead and could see the Great Forest in the night's horizon. All four courts shared the vast woods, and I felt that if I could just reach its network of gnarled trees and hidden caves, I might have a chance. Fear flushed over me as Liadan continued to catch up, and it wasn't long before she was nearly within arms distance. A banshee's scream is deadly, but its touch isn't much better. A brush of Liadan's fingers would paralyze me. I didn't want to be trapped inside my body any more than I already was.

"Body do something," I begged. My hands grabbed at the trim of my cloak and flapped the fabric as if they were wings. A thrust of air from the East hurled me into the sky and onward with blinding speed, shrinking the landscape below. Butterflies filled my stomach. The stars above and the shimmering trees below lit up the violet sky. Everything beneath me was visible, and much smaller. I could see Liadan losing ground.

"Good luck with your singing career," I jeered as the wind put distance between us. I couldn't hear her response, but I'm sure it had something to do with eating my soul.

As I tore through the sky and over the Great Forest, my nerves settled a bit. I began to think about where I was being taken. I'd had little choice in the escape so far but knew that Father was a brilliant planner. Then it hit me. *Where was Father?* He had seemingly leapt inside me, but where was he hiding now? I half expected him to reappear on the moon above me to explain part two of his great plan.

The warm stream of air I'd been riding suddenly gave way. As it faded, I descended towards the bushy tops of the Great Forest's myrtle trees. It wasn't long before I splashed into the river of leaves, branches and thorns that clawed at me as I plummeted.

"Ow, ow, ouch, whoa that doesn't belong there, ow, eek, eww," is all that came out of me. Finally, I landed. I could feel the invisible puppet strings loosen from my nerves, and as I lifted my arm to rub my head, I no longer experienced any tug-of-war to control my actions. Once my wits were about me again, I scanned my surroundings. I was now in the wilds, a dangerous place for anyone at night. There were frightening tales of bugbear packs, ogre dens and worst of all, giants, that came from the Great Forest's depths during the hours of darkness. None of it could be confirmed of course, as anyone who entered by themselves were never heard from again. Maybe it was because they stumbled upon some giant never-ending forest orgy, but I doubted it.

I'd been encased in a broad hall of thick bushes nearly ten feet tall. The trees I'd fallen through were all that was visible above the shrubbery, peeking like giants over an emerald fence. Behind me was a dead end, and in front of me was a walkway that curved left. I edged my way to the bend and found a path that lead to a single forked passageway. At once it became clear that I'd crash landed in the middle of a hedge maze.

Riddles, puzzles and mazes were the fairies' favorite method for protecting valuables. I continued cautiously, certain that there'd be insidious traps and lifelike illusions that could lead to a painful and cruel death. I tiptoed to the divide in the pathway, staring at all three corridors. Each was a copy of the other, long and winding. It appeared that once you chose your trail, it was way too far-reaching to turn back.

"What I need is a damn map," I cursed under my breath. "What I have are freaking acorns." I took a moment to think. Perhaps it was the years of boredom before this, but I decided I wasn't going to let this adventure's little snag get me down. My mind went to my comic books. *What would Wolverine do in a situation like this?* Then it hit me. While I didn't have any mutant powers to help me smell my way out, my hearing had been amplified tenfold. Too bad *Ear Man* doesn't have a better ring to it. I plucked the acorns out of my earlobes and listened. Crickets chirped. A crunch of foliage cracked in the distance, accompanied by heavy breathing. I wasn't alone. I needed to choose quickly before whatever was protecting this labyrinth found me.

But before I could make a choice, I heard a soft thump plop near my feat. I looked down to discover a simple ball of yarn that had fallen from the folds of my cape. I bent down to grab the bundle, but before I could snatch it up, the sphere rolled towards the left path. I watched as it continued to spin, wobbling almost drunkenly along the uneven lawn, a train of string unwinding behind it. I pinched at the thin twine, gathering it in my hands as I followed its trail. Step by step I slowly harvested a bale of thread in my grip, until finally the path came to another crossroad.

Despite the two pathways, the ball of string rolled left again and spun out of my line of sight. I hurried to catch up but was stopped in my track. Lying beyond the hedge's corner was an opening where a lilac garden wrapped around a silver pond. The smell of mint cloves pampered my nostrils, and a cascade of flower petals trickling from the sky took my eye. As I inspected the patch, my ball of yarn rolled to the pond. But just before it could splash into the waters, a hand from a nearby hazelnut patch caught it. Blossoming from a clove of flowers was a nude woman, curvy and alluring, with sapphire hair. She held the ball under her sheen blue lips.

"Um," I droned as she approached me, "hi, how are you?" The woman said nothing. I could see scattered bones amongst her feet along the grass. For some reason, it didn't seem to frighten me. "Say," I belted, "can you tell me ..." but my mind went blank. It was as if a thick mist of fog filled my head. I couldn't seem to think straight. *What the heck did I want to ask her?* The woman closed the distance between us until she was so near that I could feel her breath. She wrapped her arms around my shoulders, desire in her eyes. "Eh, never mind. Couldn't have been too important."

The beauty placed her lips along my neck, sending a cascade of pleasure throughout my body. My hands slackened, causing the ear-acorns I'd been gripping to fall to the grass. Perhaps, I hoped, Father wanted me to live the rest of my days hidden within this secret garden? Or maybe this creature had a helpful message, but it could only be expressed through a more ... *physical* language? Whatever the reason for her, I was happy for it. I wanted nothing more but to be with this blue haired goddess for the rest of my days.

Then suddenly, just as the woman began unbuttoning my trousers, her back recoiled in agony. I stared with confusion until she collapsed beneath my feet. As she plummeted to the ground, a new figure emerged behind her. It was Liadan, her mouth yawning as she stared at me with her bleeding eyes. *This was bad*. I looked down at the ground where both my acorns and the nymph lay. The nymph's bloody back had been pierced by Liadan's cold-iron dagger.

Then Liadan screamed.

The shriek's shrill was the mixture of a mournful mother's cry, a wounded doe's bellow and a dead man's cackle. I could feel my heart quiver while a stabbing pierced inside my chest, as if my very soul were being torn apart. I tried to lift my arms in surrender, but they were too wracked with pain. Liadan took a breath and then howled a second time. The sheer shrill caused my heightened hearing to rob me of any cognizant thought. Only torture filled inside me. My body swayed uncontrollably. She was one last scream away from killing me. That's when a bolt of tiger orange energy came darting from above us.

"Leave him alone," cried Fergal as he swooped down on the back of Tess. There was an aura around him, and as he soared past the arm of Liadan, he left a gash along her forearm. Liadan clamped her mouth shut, grabbing her wound while spinning to watch Fergal ascend. Almost immediately did the pain in my chest cease. "Adair," hollered Fergal while steering Tess around so that her nose was facing the banshee again, "get in the pond."

Fergal was the last sidhe I could count on. I had hundreds of questions for him, but I was no fool. Liadan was far too much of a match for either of us. So, as he swooped down again, slicing a lock of Liadan's hair from her head, I acted. I turned towards the pool and ran. Liadan took notice and chased after me. Her speed was overbearing, and as I neared the lip of the waters, I could feel her cold hand press along my back. My body froze before I could leap forward, stiffening me in a forward leaning position. I was but a hair's length away from escaping. *This just isn't my day.* But before Liadan could drag me from the pond to take me back to my grandmother, or worse yet, kill me with her scream, I heard a cry from Fergal.

"Unhand him you flap-mouthed harpy," he shouted behind me. Without warning, a small but forceful jab struck me along my back shoulder. I felt my body toppling forward like a chopped tree readying to fall. There was an outcry from Liadan that caused my insides to once again shutter. But before the banshee could tear my soul apart, I gained momentum and splashed into the pond.

The waters weren't bitter as I'd expected. Nor were they warm. They were neither because all sensation had been wiped away. Instead, everything was now a state of mind, like a dream or sentiment. Memories flashed before me, and emotions filled my heart, all of it arbitrary and fleeting. The face of a young woman flickered forth in my mind's eye. She had golden hair and a lovely face. She gave me a holiday smile before fading away into the void. I waded in inertness; my mind dull. I don't know how long this went on, but at last my wits returned.

***

When they had, I found that I was swimming in a cold puddle of mud within a small ring of trees, rain pouring down on me. It was still nighttime, and as I sat up, it was clear that I was in a part of the countryside that didn't look familiar. The grubby foothills were less lively than any other part of the realm. The grass was sodden and pickle in color with a ruddy sky. Beside the knolls laid a single path, paved in stone, with mustard paint striped down the center. There were no stars shining, nor did any birds sing.

I brought myself to my feet, allowing the sludge to drip off. As I stood shivering, an internal urge, like preparing for a sneeze, came over me. My stomach twisted before a sapphire light darted from my chest into the sky. I was trying to understand what was happening when a pair of beaming lights shined from atop the hill in front of me. There was a silver cart with neon yellow lines along its doors. It was as big as a fomorian, with rubber wheels and glowing eyes. I watched as the thing crawled through the granite path, stopping a stone's throw away from the ring I hid in. Suddenly, torches of blue flashed from on top of the iron wagon.

"Hey there friend," said a thick voice from a gap in the cart's side, "need a hand?" I studied the stranger for a moment. He had all the makings of free folk with his peppered mustache, funny brimmed cap, and bright yellow vest that read *Garda*.

"Uh," I hummed, "yeah. That would be nice." There was a distant crack of thunder that bellowed through the sky. "Before I do though, tell me this. What court do you serve?"

The stranger gave a puzzled look, his cheeks puffed, and his lips pursed. "What?"

"Your court," I said more clearly. "Which season do you serve?"

The stranger continued to stare at me. Then with the same tone that he'd spoken in before he repeated, "What?" *Perhaps there was a language barrier.*

"Are you Summer Court?" I asked loudly. The man looked me over. I was dripping with mud and slightly trembling. My decorative clothing and cloak had been caked in earth, concealing my autumn tunic.

"I like fishing in the spring," he said with a shrug of his shoulders.

"Okay, cool. I'm Autumn, but I'm not like most of my kind. I like the Spring court." The man furrowed his brows. "Now, if you don't mind asking me my riddle, I'll happily accept your assistance." The rumble of the man's cart continued to growl. He gawped in my direction, one hand over a round wheel near his chest and the other planted on his temple as if he'd been suffering from a headache.

"Jaysus," he cursed. After a drawn-out moment, the wild sidhe turned his attention back to me, squinting through the curtains of rain. "Listen," he said with resolve, "it's bucketing, and clearly you've had a few too many. Let me get you to a room so you can get yourself a kip. I can help you find a ride to wherever you need to go in the morning."

I contemplated his offer. I wasn't very trusting now, but desperation is a funny thing. I was cold, miserable, and confused. I needed some time to get my head straight. I wished three times that this was all part of Father's plan. If not, I was doomed.

"I accept your offer Mister …." I paused in hopes that he'd offer his common name.

"Friendly," he grunted with a half-smile before leaning over to the other side of his cart and pushing open a side door. "Officer Friendly."

I navigated through the dark and climbed inside his carriage. There was a cozy draft of heat pouring from a vent. Officer Friendly reached over to me cautiously, stretching a long rope over my chest as I shut the door. Before I could refute, Officer Friendly smiled, tobacco lodged in his teeth.

"Safety first," he insisted while latching the belt. "Now lad, relax and I'll have you in between some sheets in no time."

"I'm Adair," I offered, "and I appreciate everything you're doing for me." Officer Friendly nodded as he grabbed at the wheel in front of him. With a kick from his foot, he sent the carriage moving forward along the stone road. I watched from the glass in front of me as we cantered with alarming speed. Then it hit me. This wasn't a carriage. *It was damn a car.*

"Um, Officer Friendly," I said in my calmest tone, "what inn are you taking me to?"

"Oh, it's just outside the Ring of Kerry," he said gaily as he steered the wheel of the cart. "My cousin owns it. It's been in our family for generations. The Bleeding Wolf Inn," he carried on through a smile, causing my innards to twist. "The best place in Killarney, if not all of Ireland for suckin' down diesel."

Chapter 6

My mind continued to stir. The pond must have sent me to the land of the Firbolg. I was back to where it all started. I cycled through what I knew about Earth, separating facts from the fiction. After all, most of what I'd known was what I read in comics. Uncle had mentioned Ireland, as well as a bleeding wolf. *Did he know I'd end up here? Could I trust his intentions?* Ultimately, it was his betrayal that forced Father's confession. Then it hit me. I'd been so distracted by the day's chaos that I never really contemplated Father's fate. He had said that he would forfeit his life, but not to the courts. Instead, he insisted that he'd surrender it to his son. *Me.* Father wasn't in hiding. He'd sacrificed himself, bequeathing his mantle of power to me to aid in my escape. He was … *gone.*

Tears welled up. My lungs filled with fire and I couldn't help from sobbing. Officer Friendly gave me a quick glance from the corner of his eye. I could tell that he wanted nothing to do with my grief. I watched from outside the car window for what seemed like an eternity, tears still fogging my vision as we drew into a village. There were strange stone homes, tarnished road markers and glowing signs along every street corner. *Light bulbs.* As we pulled up to one of the dirty stone houses, I noticed a sign hanging over the entrance, a lone wolf with a spear driven through its backside. *The Bleeding Wolf Inn* read the words above it. Officer Friendly parked his car next to several others before escorting me out. He gave me a moment to collect myself before we went inside.

This wasn't how it went in the comics. The hero never melted down or began crying. No. They acknowledged their circumstances and moved on to become stronger. They used their new found powers to exact vengeance on evil doers and help those who needed it. So, why couldn't I do the same? Why was it that after wishing for adventure for so long, I now detested it?

A much-needed blanket of warmth swathed over my damp body as we entered the inn. Clinking glasses, mumbling voices, and a crackling fire drowned out the guitar music in the background. There was a half dozen browbeaten Firbolg sipping on foamy drinks. All at once they stopped what they were doing and looked up. On the patron's side of the bar was a ragtag motley of men in dirty clothes. Next to them was a balding fellow in a long coat who seemed to be talking to himself, and a blue ghost with a flat cap. At the server's side of the bar was a middle-aged chubby woman pouring drinks. She smiled when she saw us.

"Liam," she greeted, hurrying over. Officer Friendly held out his arms. He gave a tight hug and laugh as the barkeep entered his embrace.

"Ah Brigid," said Officer Friendly as he released his grip, "how's my favorite cousin?"

Brigid slapped him on the chest. "Oh, don't be a hard neck," she teased. "If I were your favorite, then you'd come and visit more often, wouldn't you? I could use your help with the likes of these hooligans," she added while pointing towards the men drinking at the bar. The two of them smiled before hugging one another again. I watched as the tall ghost inspected us from his stool. He had a plane face, yet every crease along his nose and brow furrowed. "And who is your muddy friend here?" Brigid inquired.

I was broken up about Father and being on Earth, but I knew that Officer Friendly already thought that I was nuts. Not wanting to draw any more attention to myself, especially with Grandmother and Liadan still somewhere out there, I decided to try and blend in as much as possible, which was going to be difficult for a guy who hadn't been on Earth for centuries. What would Clark Kent do?

"Adair," I said as warmly as possible, stretching out my arms to embrace Brigid as Officer Friendly had. The woman gasped as I hugged her.

"Oh my," she laughed as I pulled away. "You're a friendly one aren't you?" A line of slop from my clothes drew a wet line along her apron.

"Forgive me," I apologized. Brigid gave a wave of her hand while swatting at her apron.

"No worries lad," she laughed. "It's just dirt."

"I found this strange fella hiding in the Fairy Fort near Ross Castle," said Officer Friendly. "He must have gotten langered on a hike." He leaned in towards Brigid and whispered, but my keen ears picked up on it. "I think he's Canadian." Brigid looked me over one more time.

"What do you say Brigid," he asked while rubbing her back, "can you hold him up for the night?" Brigid considered it for a moment, taking a deep breath.

"Of course," she exhaled. "I love strays. I'll put him up next to the American lasses who are hunting for ghosts. Such nonsense," she muttered to herself, "believing in spooks". I turned my head in consideration to the spirit. The phantom put his hand to his temple and shook his head. I turned back to my hostess.

"Thanks Lady Brigid," I said with a bow of my head. "That's very nice of you. I'll owe you a boon."

"Oh," she said with delight. "Fancy that, *Lady* Brigid. We might have to keep this one around Liam. Now," she continued while tugging at my arm, "let's get you cleaned up. I have a few of my late husband's things stowed away. You look about his size."

"Thank you love," said Officer Liam Friendly. "I'll check in on him in the morning."

"Not staying?" she hissed while taking my hand and dragging me up a set of nearby stares.

"Sorry my dear," he apologized as he tightened his coat before opening the inn's door. "Still on duty."

Officer Liam Friendly tipped his cap and then headed into the storms. Brigid's thoughts must have frozen her in place, as a strained stare locked her eyes on the entrance. She sighed and then guided me up the steps into a hallway with a half dozen numbered doors. We entered 1A, where a tawny room with a single window awaited. There was a scruffy bed with stacks of sheets folded across it, and boxes scattered along the floor. Brigid began clearing the blankets before entering a white side chamber. There was an ivory seat and curtained closet. She turned a knob inside so that a fountain of water poured from its walls. Steam began to mist within the cool chamber as the indoor fountain rained down onto a drain in the floor.

"1A is usually my storage room," Brigid disclosed. "Apparently, it's where I keep stowaways as well." I tried to smile, but my nerves were too frayed. Brigid seemed to read my face and frowned before hurrying towards the doorway. "There's towels hanging in the bathroom. I'll go get some of Sean's clothes. I don't have any sweaters," she said in consideration, "so you'll have to take one of his old jackets. Once you're settled, come down for tea."

I was trying to use whatever guile I had in me, but every time I'd opened my mouth so far ended in disaster. So instead, I donated another quick bow of my head.

"Thanks Lady Brigid."

"Ha," she snorted while leaving the room. "*Lady* Brigid he says. This one is gone in the head—a charmer but gone in the head." And with that she closed the door.

I walked over to the shower, touching the fountain a few times in order test it. The waters were warm. I unrobed and entered, letting the stream clean the caked mud from my skin. As it did, a volcano of fear and anguish surfaced from inside me. I leaned my head along the wall and began to cry again.

It took some time to get completely clean, but once I was done scrubbing off the muck and had calmed myself, I turned the knob to stop the water. I toweled off and entered the bedroom once more. Strewn across the bed were fresh blankets and a bundle of clothing. Brigid must have slipped back in as she'd warned. The pile of clothes reminded me of my last morning in Havgan, Grandmother's handpicked garments waiting on my table, followed by Fergal's delivery of my Father's cloak. *Was this all going to plan, and if so, whose?* I tried to shake off the thought knowing that I wasn't in the right state of mind and began going through my new clothes.

There was a pair of sturdy denim trousers, a white cotton shirt and walnut leather shoes. At the bottom of the pile was a slim fit brown leather jacket, worn, with a short neck collar, breast pockets, and thin shoulder flaps that made the coat appear slightly soldierly. I dressed myself in the dry clothing, and then, remembering that there was a mirror in the bathing room, hurried to inspect myself. It was the first time I'd seen my mirrored reflection in a long time, and after wiping the mist from the surface, I noticed that I looked more like a Firbolg already. The ghost from downstairs, who rose from the floor behind me, seemed to take notice as well.

"You almost look as good as I did in them," said the spirit as he hung his head over my shoulder. He was tall and thin, with a broad jaw and big ears that pointed forward.

"Thanks," I replied. "You must be Sean, Lady Brigid's husband?" The specter looked at me uncertainly.

"Why aren't you afraid of me?" he challenged. His question seemed a little silly.

"Why would I be?"

"Well, for starters I'm dead."

"And?"

"Well, that tends to frighten people."

I gave a light chuckle. "Why?"

"Hmm," he hummed, "I never cared to consider it." There was a pause while the figure rubbed at his translucent chin. "I guess because the dead aren't supposed to mingle with the living."

"Ha, maybe on Earth," I said good-humoredly while flapping my long bangs out of my eyes, "but where I'm from it's a pretty normal."

The ghost floated over to a wall cabinet within the washing room, removing a small metal cylinder and floating it over to me. It took him sometime to balance the tin container over to where I was standing, but once he had, he placed it in my hand. "Here," he said helpfully, "try this for your hair." I twisted off the top and found ivory putty similar in consistency to clay. "So then," he said while pointing at the paste and then pointing to my mane, "where are you from?"

"Sorry Sean, but how do I know I can trust you?" I tested, still a bit on edge.

"Not sure," he said thoughtfully. "Once again, I never considered why someone wouldn't." I smeared my fingers into the hair cream, taking a nip and spreading it across my scalp. "You'll need far more than that," he said after a quick assessment. I dabbed another large glob in my hands and then smeared it across my strands of orange. "I guess I have no way of making you trust me, but I've never met anyone who can freely see me before. It's a bit exciting." He tapped on his chin. "Perhaps, if you find it in your heart to confide in me, I can help you?"

"How can you help me?"

"Well for starters," he said while flying over to my side so that I could focus on my reflection while speaking with him, "might I advise that you stop speaking like you work for a Renaissance Faire."

"But that's how I speak good sir," I said defensively.

"Aye, exactly."

"Fair enough."

I had to remind myself that this ghost wasn't sidhe, but Firbolg. Humans weren't supposed to be as shifty as our kind. I could imagine being pretty lonely sitting at the tavern each night, hoping someone might get a glimpse of him. Maybe a little trust wouldn't hurt. Besides, what did I have to lose? It wouldn't be long before Grandmother's hounds found me.

"I'm from The Lands of Change," I confessed. The ghost didn't seem to understand. "You know," I said hopefully, "The home of the sidhe."

The ghost's jaw dropped nearly four sizes too wide. Apparently, not even the dead believed in us. "You mean to tell me," he said with excitement, "you're a fairy?"

"Well," I considered, "I'm a half child, so half-fairy." I paused to think about what happened during the assembly. "Although my Father kind of lives inside me now, so, I'm not quite sure exactly sure."

"My Grandmother used to tell me stories about the Good People, but I thought they were just tall tales."

"No Sean," I said while standing my gloppy hair up like a spike, "we're as real as the air you breathe." Sean gave me a slight frown. "Sorry."

"It's all right," he replied. "So how come I don't see your kind more often?"

"We're not supposed to consort with your kind any longer."

"Why not?" he begged. I gave him a suspect look.

"I'll tell you what," I said while trying to untangle my hair from the horn I'd sculpted. "Help me fix my hair problem here and I'll tell you all about it."

"Of course," he said excitedly. "Any requests?"

I shrugged. "Something appealing I suppose."

"Appealing aye?" he said while stabbing his cold ghostly fingers into my scalp. "I think I might have just the thing." He started to shove my bangs forward. "Tell me, has the legend of Elvis reached the fairyland yet?"

Sean wanted to know everything there was about The Lands of Change from the courts to their tendencies. Like cutting off the head of a hydra, any explanation I had only led to two more questions. Finally, just as I'd finished the story on how I'd fell through the pond, a knocking came at the door.

"Adair," called out Brigid, "are you all right in there dear?"

"Damn," fizzed Sean, "it's my wife. Don't say anything strange." He tapped at his chin again.

"What should I say?" I whispered.

"Just tell her you'll be down in a moment," he hummed, "and that you're feeling much better."

"I'll be down in a moment," I called out. "And I'm feeling much better."

"Oh good," Brigid said in relief through the door. "I thought a shower might help." There was a pause. "A few of the bogtrotters are eager to meet you. They can't stop blathering about the mud man. When should we expect you down?"

"Tell her you'll be down shortly," instructed Sean. "You're just getting dressed."

"Thank you so much Brigid. I'll be down shortly," I continued. "I'm just getting dressed."

"How long do you think?" asked Brigid.

"Janey Mack," yelled Sean.

"Janey Mack," I shouted in repetition.

"No," Sean winced. "That wasn't meant for repeating." There was silence on the other side of the door. "Uh, sorry my la ..." Sean shook his head. "Sorry Brigid. I'll be down soon."

"All right then," Brigid surrendered, uncertainty in her voice. "I'll have some sandwiches ready for you." The sounds of short but heavy footsteps walking along the hall and down the stairs let us know that she had yielded.

"She's a splendid woman," Sean defended as he floated near the door, "just a bit lonely. I guess that's why I'm still here, you know, to keep an eye on her."

"Well Sean," I said while taking a look at my freshly shaped hair, "unless there's any other immediate questions, it seems we're needed downstairs. Shall we?"

"Yes," said Sean in agreement. "But try to listen to me before answering anyone. I'll make sure that you don't drop the ball."

"I'm hoping that's a metaphor?"

"It is," Sean confessed. "It means that I'll make sure you don't put your foot in your mouth."

I gave a puzzled look before heading the door. Upon arriving downstairs, I noticed that the music had gone silent, and that the handful of men at the bar were now huddled in a circle. They stared at me as I reached the last step. Brigid, who was the only one smiling, came from behind the bar and escorted me to an empty stool.

"Well, don't you clean up well," she commended. "You look like a ginger haired James Dean. Jimmy," she called out to one of the men at the bar, "doesn't he look like James Dean?"

"Huh," grunted the man.

"Oh yes," Brigid continued. "Sean adored that sort of thing. Elvis, leather jackets, motorcycles." I gave a brief glance at her husband who nodded with pride. "Now come with me," she continued while shoving me down into the tall chair. "I have a nice couple of sandwiches to help sober ya' up."

"Tell her she's an angel," Sean jumped in.

"You're an angel," I echoed.

"Aw, my Sean use to say that," she frowned. "Now, I'll go get the kettle. You stay right here." Brigid ambled through the doors leading to the kitchen. I hung my head and inspected the sandwiches staring at me.

"Would you please stop having me say things that remind her of you," I whispered. "She's going to break into tears."

"Say something lad?" called out one of the bigger men amongst the huddle. The group of red nosed, grimy villagers were glaring at me now. I had to remember to be careful, as sidhe were known for stirring up emotions in Firbolg.

"Easy now," warned Sean. "That's Hugh. He's a moldy bastard who loves a good fight."

"No, I didn't say anything," I squeaked before picking up a sandwich and stuffing it into my face. *Not what Batman would do.* I could taste the flavor of tomato, but everything else was far too salty to make out. I tried not to gag before swallowing a mouthful, gathering my thoughts as I chewed. Then, just as the stillness of the bar had settled, a shrill voice broke the silence.

"Good evening young man," hooted someone in my ear. I'd nearly jumped out of my skin before spinning around in my chair. The balding man in the long coat I'd seen earlier was now at the barstool next to me. He was middle aged with frizzy gray hair around his temples that surrounded an otherwise bald head. He had a scruffy short beard to match and large saucer eyes and puckered lips. He dug into his coat pocket. "Now isn't this a lucky meeting."

"Oh no," Sean sighed.

"I can tell by the twinkle in your eyes," the stranger continued, "that you're in search of something."

"I am," I agreed.

"And what is the name of this *something*?" the stranger inquired.

"I'm not sure," I confessed. I knew that Father had a plan, and that he wanted me to follow it, but because of the Rule of Three, he wasn't able to tell me any of it. I was wandering blind.

"Well, what's in a name?" he asked rhetorically. "Mine is Eamon, but I really can't stand it."

Eamon huh? What were the chances that this was Uncle's Earthly contact? To put it bluntly, there are no coincidences with fairies. I contemplated if this was a trap, and in preparation, balled my fist underneath the bar. "Well, I think I know what it is you're searching for, and I have it right here in my pocket."

Sean slapped at his forehead, before flying through Eamon's head with his own. "Don't listen to him. He's a con artist and cheat. I don't know why Brigid still lets him in here."

"And what exactly do you have there Eamon?" I probed. Eamon pulled out a silver square with a small pane of glass fused along its face.

"This my friend," he said in a showy voice, "is the latest in phone technology. It texts, e-mails, maps your destination, plays videos and calls people without interruption. I guarantee the best signal with this beauty. Here," he spat while pushing the mechanism in my hands, "I insist you have it."

"Well, that could be useful," I said while holding up the latest in phone technology up to the light and inspecting it. "Thank you."

"Of course," Eamon replied before standing up and starting to walk away. But before he'd taken the first step, he quickly spun back around to face me. "And, it's because you're such a fine young lad, that I'm only going to ask you to pay me what I bought it for."

"Sorry," I apologized. "I don't carry Firbolg currency."

The pack of men at the bar laughed to one another, mean smiles across their faces. But Eamon wasn't smiling. His salesman's face bled sober, fear replacing confidence.

"What was that you said?" he asked with a shaky voice.

I thought about what I might have said. Then in a moment of clarity, I realized that I'd accidentally used the term Firbolg. Eamon recognized it. It was no secret that sidhe were sly and nasty, mostly because … well, they were. If Eamon had dealt with the likes of Uncle, then he'd surely be familiar with the destruction they could cause. Convinced that I had the upper hand, I decided to use his fear to my advantage.

"Trust your ears, Eamon," I warned. I didn't mean to, but as I leaned in, a sourceless breeze blew through the inn, propelling napkins and paper onto the floor. "Uncle says you owe him a boon, and that it's time for me to collect."

"Tuatha Dé Danann," Eamon mumbled as he hurried towards the main door. "You tell Mr. Goodfellow that I don't owe him anything," he said while prying the entrance's doorknob, letting the rain slip inside the tavern. "He tricked me," Eamon cursed as he ran through the threshold. "He tricked me." Then with a slam of the door, he was gone. *Clearly, I wasn't the only one who didn't trust Uncle any longer.*

"Well," I gasped while shaking my head towards Sean, "it appears that not everyone thinks fairies are tall tales."

Chapter 7

Long ago, when pigs were called swine and stories were still told by the fire, there was a humble town called Killarney. Now this isn't the town that people know today—*oh no dearies*. This was before widened roads, luxury hotels, and golf outings. This was when the town thrived on strong backs, humble hearts and ancient tradition. It was a time when buttermilk was left on doorsteps for the *Good People,* and songs were played for them in the fields of Ross Castle.

Now amongst the many Killarney townsfolk was a boy with patchy pants and undone hair named Sean. Born the seventh son of the seventh son, Sean was said to be favored by stars. But he didn't see himself as favored. Indeed, he felt the opposite. That's because ever since Sean was a boy, he had premonitions of his own death. They always began the same and ended just as unwell. Sean saw himself ten hands taller and older than his father. In his mysterious dream, he coughed up smoke upon the lap of a solemn angel within a wolf's den. The angelic figure let Sean drink her tears while she pet his head until he breathed his last breath.

Now as time went by and Sean became older, he began to have his dreams less often and worried about them very little. In his mind he resolved that *if it happened it happened,* and there was no use worrying. This was all good and well, as Sean had more immediate things to care for than mysterious premonitions. He was barely a man now and was expected to provide for himself. So, Sean took to cleaning chimneys in order to make a decent wage. He traveled door to door through Killarney offering his services for a fair price. Before long, he had enough for an old car that sputtered black fumes and room of his own that he rented from his cousin. And that's how Sean lived, and happy was he, or at least so he thought.

It was the first day of October and Sean stayed busy cleaning chimneys after Autumn's cold first kiss. Upon heading to a local inn known as The Bleeding Wolf however, Sean's stars decided to prove their favor for him. For a woman as old as he answered the door. She had eyes like a saint and the character of an angel. Her name was Brigid, and she was the innkeeper's daughter. The two sparked an interest in one another and met often. Even after Brigid went away to nursing school, the two wrote and called so much that the mail person's shoes wore thin, and the phone lines were busier than worker bees. Since Sean had made himself the best chimney sweep in Killarney, he was used by Brigid's father often. And because Sean's stars kept an eye out for their seventh son, Brigid always happened to visit home during Sean's cleanings.

Then one day, time came to collect its dues, and Brigid's father became ill. Brigid was forced to return home to help her mother care for her father's failing body. And though a part of her heart was heavy for her father's fate, Sean made sure he lifted the other half up to the best of his abilities. He lent a hand at inn, keeping the nails in the wood and supplies in the pantry while Brigid cared for her Father. And at night, when everyone was asleep, Brigid and Sean spent their nights together under the stars—the same stars that continued to due Sean favors. For a year and a day after Brigid came home, Sean begged for her hand in marriage. And much to his hopes, Brigid agreed to be his until death did them part. The two were married at the stairs of inn so that Brigid's Father could attend.

Not shortly after tragedy struck, and Brigid's Father died. The death caused Brigid's mother to move away and live with her sisters. Brigid inherited the Bleeding Wolf Inn, and together with Sean, they moved into room 1A. The Bleeding Wolf Inn was now their home and livelihood. For years the two cared for the keep and in return it cared for them, too. Sean cooked for the locals while Brigid poured them ales. Sean smoked with the town folk while Brigid gossiped with the locals. It was all that Sean could ask for.

But Sean's stars were running out of favors. Soon an itchy throat became a cough, and Sean was short of breath. After a visit to the doctor, it was deemed that Sean's lungs were black and failing. Brigid was devastated, but for Sean, it was expected. After all, his premonitions had told him his fate long ago. And on a day when mirrors didn't cast reflections, Sean began to die. For the rest of his days, he lay in 1A, coughing on Brigid's lap as she wet his lips with sopping tissue. Brigid stroked Sean's head, her eyes never going dry, until he breathed his last breath. And although Brigid felt alone, Sean never left her. After all, true love is a ghost, unseen but always present.

Chapter 8

"Eamon wait," I called out as I chased the shaggy old man through the rain. I'd just dried off, and the bitter shower was already making me miserable. Eamon ran to a schlocky looking car, jabbing a key into its side door. "Wait, Eamon, I'm sorry," I cried. "I was bluffing." Eamon continued to stab at the keyhole, but his shaky hands were working against him. I caught up, grabbing him by the shoulder. He spun in a clumsy half circle, throwing his arms up in a silly pose.

"Don't try me fairy," he spat timidly while chopping at the air, "I'm a black belt in Taekwon-Fu."

"What?" I asked through a repressed smile. Eamon swung his stiffened hand at my neck like an axe.

Crack!

Eamon grabbed at his fingers with a pain-ridden grimace. I felt the pressure of the blow, but there was no pain.

"Bloody hell," squealed Eamon as he cradled his hand, "I think you broke my fingers."

"Eamon, listen, I'm sorry. My Uncle didn't send me. I was trying to scare you."

"Like hell he didn't," Eamon hollered while trying to wiggle his fingers. "He's always trying to trick me."

"He tricks everyone," I said flatly. "It's kind of his thing."

"Well, better to understand a little than to misunderstand a lot. I don't know much about fairies, but I know they're always saying one thing, but meaning another. In fact, how can I be sure that you're not Mr. Goodfellow?"

"Ask yourself this," my voice raised, "if I were Uncle, wouldn't I have gone about this with more guile?" Eamon considered, bobbing his head back in forth. "Now, I don't know what Uncle had done to you, but I do know what he's done to *me*. He's a traitor, and my Father is dead because of it."

"Let's say that I believe you," Eamon said suspiciously, "what do you want with me? I don't stand a chance against your Uncle."

Just then, a car pulled up along the inn. Eamon and I went mute as a pair of young ladies with jackets shielding their heads hopped out from the back and retreated to the tavern. Once they'd made it inside, the car drove away. I returned my attention to Eamon. Even if the tapping rain muffled our conversation, this was a bad place to talk about fairy matters.

"Can we talk somewhere a little more private," I suggested, "and perhaps more dry?"

"Care to have a seat in my office?" asked Eamon in a calmer tone.

"Your what?"

"My car," he groaned while pointing at a vehicle behind me.

"Oh. Yes, please." I slogged through the wet lawn towards the passenger side door and hurriedly entered. The smells of tobacco radiated from the seats that were stained by coffee and singed with burn marks. Eamon jabbed his car key into a hole near the driving wheel, causing the vehicle to rumble with life.

"It'll take a moment to warm up mind you," he said while huffing hot breath on his hands, "but we should have some heat soon." We sat inside the car for some time, listening to the raindrops as they defiantly escaped their cloudy master. After a few moments, Eamon turned some nobs and heat poured from the outlets of the dashboard.

"Listen Eamon," I finally said, breaking the silence, "I can tell you hate Uncle just as much as I do. Unfortunately, I don't know how to get you to trust me without telling you the truth. So," I said with resolution, "that's just what I'm going to do."

"You're going to tell me everything about?"

"About who I am," I said while counting on my fingers, "where Uncle comes from, and whatever you want to know."

"I'm all ears."

It was a major risk to tell Eamon everything, from Father taking me to the fairy realm as a boy, to my grandmother's schemes. Most sidhe are secretive creatures, hoarding and trading information for other services. I'd hoped that my honesty would be enough to convince him that I wasn't like Uncle. He could trust me. While I wasn't as good of a storyteller as Uncle, I told a tale that started with *hello* and ended in *goodbye*. It was a story that I hoped was just good enough to get Eamon to pity my circumstances, but not enough to think I was too weak to help him. By the end, the car was warm, and the rain had slightly let up. I tried to read Eamon's body language. While he still seemed suspect, I could see from his loose posture and fifth lit cigarette that he'd managed to ease up, if not just a bit.

"So," I said after my longwinded account, "now you know everything about me. Please, can you help?" Eamon, who was now warming a hand on the vent, looked down the road. With his eyes still locked in their direction, he pointed towards the hills that lit up with every flash of lightning.

"I was peddling to some tourists by the fairy fort when I met Mr. Goodfellow," he lamented. "Your Uncle was a strange site, but as smooth as summer cherries when he flapped his damn lips. We started talking and before long, he'd convinced me that he was my fairy godfather. He said that in return for my mortal servitude, he could trade a bit of himself in me so that I never lost a wager. Cards, bones, you name it, he promised that so long as there was a profit on the line, I'd win." Eamon sighed. "Of course I agreed, and before long I was signing some fancy contract."

"And then what happened?"

"What happened was the bastard tricked me," he shouted. "While it was true that I couldn't lose a hand, no one in Killarney trusted me anymore. They always thought I was cheating 'em. It was as if I had Lucifer's aura around me. I was an outcast by my own people."

It was a classic sidhe ruse. Negotiate a contract that gives you the upper hand. It's why some fairy arrangements take centuries to barter. If Eamon ever wanted to cure himself of his curse, he'd need to consent to more terrible promises until he was practically Uncle's slave. As terrible as it was, the contract was also a risk on Uncle's part. A piece of Uncle, no matter how tiny, was now in Eamon. Technically, it made him responsible for Eamon's actions. A scheme began to form in my head.

"Eamon, I think I might be able to help you," I said confidently. "I can't interfere with your contact, but we may be able to use it to our advantage."

"In the words of my Mother when she met my dear old Dad, 'Give me what you got young man.'"

"If you promise to help me get revenge, I'll help release you from your contract."

"And how might I ask, do you plan on doing that?"

"It's complicated, but I have a plan. Get an axe and meet me back here before sunrise."

"A what?"

"An axe," I sighed. "You know, they cut down trees and split logs."

"Now listen here lad," Eamon demanded, "I take great pride in how modest I can be." I raised a brow. "But I think I'm going to need more. Before I go get you the weapon, you're going to murder me with, I'd like an explanation."

I pressed my hands to my eyes for a moment and massaged them. Working with Eamon was already becoming taxing. "Our worlds are closest at dusk and dawn. Come morning, you and I will have a visit to the fairy fort. Axe plus trees. You do the math."

"Ah," said Eamon with a little more understanding. "I see said the blind man."

"Now it's been a long day, and I still need to speak with Sean."

"Who?" Eamon asked curiously.

"Never mind. Just make sure that you're here before dawn with that axe. And if anyone suspicious comes along your path, run. I know enough to tell that the courts will send some of their own soon."

"But didn't you say time works differently where you're from."

"Exactly. I have no idea if the Queen's hounds will be here in five minutes or five years."

"Right then."

It had been an exhausting day, and although I wasn't sure how much time passed back home, the clock was ticking. If Liadan was clever, she'd get the courts permission before pursuing me. Then again, I didn't put it past Liadan to break the court's rules in hopes to kill me immediately. It's kind of her thing. I'd need someone to watch my back tonight, especially if I were going to get any rest. Luckily, I knew just the guy.

I entered *The Bleeding Wolf* in search of Sean. The once heavy atmosphere had completely changed. Instead of scowls and growls, the men of the inn were smiling and bumping mugs while surrounding the table nearest the fire. Amongst them, the two young ladies that I'd seen running side the inn were now seated, smothered in patron affection. One of the young women, a dark girl with short hair and thick framed glasses, could have easily been mistaken for Winter Court with her drab clothing. Contrary to her appearance, she was animated, singing with the men while slapping them on their backs. Her partner, who was quietly sharing a large wood chair with the woman with glasses, was something different all together.

Her honey colored locks cascaded down to her neck, a tiny braid capturing the wisps at her temple and tossed to the side of her thin face. She had sapphire eyes with a light splash of frost around them, and long elegant lashes. Her delicate features and clever smile hung beneath her button nose, giving her an almost ethereal quality. She wore a simple knitted sweater with a collection of charms, rings and necklaces along her arms and neck. Our eyes locked as I strode to my stool, causing her smile to grow larger. Time did me a favor and paused long enough for my heart to do a quick little summersault. I tried not to trip as I took a seat next to Sean at the bar. Brigid was pouring a new round of ales along a tray.

"Thank Mary and Joseph you're all right," Brigid said in relief. "I thought that Eamon had done something terrible to you. Not sure why I still let him in here."

"Oh, I'm okay," I said absentmindedly, keeping my gaze locked on the young woman. The summer flower was conversing with one of the men, but occasionally glanced in my direction. Each time our eyes met, sugar wine poured through me. I must have been hit by Thor's Hammer because my mood leapt from pure hatred for Grandmother to pure desire for some strange girl I'd never met. *Some beautiful, strange girl.* I took a second to consider whether my newly inherited sidhe abilities had come with newly inherited sidhe emotions? And more importantly perhaps, lust. Unpredictable, impulsive—these were the ways of the free folk. I didn't think it worked like that, but then again, what other explanation was there? I tried to put the thought in the back of my mind.

"He's not so bad," I mumbled to Brigid.

"Eamon? Like hell he's not," Brigid warned before lifting the tray of drinks and walking them towards the group by the fire. "That man is crooked as a witch's teeth. Everyone knows he's a cheat."

Sean watched me stare. "The lass with the glasses is Lidia," he said with a grin. "But I'm supposin' that you've got eyes on her friend." I smiled uncontrollably. "Ah, yes. That's Evie."

Evie. Whoever said that humans couldn't compare in beauty to the fairies never looked at this woman. I'd never seen anyone so lovely. Her quiet laugh colored the room. The subtle way she rubbed her earlobe forced my jaw to slacken. And that smile—*oh, that smile.* I'd dreamt about dozens of comic book women as a boy, but none of them paled in comparison to Evie. It was perhaps only a few seconds after Brigid had returned from the table, and Evie and I had gone on our fifth date in my head, that a heavy stomping came plodding next to me.

Sean tried to warn me. "Adair, Adair, heads up lad."

"Don't you know that it's rude to gawp?" growled a heavy voice breathing above me. I turned my head to find Hugh, his strapping chest and bulging arms ripping from his oil stained work shirt. "Even if it is at a fine thing like that." Hugh reeked of sweat and ale. I could tell that he was looking for trouble, as his hands were already balled into fists. I reminded myself of what Uncle had told me. Human minds were feeble. I needed to avoid using Father's gifts, especially if I didn't want to draw any more attention to myself. However, it didn't mean that I was going to allow myself to look like a coward in front of Evie.

"Sorry," I apologized, "but I don't speak buffoon." Hugh's eyes widened. "Say, who let you out of your cage anyway?"

Unfortunately, Hugh didn't have such a good sense of humor. He grabbed me by my collar and began punching my head. *So much for that approach.* Though the blows caused my brain to rattle, there was no pain. I wondered if perhaps Father's gifts were in play. If, like other fairy, I could only be harmed by cold iron and special magics. Eager to help me test this theory, Hugh lifted me above his head and hurled me over the bar.

"Wee," I shouted as I flew into a row of bottles stacked across the tavern counter. Brigid screamed in terror. I pushed off the floor, staggering to my feet. As I did, Hugh closed the distance, his teeth grinding as he reached for my neck. But before he could wrap his hulking hands around me, a sudden sizzling noise came from his backside. Hugh's body froze, though his eyes widened and watered.

"Gah," he finally belted as a light waft of smoke came from his spine. Hugh retreated towards the tavern door, a singed hole and brand mark burned into the center of his back. I hadn't noticed at first, but Evie was standing where Hugh once had been, a smoldering fire poker gripped in her hand. As Hugh ran out into the rain, his mates chased after him, Brigid trailing close behind. Once the men exited, Brigid slammed the entrance shut, locking a brass bolt.

"That's it," she growled as she stared at the broken bottles, "we're closed." She shook her head in frustration as she made her way to a broom closet and removed a mop. "Damn gurriers."

Evie, who was now closer than she'd ever been before, gave me a glance over before brushing some glass off my shoulder. "Are you all right?" she asked.

I wanted to say something considerably debonair, but as I went to lean on the bar all that came onto my tongue was, "My hero."

Chapter 9

As Uncle use to say, *A closed mouth gathers no foot*. I wasn't sure why Brigid was being so kind, but I wasn't about to ask. Not only had she donated me clothes and a room for the night, but she also insisted that Lidia, Evie, and I sit and enjoy the last of the fire while she cleaned up Hugh's mess. I was eternally grateful. Evie invited me to her table where a round of unspoiled ales were eager to be drunk.

"Come have a drink with us," she said as she grabbed my hand and walked me over. "You earned it." I sat down on the wobbly chair and tried not to look like a fish out of water. "This is my best friend Lidia," Evie added, unbeknownst that I'd already been introduced by a ghost. Lidia finished her pint before wiggling her fingers at me. "I'm Evelyn by the way, but almost everyone just calls me Evie."

"Adair," I greeted. "But almost everyone just calls me Adair." Evie's mouth went sideways, and she blinked several times. It framed an expression that said she thought I was teasing her. *Damn, I was already screwing it up.* Sean floated over, pulling up his ghostly sleeves.

"All right young fairy boy," he said as he cleared his throat, "you're going to need my help to not muck this one up. Luckily for you, I was quite the ladies' man before Brigid." Relief swam over me. Although I didn't respond as Evie handed me a glass, I was thankful for Sean's aid.

"So Adair," Lidia called out after a tiny burp, "why is a stud like you getting roughed up in a town like this?"

"Lidia," Evie scolded, "would you stop embarrassing yourself?"

Sean gave a chuckle. "Oh, I like her." He glided between the two young ladies, rubbing his ghostly blue chin. "Okay, let's play it smooth. Tell Lidia that there's nothing wrong with being a little curious."

"Oh, that's okay," I said politely, trying to slip in a sincere laugh. "There's nothing wrong with being a little curious, Lidia."

"Now mention that you're doing a little research on your ancestry," Sean continued. "Tourists do it in Killarney all the time."

"Actually," I added while taking a sip of the ale. I'd never had spirits before, and the bitter flavor left much to be desired. "I'm doing a little research on my ancestry."

"No way," shouted Lidia as she slapped the countertop. Her words were slurred, but my ears noticed an accent similar to Evie's. It was light, fluent, and a bit nasally. "That's why we're here, too. Evie is tracing her family tree." Sean puffed out his see-through chest proudly, as if everything was going as planned. "So naturally she took her bestest friend ever. Apparently," Lidia continued after taking a mouthful from a new ale, "Evie's dad grew up here." Evie gave a nod as she tucked her hair behind her ear.

"Huh," Sean muttered, "I wonder if I know him? Ask what her Father's name is?"

"Really?" I said while changing my focus to Evie. "What's your Father's name if you don't mind me asking?"

"It's Tom," said Evie. "Tom O'Kane."

"Ah, Tom," Sean snorted. "I trained him in hurling. I wonder how he likes the States?" I turned to Sean and blinked several times. "Oh right. Tell her that the O'Kane family has quite a bit of history here. Her grandparents helped organize the sanctuary that protects Killarney's parks and wildlife."

I turned my head back to Evie, shifting my weight. She was staring at me with a half-smile that could repel storms. My lips involuntarily returned the favor. "Now that you mention it, I came across your grandparents' name in my research. Did you know they helped coordinate the sanctuary that protects local sights and wildlife?"

"That's what we heard," spat Lidia before Evie could speak. "Some of the locals say Evie's grandparents were trying to keep the *Good People* happy." Lidia walled her hand along her mouth. "That means fairies," she winked. "Rumor has it that if you tick off the fairies, they'll make the waters recede overnight." I made note. Lidia hiccupped. The gulp of air must have brought a new idea, because her mouth twitched before giving a lopsided grin. "Evie," said Lidia, "maybe we can get Adair to help us out?"

"Lidia," sighed Evie, "you're drunk."

"That's true," Lidia agreed. "But it doesn't mean I'm not right. We need a guide. In fact, we've needed a guide since we got here. Maybe Adair could help speed things up."

"Well," said Evie shyly, "no. I mean," she corrected herself, "I'm sure he has things to do. I wouldn't want to trouble him."

"I'd love to," I said a bit too enthusiastically. Sean slapped at his ethereal forehead in frustration. "I mean, like I said before, I'm doing research, too." I tried to calm myself and recover. "I'm sure I've come across some information that would help you. I'd be happy to share it. Maybe we could even learn a few new things together."

Sean pushed his open palms forward as if trying to talk me off a ledge. "Easy now," he petitioned. "You might be biting off more than you can chew."

"Great," said Lidia while raising her glass. "We're headed to the fairy fort tomorrow. Perhaps you could come with?"

Oh no, not the fairy fort. The plan was to have Eamon cut down the patch since it was sidhe property. Defacing it would get Uncle in trouble with the courts, as it would be *his* mortal servant who'd committed the crime. Fairy justice was nothing short of merciless. With Uncle out of the way, I could concentrate on Grandmother. But, if there was no tree, there was no Evie. And at the moment, I wanted there to be Evie. I'd need to come up with another plan.

"Sure that would be great," I said as affably as possible.

"Cool," said Lidia as she swayed to the music playing in her head. Evie continued to stare at me as she fiddled with her bracelet. I couldn't tell if it was something I should welcome or if she was staring because I was coming off odder than a wingless bird. "That is," I paused, "if you don't mind of course?"

"No, I'd like that," she answered quickly. "I mean, it would be nice to have a native helping us."

"Ha," Sean laughed. "She thinks you're from Killarney."

"Great," I said while ignoring Sean. "I'm in room 1A." Sean's face went sober, his gaze focused on staircase that led to the inn rooms. "If you'd like," I invited, "just come and fetch me tomorrow. We'll go together."

"Don't sound too desperate," Sean butted in, shaking out from his spell. "Tell her something about squeezing her into your busy schedule." I brushed him off.

"Besides," I said with a playful smirk, "I think I owe you my life."

Evie snorted. Finally, she'd liked something *I* said. Maybe I didn't have to filter myself as much as I'd thought. Maybe I just needed to be me.

"Well then," she said as she chewed at her lip, "it's a date. Well," she stopped herself, "not a date, but, well, you know I mean."

"You know something," said Lidia as she leaned on the table, as if ready to take a nap. "You two would make a cute couple."

"Lidia," Evie barked. My stomach twisted. I looked towards my feet. I could see from the corners of my eyes that Evie was giving Lidia a look that could melt cold-iron.

"All right ladies and gentleman," Brigid called out from the bar, a mop tightly pressed in her hand. "I think I have everything sorted out. Time for you hooligans to get to your rooms." Lidia, Evie, and my eyes all met. "Oh, and bring me any empty pints please." Lidia pushed from her chair and stood up. She tried to balance herself before swaying her way to the stairs as if dancing.

"Good night Uh-Dare," Lidia annunciated. "I *uh, dare* you to sleep tight," Lidia giggled. "Ha, your name is funny." Evie shook her head but laughed.

"I'll be up after I clean your mess," Evie jabbed while gathering Lidia's empty glasses.

"Yes Mom," Lidia mumbled before disappearing into the hall.

"And don't forget to brush your teeth," Evie added. I lingered, helping collect empty pints. It was an improvised ploy that I'd hoped would help me steal a few more moments with Evie. Brigid, who was counting her earnings, gave me a glance before digging her head low.

"So," Evie said as she returned the hot poker she'd used on Hugh from the table, "I hate to put you on the spot, but is there any chance you know anything about my Mother?"

I waited for Sean, who double-checked his wife's math. He looked up and shook his head. "Say you don't know anything," he commanded. "I'll tell you later."

"I'm sorry," I apologized with a shrug, "I'm afraid I don't know."

Evie frowned. "Darn. No one seems to have any information on her."

"Is she from Killarney?" I asked.

"Don't know," Evie sighed. "She met my dad here, but my Mom never talked about where she was from. They were only together a short while. She disappeared shortly after I was born. Dad doesn't like to talk about it much."

"I know how you feel," I said after a moment. "My Father took me from my Mother when I was little. I never saw her again. I try not to dwell on it, but it can feel as if a few chapters of your life are missing." Evie's shoulders slackened and her brows arched. Then with a soft pat on the arm she smiled.

"Exactly."

Just then Brigid stepped up and pressed between us. She shot me a subtle wink before turning to Evie. "Well, I'm off to bed. Take another minute if you need. Just turn the lights off when you're done."

"Thanks Brigid," I said appreciatively.

"Yes, thanks Mrs. Callahan," Evie agreed.

I watched over Evie's shoulder as Brigid clambered up the stairs. She turned at the top step and gave me a thumbs up before walking out of view. Evie didn't seem to notice. She was rocking back and forth on her toes while staring at her shoes. After a moment, she looked up and grinned. I didn't want to think about what it took for the universes to construct that smile.

"So," she spoke up, "do you enjoy living in Ireland?"

There was a moment of hesitation. Though her intent seemed innocent enough, there was also a slight daringness to her inquiry. It was the same tone sidhe used when trying to seduce truths out of someone.

"It's starting to have its perks," I smirked while meeting her gaze. Evie went flush, her pale cheeks turning strawberry.

"Oh?" Her voice lifted.

"Oh," I repeated.

"I bet you say that to all the American girls who stab your enemies in the back with a hot poker."

"No," I argued with a half smirk, "just the pretty ones." Evie rolled her eyes, though her smile contradicted any disapproval.

"Are we flirting?" she asked.

"I'd like to think so."

"Don't screw it up," she warned. "You only get one chance."

"Okay," I continued, bobbing my head while accepting her challenge. "I'm going to fight my desire to ask you why you're still down here."

"Good call," she said while tucking a lock of her bangs behind her ear. "But I don't recommend resisting all your desires. "

"Well then," I continued, my wits in full drive in order to match Evie's coquettish contest, "let's just get to the good stuff shall we. Favorite color?"

"Hmm," she hummed in pleasure, "grass green."

"Favorite superhero?"

Evie's nose crinkled. "The Unbeatable Squirrel Girl of course."

"Doreen Green?" I laughed. "That's nuts. Okay, favorite season?" I probed before she could ask a question of her own.

"Oh dear," she said while grabbing at her heart, "that's not fair."

"Pass then?"

"Yes. Come back to me on that one."

"Okay, favorite thing about yourself?"

"Now that," she said while petting the nape of her neck, "I can happily answer. I'm fearlessly assertive."

"All of the time?"

"No," she said simply. "It's not a good idea to be assertive *all* of the time."

"Then when?"

"Only when I see something I want," she answered, a suggestive tone in her voice. I tried hard not to swallow the lump that swelled in my throat. It appeared that I was playing with fire.

"And *do* you see anything you like?" I said, trying hard not to let my healthy fear of rejection pour through my words.

"Let's not get ahead of ourselves," she warned. I fought a frown that strained in my face. Evie must have saw through it. "Though, I don't invite just anyone to help me research my family tree," she added. The two of us went quiet, continuing our conversation through smiles and shifting bodies. *Communication at its finest.* Sean, who was watching, shook his head in disbelief.

"Well," he said in astonishment, "it appears you have this one sorted out. I'll just go check on Brigid then." He floated up through the ceiling, evaporating into the wood.

"Okay," I said while combing my hand through the side of my greased hair. "What do you like least about yourself?"

Evie bit at her lip. "I think I may be a bit too curious for my own good. I had a sheltered childhood," she added as if defending herself.

I was liking where this was going, but there was far too much to do. I still had to plan my revenge, get Eamon out of his contract, and drink out of the skulls of my enemies. Since I'd already secured a day with Evie tomorrow, I decided to start wrapping up the conversation while I was still ahead.

"Well," I continued, "I think I'm starting to learn who I'm dealing with here. Perhaps it's time to retire?"

"Wait," she cut in. "I haven't answered your question yet."

"Oh?" I said matter-of-factly. "By all means. What's your favorite season?"

"Summer," she belted. My spirits dropped as if Grandmother tap danced into the room and popped my bubble with her middle finger. Then, as if a damn had broken inside me, I thought of Father's death, Uncle's betrayal and Grandmother's desire to kill me. Evie, who seemed to take notice, frowned.

"That wasn't the answer you wanted?" she asked.

"No," I tried to say as if unaffected, "summer is good. There's nothing wrong with summer." Evie lightly punched my arm.

"This was fun," she said after a moment. "Wanna continue tomorrow."

"Yes," I said hopefully. "I'd like that."

"Off to bed then?" she whispered, her flirtatious voice receding and being replaced by a rational one.

"To bed."

The two of us walked up the stairs together, almost close enough to hold hands. She took the lead, guiding me to my inn room. Lidia could be heard singing drunken lullabies in a suite nearby. Evie and I tried to swallow our laughter.

"Well," whispered Evie while rubbing her hand over my room number, "this is you."

"So it is. Goodnight," I said quietly. Evie leaned in, pressing her lips onto my cheek. It was as soft as lily petals and warm like the sun. I could feel fairy fire bubbling inside me.

"Goodnight Adair," she whispered back before turning and walking to her room. My thoughts were dizzy, as if a confusion charm had been cast over me. My hand grabbed for my door handle, opening it clumsily so that I could step inside.

The room was cold, and although I was worn out, the excitement of the day must have blocked my mind from surrendering. After taking off my jacket and shoes, I cuddled under the stale blankets and tried to get some sleep. I would have a long day tomorrow. My head was a ballroom, and all my thoughts were dancing around. Queen Orla, Uncle, Grandmother—friends may come and go, but enemies tend to accumulate. I stared at the ceiling for what seemed like forever. For some reason my mind was weary, but it was unable to persuade my body to rest. *Why couldn't I fall asleep?* Then it hit me.

"You have to promise me at least one trick a day," Uncle made me guarantee three times. *Damn you Uncle.* I couldn't escape his hold over things, even in the Firbolg lands. It appeared our agreement carried over. I would need to follow through with a prank a day if I wanted rest.

I left my room in my bare feet, creeping down to the bar. I shuffled over to Hugh's stool and took the time to twist several of the screws loose. When I was done, I placed them in my pants pocket and went back upstairs. Sure enough, as I opened my door, drowsiness and sleep deprivation punched me harder than Hugh. As I fell onto the bed, my eyes shut, and I fell asleep. The day was finally over, and as I drifted into dreamland, I wondered if it was possible to have both the worst and best day at the same time.

Chapter 10

Many years ago, at a time when rivers flowed with honey and wishes all came true, there was a young girl who lived in a snow globe. Her name was Evie, and her fate was something of a contradiction. By day, she was trapped in her bed, the air around her too harsh to breath. But during the evening hours, when it was so late that even cats fell asleep, Evie visited a most fantastical world in her dreams. It was a land filled with colors brighter than a pair of suns, and grander than the deepest ocean. It was a land where she danced alongside girls of gold and smiled from afar at boys of fire. So enchanted was she, that Evie swore she'd one day find it, if only for a day.

Months would pass, and Evie grew impatient. Her want became need, need became obsession, and before long, Evie filled every waking hour consumed by her dreams. Unicorn trinkets adorned her bedroom shelves, elf sketches pasted crookedly along her walls, and costumes stitched with glossy wings filled her closet. Every morning was spent imagining great castles or forests, and every night Evie wouldn't sleep unless her father read from her favorite fairy tale books. No doubt, Evie was a fairy, if only in her head.

As time moved along, and Evie's lungs grew stronger, her dreams began to fade into a leisurely pleasure. Trinkets became decorations, sketches were filed in garbage cans and little dresses with glossy wings took flight into the confines of the attic. For now, that Evie could venture outside her snow globe, she had a lot of living to catch up to. She learned to laugh, love, and sing. She learned heartache, heartbreak, and grief. But as quickly as life poured into her cup, Evie emptied it even quicker. So thirsty was she, that her heart called to leave its nest, if only to see past the horizon.

Fate, receiving word that its little girl in the snow globe had become a woman, decided to intervene. It whispered in the appropriate ears, and shortly after, Evie received a letter in the mail. The correspondence, meant for only Evie's eyes, promised great adventure, far away travel, and the appropriate means to do so. And all the while as these promises of excitement swirled in Evie's head, an even deeper thought awakened.

It was a voice from her past, one filled with colors brighter than a pair of suns, and grander than the deepest ocean. Evie would trek to the land of Emerald, where she'd find the answers she'd been looking for since the days of her snow globe, if only she wished it.

So, the little sick girl that transformed into the lovely adventurer took to the skies. Though she told herself that she was merely taking a holiday, she knew it to be more. For the time when rivers flowed with honey and wishes all came true had returned. And Evie, whose fate was something of a contradiction, was no longer trapped in her little bed, the air around her too harsh to breath. It was time to once again visit a most fantastical world, this time while awake. It was time to dance with girls of gold, and smile at boys of fire, if only Evie wished it.

Chapter 11

I watched from the treetops as leaves rained down in the forest like a storm. Several hundred of them nestled together to weave a quilt along the roof of the cottage. Smoke billowed from the chimney as embers flew up into the grey sky. I could see movement from the cottage's window, though the foggy grid of small pains made it difficult to make out. Suddenly, as if by its own will, the ivory smothered front door swept open. After waiting momentarily, I used the wind to glide into the cabin's entrance.

Inside was a gingerbread-brown room bathed in firelight. To my astonishment, dancing within a small chamber cluttered with blankets, sitting cushions and a cast iron stove was a pair of young lovers near the chimney's hearth. They stared in each other's eyes as if centuries had torn them apart. The woman, who looked vaguely familiar, wore a gown of simple rose. She stared up at her partner as they spun in a sweeping circle. Her fire colored locks were braided into a long rope that sat lazily over her shoulder. Her lover, who stood a near half-foot taller, wore a cloak of autumn foliage.

As they spun in slow circles, I could make out that the man in the Autumn cloak was Father. I tried to call out to him, but my voice had no effect. I was but a spectator. I stood there watching as Father and Mother continue to dance. There were no words between them, only smiles. My heart tugged as I watched them sway, that is, until a stiff set of fingers gripped onto my shoulder.

"Adair," cooed a voice in the dark. "Wake up."

I leapt up in fright, grabbing the hand on my shoulder and twisting it.

"Ouch, my bloody fingers," cried the man hovering over me. My senses returned. Though I'd half expected to wake up in the confines of my tree hut, my mind reminded me that I was on Earth. I was in a chilled room at the Bleeding Wolf Inn. Eamon, who was wincing, pleaded for me to let him go.

"Eamon," I called out as I released him. "I'm sorry." Eamon cradled his hand and rubbed at his fingers.

"I was just doin' as you'd instructed young fairy," he hissed, "and waking you up before dawn."

"I know," I apologized as I sat up from bed. "I didn't mean to."

"It's my luck that I try to break the mold and be decent, and I get my hand crushed for it." I ignored him and looked outside the room's single window. Though the sky was still a pinched shade of purple, a light haze of blue began crawling up over Killarney. It wouldn't be long now before the sun rose.

"Do you have your car?" I asked. Eamon nodded. "Good, then let me get dressed."

"I brought the axe, too," said Eamon through his naturally puckered lips.

"We won't be needing that anymore," I informed him as I slipped my jeans on. Eamon narrowed his eyes.

"I'm sorry," he grumbled, "but I'm a bit hard of hearing. It sounded like you just said we won't be needing the axe anymore, which means unless you plan on using foul language, we won't be cutting down any trees."

"That's right," I confirmed as I squeezed into my shoes. "We aren't cutting down the tree anymore." Eamon's eyes bulged. "Don't worry, we're getting our revenge. It's just a change in plans."

"Oh, well forgive me if I don't seem ecstatic by your change of heart," Eamon growled, the creases in his forehead thickening, "but your shiftiness sounds a bit familiar."

I looked at Eamon flatly before sliding through the neck hole in my shirt. "Eamon," I said in a stern voice, "let's get this clear. I am not my Uncle. You and I don't have to be friends, but if you want me to help you fix what Uncle has done to you, you must trust me, at least temporarily. Now, we don't have much time until the sun comes up, so let's hurry. I promise I have a plan."

"Oh yeah?" he challenged. "Then promise me three times." Clearly Eamon knew a bit about fairy culture, as eschewed as it was.

"Eamon," I laughed as I slipped on my leather jacket, "that only works on the other side."

"Well," he said suspiciously, his eyes narrowing, "say it does, I want you to do it anyway."

I sighed. "Fine, I promise that I have a plan that will help us both out." Eamon rolled his hand in a circle motion as if to say *again*. "I promise that I have a plan that will help us both out." Eamon crossed his arms, as if ready for me to do something dubious. Frustrated, I belched out the words one last time. "I promise that I have a plan that will help us both out." Though I was sincere, there was no strong urge or enchantment that forced my will. As I'd expected, the Rule of Three had no grounds on Earth. Uncle had taught me early on that although the rule can carry over to the human lands, it could not be birthed here. But if it made Eamon happy, I was fine with saying it.

"Now," I continued, "if you're ready to take us to the fairy fort, I can get on with my new plan."

"Oh," he cooed, "I'd like nothin' more."

We slipped downstairs where the smells of fried potatoes and cooked meat wafted. I concentrated on the sounds all around me. My ears twitched. Eamon's lungs rattled out air. Beyond that, I could hear Brigid banging pots behind the silvery doors of the kitchen and the crinkle of paper by the bar. My eyes followed the crumpling noise. Sean hovered over a stool while reading a newspaper.

"Going somewhere?" Sean inquired while trying to turn the page.

"We're headed to the fairy fort," I said while zipping up my jacket. "Would you like to come with?"

Eamon frowned. "Did you forget to take your pills this morning?" he hissed. "I'm the one taking you there."

I grimaced at Eamon. "I'm not talking to you. I'm talking to Sean."

Eamon's eyes went wide. "Sean," he said curiously, "as in Sean Callahan?"

"Yes you slippery boob," Sean answered. Eamon didn't react.

"Yes," I confirmed, "Sean Callahan. Brigid's husband."

"Jesus, Mary and Joseph," Eamon hollered while narrowing his eyes towards the bar. "Sean, it's me Eamon."

"I know who you are you damnable cheat," Sean sizzled.

"Sean," I cut in. "Sorry to be rude, but I need to beat the sunrise. Care to come with us or not?"

"Afraid I can't lad," Sean frowned. "I'm trapped here. I've tried leaving before."

"Sorry to hear that," I apologized. "On that note, I need to hurry. I'll be back shortly."

"Oh," Sean smiled, "I know you will. You've got to come back for your lass."

I gave a quick smile and headed towards the door. Eamon lingered for a moment. "Well Sean," he said loudly as if Sean was deaf, "we have to be goin' now, but I'll be sure to check up on Brigid now and then."

"Get out you slimy plonker," Sean shouted as Eamon followed me out of the door.

The two of us hurried to Eamon's car and raced our way to the fairy fort just outside the Killarney strip. Though Officer Friendly had taken me through the roads last night, everything seemed a bit livelier this time around. The colors weren't as trashcan dull as they'd once been, and the city had a bit more charm with its welcoming storefronts and homes. Perhaps my dream of Father and Mother helped lessen the melancholy, but I didn't have time to stop and think about it. I was already on borrowed time.

Once we made it near the fairy fort, parking alongside the road, we slogged through the muddy grass in order to beat the sun up the knoll. Eamon gasped for air as we reached the top, leaning on a tree for support. I studied the horizon. The sun had already peaked its bald top over the lands, glittering light across the hills. Eamon looked up at me expectedly.

"So," he said between gasps, "now what?"

"Shhh," I hissed with my finger at my lips, "just keep your eyes open."

Slowly, the sun stretched its domain over the hills. The blinding rays caused us to shade our eyes with our hands. I somehow managed to stare on ahead, my irises burning with fire. As I did, a pinkish twinkle glittered nearly a stone's throw away within the ribs of a small hill. At first, I thought it was just a trick of the light, but as I continued to watch, I saw the glitter strengthen. I focused my hearing. The faint hint of a pan flute and violin whistled through the hills. I grabbed a blinded Eamon by his wrist and tugged him forward.

"Come on," I hollered, "follow me."

Eamon clumsily obeyed, tripping on random rocks and dirt mounds along the way. We had to hurry before the sun fully rose or else the seams of the veil would vanish. I picked up the pace until we were just inches from the glow. A faded radiance glittered in the shape of a door. I reached forward, pushing at the enchanted entrance with one hand, while grabbing at Eamon with the other. Surprisingly, as I pulled him through the threshold, the bright rays of the sun were snuffed out in an instant.

An electric guitar, hand drum, and familiar pan flute and violin flooded my sensitive ears with a familiar Firbolg song. It was Judas Priest's *Riding on the Wind*. I let my ears relax. Eamon and I took a moment to absorb our surroundings. We were now in a *Foresworn* tavern, and one of the worse kinds. The barkeep, a brawny green man with a foliate head, rained sweat along his mossy brow as he feverishly poured drinks. He wore a leather vest with black jeans and had dozens of tattoos riding up his strapping arms. His patrons, a collection of hobgoblins in leathers, bugbears with spiked shoulder pads and other unsavory types, ignored us as we entered. I took inventory, searching for signs of Grandmother, Liadan, or Uncle. While there was an odd assortment of sidhe dressed in mismatched Firbolg clothes that caught my eye, none of them looked familiar.

One particularly conspicuous patron, a lean and androgynous fellow, had spring green hair shaped like rising flame and a smile to match. His yellow cat's eyes clashed with his pale skin and ruby painted lips. He wore a candy cane striped suit coat with matching tie, a gray kilt and high heels. There was a silver chord around his neck clasped to a flickering light bulb. His partner wasn't any less peculiar. He had long locks of greasy sable hair that draped over his face, concealing any features. He wore a tattered black tuxedo with a ruffled lapel and red bow tie. His hands were bound in white dress gloves and his two-tone shoes were covered in muck. In his hand, he held a thick brass key, the bow at the end shaped like kitten's head.

"What on God's green earth am I staring at," said Eamon, his eyes locked on a nude selky who was dancing by the band.

"It's not so much God's green earth as it is a pocket in between," I replied.

"Oh happy day."

This was Eamon's first encounter with any sidhe besides Uncle. It must have been alien to him. The bar was nothing like Brigid's. Instead of memorabilia along the walls, there were only mounted ogre heads with beady eyes staring down at patrons. One of the guests, a fearsome looking redcap adorned in a crimson tricorn hat and plague doctor mask, rested on a tree stump bar stool, his scarred and knobby hands gripping onto a silk rope. Connected to the other end was a scantily clad nereid who smoked a thin cigarette. Within a nearby booth, a Gristlegrinder licked the tears off a Darkling's cheeks. Meanwhile, the band of brownies wore bright children's clothing and sported false fox and rabbit ears. Their fingers moved onto their instruments with inhuman speed.

Eamon's addled grimace said it all. I'd never visited a Foresworn tavern before, but Uncle's stories had slightly prepared me. The oddly dressed sidhe, their even odder habits, and the bizarre decor were probably something out of a *Fables* graphic novel. I watched as Eamon gawk at a pair of cloaked cradle-thieves playing cards with changeling babies as the ante. The little ones were no more than a year old. One, a dark-skinned child with dimples, gleefully grasped at the air in order to capture a flying sprite, while the other toddler, a flaxen blue-eyed boy, silently cried, tear stains fallen down his cheek.

"Please don't tell me that they're plannin' on eating those wee ones, are they?" Eamon asked with outrage.

"No," I replied, putting my hand on his shoulder. "Though it might be better if they did." Eamon shot me a curious look; his eyes desperately wide. "They're taking those babies to the fairy lands in order to sell them." Eamon's frown sunk into a deeper half-moon shape.

"Fairies are sick," he spat.

"Yes," I concurred, "yes they are. Trust me, I don't like it either, but we need to stay focused. If we don't blend in, we're going to get ourselves killed. Let's go get a drink."

The pair of us made our way to the bar where the barkeeper was filling glasses of spiced dew. His stone eyes met ours before he grunted.

"I'll have a green muse," I ordered with false conviction. Green muse was a favorite of Uncle's, and I hoped it would help me earn face. It must have worked because the plantlike keeper nodded before turning to Eamon.

"Oh," Eamon belted sweetly, "I'm fine for now." The barkeep shook his head before turning to put together my tonic. "Kindly remind me," Eamon said in a hushed tone so that only I could hear him, "what we are here for?"

"Lidia made mention of glades that can recede overnight," I said as I tucked my hands in my pocket while squinting to look mysterious and tough.

"Who?" Eamon asked with a puzzled expression. I raised my brow at him as if to say *just shut up and listen*. Eamon shrugged.

"She's a mortal. I met her at The Bleeding Wolf."

"Oh yes, the Americans. Is Lidia the dark-haired slapper with the knockers or the pretty blonde?" I did my best to shoot ice from my eyes. Eamon cowered as if I were going to strike him. "Okay, never mind. It's not my place," he apologized.

"Anyhow," I persisted, "glades don't just recede on their own in a span of one moon, even on the other side. Someone, or should I say some sidhe, is moving the current. And if it's water, then it's most likely the Winter Court."

"As my dear old mother use to say when she posted me out of jail, 'Please explain yourself?'"

I sighed. "There's four seasonal courts. Everyone is associated with an element. The Winter Court pursues the pledge of water. If entire glades are disappearing and then reappearing overnight, then I bet a winter court member has something to do with it."

"Oh," said Eamon as if he understood exactly what I was getting at. He quietly continued to brood and hum, his arms crossed. But just as I was about to speak up again, he butted in. "And that helps us how?"

"It helps us because we can use someone to help us. Whoever this person is, they're bold, and they're quite powerful."

Just then the barkeep slid my steaming mauve drink across the bar. I'd forgotten that I had no real way to pay for the tonic, but what little guile was still stirring in me helped me think of an idea.

"Please put this on Mr. Robin Goodfellow's tab," I requested.

The barkeep gave me a once over from head to toe and then grunted. Places like this were Uncle's favorite. Though the courts muttered the name Robin Goodfellow with disgust, any sidhe of the Underworld thought differently. He'd told me stories of his misdeeds, and even if only half of it was true, he was a force to be respected amongst the foresworn. I'd just always assumed that I was an exception to his mischief. *Apparently, I was wrong.*

"Now what?" Eamon said while trying to act casual.

"Well," I answered after taking a sip from my drink. The essence of the liquid numbed my lips and made my heart feel a quick ting of mirth. I could hear children laughing in my head before the effects wore off. "Unless you have a decade to blow, we won't be getting straight answers from fair folk in a place like this."

"Oh happy day," Eamon said in a flat tone.

"So," I continued while grabbing his coat sleeve and tugging him towards the cradle-thieves, "you'll just have to win answers for us."

"Wait, what?" Eamon asked as he surrendered to my force, allowing me to drag him to the gambling table. The cradle-thieves looked up at us as we approached.

"Good day," I greeted, "my associate here would like to join you for a hand of cards." Eamon gave a limp waive of his hand. The pair of fairies lowered their heads in disdain, continuing to pass cards to one another. "He offers his eternal service as wager."

"I what?" Eamon objected. I gave him a brief nod and then returned my gaze to the gamblers. The pair of had gone still, though their eyes exchanged a hundred words to one another.

"And in return?" asked one of them in a toad like voice. The stitches in his cheek were now showing from his cloak's hood.

"In return," I challenged, "I want you both to escort us to the Ring of Kerry's glen-spinner." The pair gave each other another dangerous stare. Stitch-face's lip twitched. Apparently, the water wielder's identity was something of value.

"Deal," croaked Stitch-face after a moment. The two cradle-thieves made room for Eamon at the table. Eamon sat down reluctantly, turning to me briefly as cards were shuffled, his expression as apprehensive as an amateur cliff diver. I gave him a reassuring pat on the shoulder, though it only forced him to tremble. Card after card was passed to each of the players. The dealing cradle-thief, a kelpie with slimy skin, webbed hands and a long maw, gave a rancid spinach colored smile as he stared at his hand. Stitch-face was less pleased, and immediately placed three cards down for trade.

I watched over his shoulder as Eamon organized his own cards. He'd only managed to produce a pair of red aces and a trio of random off-suit numbers. Boldly, he put down his entire hand for trade. I was no cardsharp but giving up his only matching pair seemed like a bad move. Perhaps Uncle's enchantment wouldn't work in a place like this? And if that was the case, I'd just sold Eamon to fairies for eternity. *Shite.* The dealer tossed Eamon a new set of cards. He lifted the corners so that only he could see them. I strained to peak, but Eamon's stumpy fingers hurriedly pressed the cards back down onto the table.

"Show your catch," belted the dealer to Stitch-face. The scarred cradle-thief laid down his hand to reveal three tens. "Ha," laughed the dealer, "thirty miles won't beat me." Hurriedly, the dealer plopped down his own hand, revealing four queens.

"House of whores," the dealer tooted boorishly. "I win."

"Not so fast," Eamon cut in, laying down four kings over the dealer's hand. "Quad Kings," he said merrily. The dealer blinked a few times before growling. Clearly, Uncle's enchantment was still in order.

"You cheated," he accused.

"No," Eamon retorted with his pucker lipped smile, "I'm just lucky as a four leaf clover."

I stepped forward, trying to look imposing. "Now gentlemen," I barked, "fair is fair. You agreed to show us where the glen-weaver is. Are you going back on your word?" The pair scowled, knowing that they couldn't.

"We shall honor our agreement," said Stitch-face with a hint of mischief in his voice. "So long as you can leave now."

Of course, there was a catch. "We can," I answered.

"Good," Stitch-face replied, a cackle wove in his voice. "Then we will take you to her."

Her. I wish I knew who *her* was so I could tell what we were getting into. Judging by Stitch-face's tone, Eamon and I were in over our heads. We were powerless to alter the terms now. We'd just have to be on our toes. I had to remind myself that if we could survive the trip and gain audience with the glen-spinner, I might just be able to convince *her,* to help our cause. Eamon seemed to be just as nervous, and as he shakily stood up from the card table, I noticed that he made a straight march towards the bar.

"Before we go," Eamon said with a wobbly voice, "I think I may have a drink after all."

"Just a minute gentlemen," I apologized to our new guides. "We need to talk briefly before we go." I didn't stop to watch their reaction, instead following behind Eamon. He dropped onto a tree stump barstool, catching his breath.

"Are you all right?" I asked as Eamon tried to get the barkeep's attention.

"I just bloody played a card game with a bunch of child slavers for my eternal servitude," Eamon said bitterly. "What do you think?"

"I know," I apologized. "You must understand that sidhe are only interested in taking chances when there are big stakes at hand." Eamon shook his head. "Trust me, though, Eamon, if I can persuade this glen-spinner to help us, we'll be able to annul Uncle's contract with you. Once he's out of the picture, I can focus on my grandmother."

"And why would this glen-spinner help you anyhow?"

"Because if she's living on Earth," I said confidently, "then she probably had issues with the Courts."

"You're taking a lot of risks for just a few *ifs*."

I dug deep to try to get Eamon to understand. "True luck isn't holding the best hand Eamon. It's knowing just when to play the best hand you have."

Eamon stared at his feet for a moment. "Okay young fairy," he said with conviction, nodding his head slowly. "I'll play along. Let's go speak with this glen-spinner."

"I'm afraid you won't be going anywhere," a grim and scratchy voice next to us cut in. We turned to look over our shoulders. Slouched over the bar was a hulking mass adorned in a long yellow raincoat with a matching hat and tall rubber boots. The creature turned around from its stool to reveal a wart-faced beast with a long nose, red eyes and serrated teeth. Slowly, the monster removed its cap to reveal a braid of pink hair. Rundura had always been one of the nastiest trolls in the Autumn lands, and she prided herself on her reputation. Now consider that Uncle and I had made it our personal hobby to torment her, and you quickly realize how bad of a position I was in.

"Rundura," I greeted with false hospitality, "how good to see you. You're looking lovely." Rundura stood up, towering over Eamon and myself. Drool slavered from her jaws, dripping on Eamon's shoulder.

"The courts want your head," she seethed through her row of alligator teeth.

"Why?" I asked, trying to buy time. "There's hardly anything in there."

"You turned my hair pink," Rundura growled before lifting her enormous razor claws above her head. I noticed that the tips had been laced in the silvery-blue shine of cold-iron. "And now I'm going to turn yours red."

Eamon bravely screamed as the troll's talons dropped down on us. I winced and readied for the blow. *This was going to hurt.*

Chapter 12

Rundura's claws came down hard and swift. I leapt onto Eamon, who was frozen in terror, tackling him just in time to dodge the troll's blow. The bar behind us splintered into pieces as Rundura raked the surface. I must have knocked the wind out of Eamon, because he gasped for air. Wait ... *wind*.

My instincts kicked in. I took a deep breath while rolling to my knees. As Rundura prepared her talon for another swing, I released the breath from my lungs, blasting a spiral of wind from my lips into her belly. The force took the troll off her feet, sailing her into a stack of barrels behind her. The casks crashed down, burying the beast in wood and spice wine. I grabbed Eamon by his collar and brought him to his feet. He was wincing, but otherwise intact. He limped with as much haste as he could muster away from the bar towards the front door. The cradle-thieves, seeing our eagerness to leave, handed the children off to the nearby selkie and headed towards the exit. The nude selkie took the children by their little hands, corralling them to a set of winding stairs. I turned to apologize to the barkeep, but as I did, a loud roar burst from the pyramid of barrels.

Rundura thrust herself out of the cask pile and back onto her feet. She was now drawing deep breaths as she set her sites for me. There was murder in her eyes. In a rage, she grabbed at the lapels of her yellow jacket, tearing it completely from her otherwise stark body. The berserk troll's pink braid and saggy breasts flapped violently as she kicked over half a dozen barrels in a charge. *This was bad.*

I studied her body language. She was about to stomp her way to me, crushing anything in her path. I was physically no match for her, even with my newfound powers. I wondered if she was dull enough to fall for the same trick that Uncle and I had pulled on her during our last meeting, and with little time to second guess myself, I leapt into action. I waited for Rundara to close the distance before hopping over the counter towards the barkeeper. Her claws clipped the corner of my shoe, slicing off a sliver of rubber sole. While I had planned on landing on my feet, Rundara's strength caused me to instead crash on my back.

I could hear the barkeep's biker boots stamp near my head, and as I glanced up, I saw him staring down. He gave a disapproving grunt. It was a bad idea to start trouble in a sidhe's ward. But to my surprise, he offered his thick hand. Before I could grab hold, Rundura vaulted over the bar, crashing into him.

Though the troll didn't seem to notice, the barkeep did. He stretched his hand out and snarled, causing his fingers to grow like snaking vines. The coiling appendages slithered around Rundara's neck, jerking her head backwards. The troll spun around, grasping the green ropes and tugging them violently. Unable to match Rundara's momentum, the bartender was hurled over the troll's shoulder and onto a set of stools posed opposite side of the counter.

I pointed my own hands towards the ground and attempted to breath air out of them. A gale of wind poured from my fingertips, jutting me up over the bar towards the entrance. After landing, I hurried through the crowd towards the front of the tavern. Several patrons cleared the way as Rundura hurdled over the bar again and stampeded after me.

"Go," I shouted to Eamon, who along with the cradle-thieves, were waiting near the glittering pink doorway. The thieves took their clawed fingers and drew invisible symbols at the door before jumping through. Reluctant to follow, Eamon paused before realizing Rundura's frightful proximity. He jumped through the threshold with a scream, disappearing. Rundura, who was so close that I could smell her garbage breath, grabbed me by the shoulder with her cold-iron claws, forcing a jet of pain to burst from my arm socket. I hollered while trying to inch closer to the exit, but the troll's grasp was too much. Clenching me, she opened her maw, ready to clamp down and twist off my head like a wine cork.

But before she could take a taste, a noose of green flame wrapped around her thick neck, jerking Rundura backwards. The troll tried to shout, but it came out only as a gurgle. She struggled for several moments before releasing me to try and scratch the strangling flames. I looked behind her to see the androgynous man with his hands extended, his lasso of green fairy fire jutting from his palms as he continued to restrain Rundura. He gave me a quick wink with one of his cat's eyes before returning his attention to the troll. I didn't stop to thank him. Instead I just leapt into the doorway and let it do its work. There was a moment when the exit's radiance caused my skin to feel as if it was covered by a hundred cold-legged ants. Then, I was spat onto the other side.

I half expected to land on the wet grass of Killarney's knolls, but was instead spewed out onto a hard-rocky floor. I could hear flowing water, and as I glanced up, I found that I was in a domed cavern. The cave walls were flaking like an old scab about to shed. A thin icy river, which ran through the cave's spine, glowed teal along its bed, illuminating the ceiling with fluttering light. The cradle-thieves lingered along the water shores, waiting for Eamon and me to join them. Eamon took in his surroundings, mumbling as he stared at several blood colored ruins shaped like spiders within our stone prison.

"Oh, happy day," he maundered. I gave Eamon a grim look and pointed with my nose towards the cloaked sidhe, who seemed to be arguing over the best route. Eamon nodded in comprehension and then meandered over to me so that we were shoulder to shoulder.

"What's the plan young fairy?" He whispered tensely.

"Same as it was before," I quietly answered, "we keep a close eye on those two until we can find the glen-spinner." Eamon rubbed at the back of his neck.

"Now young fairy," he deplored, "I think your uncle is a bastard of the worst kind, but your anger seems a bit dangerous. Perhaps you need ta' ask yourself some serious questions before we move on."

"Like what?" I demanded while cocking my head back.

"Like, is the life your Grandmother and Uncle stole from you worth getting back?" Eamon second guessed. "I mean, Earth ain't all that bad is it? The best revenge might be to let them keep your old life and start anew."

Let them keep my old life? Was he kidding? I'd been wronged, my Father sacrificed, and my world turned upside down all because Grandmother didn't care to have me around. In addition, Uncle, my only friend, betrayed me without even so much as a warning. *No,* there would be no room for a new life until the old one was avenged. Furious,

I cracked my knuckles and grinder my teeth, wordlessly emanating my frustrations to Eamon. He frowned.

"Fine then," he said while digging his hands in his coat pockets, "we'll do it your way." We stared at each other for a moment, letting the drops from the dripping ceiling fill the silence.

While I didn't think that Eamon understood what I was going through, I did partially agree that my emotions needed to be kept in check, at least while we were down here. I didn't know exactly how our host would take our unannounced visit, but I'm betting that a foresworn in hiding didn't take well to being intruded upon. Once the cradle-thieves plotted their course, they beckoned Eamon and I to follow. The four of us marched through twists and turns, our route trailing along the riverbed. Eamon and I did everything in our power to stay behind our guides, readying for anything they might have up their sleeves.

Finally, after a song's time, we came to a clearing. The massive opening was like a naturally made coliseum, with rounded rock walls and a center stage chiseled from earth. The river we'd been following flowed into the center, collecting into a large pond of shimmering turquoise water. There were several other rivers flowing from other entrances around the bed, all of them weaving together like a web.

"Here you are," said the toad like voice of Stitch-face as he bowed. "As promised."

"Where is the glen-spinner?" I challenged. The cradle-thief smiled.

A spew of bubbles began to froth from the pond's center. Slowly from the depths arose the upper torso of a freakishly beautiful woman. She was nude and glistening. She held her sharp chin high and paid no mind to Eamon as he stared at her bare chest. She had midnight hair bound in a compact bun that seemed painted onto her diamond shaped head. Her deep-set eyes and short nose made her face appear childlike, though her curves and proportions told us otherwise. The sidhe woman stretched out her dripping arms and yawned before fixing her gaze upon us. Her glance alone was frightening, peppered with the same frustrating glare that one gives buzzing flies.

"Who are you, and why are you here?" She asked in a vexed high pitch voice.

"My name is Adair," I proclaimed, "half child of Autumn." Winter Courts found Autumn a bit doleful, but the two seasons tended to work well together due to our common deathly bonds. And although everyone knew that Winter thought they were superior to everyone else; we were the only kingdom that were on slightly friendly terms. I'd hoped, not so much as expected, that it might help. The woman gave no indication whether it did or not. Her expression was plain and unpredictable, much like Grandmother's.

"You are the son of the Autumn Prince no doubt?" she said as if leading me into a trap.

"Yes I am," I agreed. "And you are?"

"I am Jacinda," she announced. "Ruler of the Ley Lines, Mistress of the Independent, and former wife and queen of King Wynnfrith."

King Wynnfrith of the Winter Court was as delightful as a torture wrack. His several failed marriages led to false accusations of treason that ended in court approved executions by the cold-iron sword. Jacinda was the exception. Her ingenuity during her trial secured her banishment instead of death. Though many feared her return, after many moons she was simply forgotten.

"Your Father was a very bold member of the court," she said indifferently. "Foolish, but bold. I enjoyed his addresses, especially when they thwarted Summer's conquests. No doubt such boldness is the reason you're here."

I'd always known that Father had been considered as an insubordinate by many of the hierarchy, but apparently, he had been much more of a thorn in their side than I'd known. *Had my expulsion been punishment?*

"My Father lived the way he died," I said honestly, "sacrificing himself to protect what he felt mattered." Eamon winced as if stung by a wasp, no doubt afraid that Jacinda would take offense to my audacity. But I knew better. She may be foresworn, but she was engrained with Winter. They were undemonstrative and calculated, unconcerned by words of the heart.

"As I said before," she continued without arousal, "he was bold, but respected." Jacinda glided towards the shore of the pond, allowing more of her body to rise from the surface. I could see from her now exposed belly that she had a black coat of bristling hairs clung to her waist, like a belt made of fur. "So, tell me, what is it that you require?"

"Require?" I asked innocently, trying to buy time. It was my hope to butter up Jacinda before pitching any request. With so little leverage, I was in danger of getting Eamon and I killed.

"Yes," she reiterated. "Those who know of me desperately dare not visit, and those who visit, dare desperately."

The cradle-thieves began to backpedal, tracing their footsteps until they tiptoed out of sight. Eamon, meanwhile, in an act of deranged loyalty, stepped forward so that we were side by side. He pat me on the back as if to say *I'll handle this*, before pulling the cuffs of his dress shirt from the ends of his jacket sleeves. He then combed the sides of his frizzy hair with his fingers and gave a randy smile.

"Now love," he said with a pitch of sincerity and charm, "I think you can agree that the lot of us have not a leg to stand on when in the presence of a creature as lovely and powerful as yourself. We swindle for trifles while you move entire glens. So, with that being said, I'd beg for you ta' ask why would a pair of fools like us come and disturb you unless we had something to offer?"

Jacinda's face contorted from disdain to interest as she began to emerge from out of the pool. I don't know what was more terrifying, seeing real emotion out of her or seeing her body in its entirety. She approached us in a predatory fashion as if ready to pounce. To our alarm, instead of two lanky legs surfacing from the waters was the bottom end of an arachnid. The creature's quadruped base teemed with prickly black hairs, spear-like legs and a bulbous abdomen. There were blue veins spread like cracks of broken glass along her shell and a silk thread that drew from the end of her web spinner into the pond. *She was not like this the last time I saw her.* Shocked, I turned to Eamon, who was frozen in terror, his jaw gaping downward. Jacinda towered over us, nearly double our height.

"You claim to be able to offer me something of value?" Jacinda challenged. "Make it good mortal or I will eat out your insides first."

Eamon seemed to search for words, but after a hum and smack of his flappy lips, all that came out was, "I um … you, uh, spider."

"We offer you vengeance," I shouted. "No doubt you look for reprisal after what King Wynnfrith did to you. Queen Aveline and my Uncle have committed similar acts against us. Let's join forces and lash back at the council."

Jacinda reared her front legs, ready to strike. "Why," she hissed, "would I ally with a mortal and a half child? You are weak." Her pointed front leg came down towards Eamon's forehead. I leapt in front of him, guarding my own face as I tried to protect him. Desperately, I spat out the only reason I could think of.

"Because before my Father sacrificed his life," I said between breaths, "he bequeathed to me his mantle of power. And before Uncle knew what the consequences would be, he bestowed his servant Eamon here with a piece of himself." Jacinda paused, lowering her front legs slowly until they pressed on the ground.

"Not so weak are you then." There was a still moment. "Tempting," she said to herself, her front appendages now twining together as if spinning invisible yarn. "Very tempting." There was a short pause. I could hear a symphony of small sounds, from the dripping of cave water to Eamon's heavy breathing. Finally, Jacinda resumed. "I regret to inform you that your request for my assistance will not be as you desire." I tried to restrain my feelings, but a short sigh leaked out. "I will offer you aid, but it will not be in the form of any of my resources. Instead, I shall lend you information, in hopes that it will ripple forth from you like a tide."

Information in *The Lands of Change* was a powerful thing. A name, undisclosed location or proof of a secret pact could overturn entire dynasties and had. Perhaps Jacinda knew something that would bring Grandmother to her knees. I bowed as if being knighted, my head down humbly while waiting for Jacinda's tidings.

"Though the sun should set at the beat of fall's drummer," she crooned, "a new rule begins in an All-Hallowe'en Summer." Eamon remained still before taking a second glance at Jacinda's deadly legs. Instilled with fear, he took a step backwards and clapped his hands.

"Well, isn't that delightful to the ear," he said. "I'm satisfied Adair. How about you?"

"Wait," I demanded, grabbing Eamon by the sleeve while keeping my eyes on Jacinda. "Are you saying that Summer and Autumn have an illegal truce? How?"

It sounded like something that Grandmother would do, though I was mystified on how it worked.

"My sources know not," confessed Jacinda, "though Summer and Autumn's recent interest in the Firbolg lands makes one believe that they will expose a flaw within the court's laws. This alliance would give them the opportunity to usurp the other rulers and upset the balance."

"That traitorous fly-bitten death-token," I cried. My voice reverberated throughout the caves.

"We humans," Eamon said lightly, "usually just say *shit*."

"Shit," I shouted even louder.

Within all the fairylands, there was no one as patient, deceitful and scheming as Grandmother. Though I knew that the seasons were prohibited from bartering alliances, and that muddling in the affairs of men was banned, I'd accepted the fact that she somehow managed a way to sort out all those inconvenient truths in her favor.

"Lady Jacinda," I pleaded, "do you know who or where Queen Aveline's interests have been concentrated on?"

Lady Jacinda nodded. "West of these lands is a great ocean where a continent of rebels make their home. There are a great many towns and cities there. One particular metropolis, *The City of Wind*, is where Queen Aveline's subordinates conduct their activities."

"Fitting," I mumbled. "And now what do I do?" I inquired in the direction of Jacinda.

"What *do* you do?" she asked in return. "I have given you what information I possess. Will you squander it or seize the opportunity?"

Jacinda wasn't willing to risk herself for a fool's errand. However, she had almost certainly weighed the value of feeding me this vital information. It would cost her nothing to let me in on Grandmother's plot, and in return, my drive might be enough to shake up the current state of affairs. It was brilliant on her part.

"If you would be so kind as to return us to the Firbolg lands," I requested, "then I would start my quest."

"Specifically," Eamon added, "Killarney if you don't mind." I gave Eamon a cross look. "Hey now," he said in response to my stare, "don't act like you folk don't love to expose technicalities." I nodded and then looked up to Jacinda. The spider fairy stared down at us with satisfaction.

"Very well," she said keenly, "I shall allow you passage." The silk protruding from her abdomen into the waters began to surge with life. A bright and powerful light pulsated from the webbing, causing the pond and glens to glow a sickly blue. Then, without warning, Jacinda lashed out at the legs of Eamon and I, tripping us with the dull part of her arachnid legs. Almost immediately, Jacinda dragged me towards her, further seizing me with her humanoid upper arms. A vise like grip began to squeeze at my feet, and I noticed that she'd reared upwards, and was using the chord of glowing silk to rope me in a condensed cocoon of silk.

"What are you doing?" I demanded as she packaged my arms and chest in a cluster of web. "We had a deal."

A serrated-tooth grin grew from Jacinda's mouth, though she remained mute. I tried to struggle, but the webs were too strong. She had already begun binding my neck and mouth when I saw that her back legs were sewing a similar suit for Eamon. As a blindfold of silk stole my vision, I wondered why Jacinda would go through such lengths just to devour us. It seemed illogical. Then again, I was only half sidhe, and didn't always understand the nature of my Father's kind. As my mind raced with a blend of anger, dread, and disappointment, I could feel a sudden weightlessness followed by a cold waft of icy water cool over me. Jacinda had thrown me into her pond and was trying to drown me before making me her supper.

Shit!

Chapter 13

A choir of morning birds nearly drowned out Eamon's shouts of gibberish. I could feel spongy soil against my hands and cheeks. I was on the ground and no longer bound. I opened my eyes to find that I'd been spit out onto the muddy knolls of Killarney, *again*. I rolled over and pulled myself into the sitting position. Eamon was lying flat on his back not but a stone's throw away, flailing and shouting like a man engulfed in flames.

"Ya' manky spider-bitch," he cursed, "you said you'd help us."

"Eamon," I called out. Eamon continued to swing at invisible enemies. "Eamon!" Eamon froze. He stared up at the blue sky, blinking several times.

"Oh, that damnable gowl," he sighed in relief. "She tricked us." I climbed to my feet and offered Eamon a hand.

"More than you know," I suggested as I pulled him from the mud.

"What do you mean?"

"Jacinda is using us for her own gain. She knows we're on a suicide mission," I said while wiping the dirt off my leather jacket. The mud slipped off the leathers sleek surface.

"I'm confused," Eamon confessed while digging slop out from his frazzled hair. "So is she on your Grandmother's side then?"

"No. Jacinda is on Jacinda's side." We wobbled our way back to Eamon's car before I said another word. "She wants us to succeed because she hates Queen Orla and the courts, but she's not going to help."

"So we've failed?" Eamon asked.

"Not really," I answered as I slogged through the slop to the passenger side of the vehicle. "The information Jacinda gave us about Summer and Autumn's unlawful alliance could bring everyone behind the plot, including Uncle and Queen Aveline, to the sword. We just need to figure out a way to use this information to expose them."

"Well then," said Eamon as he plucked his keys from his long coat, "it looks like you and I will be forced to go it alone." Eamon opened his car door and stepped inside. I opened the passenger door before slopping in. Mud splashed along the seat, but Eamon didn't seem to care. The rumble of his rickety vehicle thundered beneath us. Eamon looked at a clock built inside his car's steering panel.

"Well, would you look at that," Eamon said as he put the car into drive. "Either this clock is broken or we've only been gone for five minutes.

I sighed. "That's pretty normal. Our time is unpredictable, and most certainly *not* parallel with Earth's."

Eamon gave a chuckle. "If only Walt Disney knew."

"Eamon listen," I said bluntly. "You know you're not obligated to help me any longer. Things are about to get serious. I don't want you risking your life."

"Oh you mean my glorious life I endure as an outcast?" He countered. "Not even my own sister will talk to me. Everyone thinks I'm a good for nothing cheat. Trust me, as much as I'd love to stay out of harm's way, my bloody life isn't worth a farthing since meeting Mr. Goodfellow."

Eamon used his knees to steer the car while removing a pack of cigarettes and matches from his coat pocket. He placed the guilty pleasure between his lips. After lighting the coffin nail, he puffed a few times, savoring the tobacco before placing his hands back on the wheel. "No, I'm afraid I'm in it for the long run."

I had to admit that as much as I feared for Eamon, it would be nice to have some company. I'd been dealing with sidhe for nearly my entire life, and they still frightened me. Eamon was an odd, no doubt, but I needed someone with his sense of humor, if not knowledge, for what lay ahead. He wasn't exactly Bucky Barnes, but then again, I wasn't exactly Captain America.

"All right," I said with a nod. "Then we'll need a plan."

"Right," said Eamon through clenched teeth that were biting the end of his cigarette. "Tell me how I can help?"

My mind went into objective mode. "First, we'll need to find out where this city of wind is. Once we do, we'll travel there to investigate what Queen Aveline is up to. We need to prove that what Jacinda is saying is true."

"How will we do that?"

Justin Alcala

"Sidhe are slippery, but I know a couple of tricks. If I can find the trail to Queen Aveline's underlings, we may be able to barter with them. If we can get them to attest to the alliance in front of the courts, Queen Aveline and Uncle are done for." I tapped my foot on the carpeted floor of Eamon's car. "We'll also need more of your human currency." Eamon raised his brow. "I'm assuming crossing an ocean isn't free?"

"No, it most certainly is not," he agreed.

"Maybe Sean can help?"

"He's dead."

"So."

There was a pause. "Not sure what I can do about the money, but I'll look into this city of wind," Eamon volunteered.

"How?"

"Young fairy," Eamon laughed, "Do you honestly not know about the Internet?" I tried to think back. Eamon cut my thoughts off. "It's a place of endless information, games, and porn."

"Really?"

"Oh yes. There's *Red Headed Hoochies, M.I.L.F., mania*—"

"Damn it Eamon, I'm not talking about the porn."

"Oh."

"You mentioned games," I said curiously.

"Yes."

"Can you gamble on the internet?"

Eamon's eyes went wide. He stood there for a moment, staring at nothing, before addressing me again. "Never thought of that," he said thoughtfully, "but let me worry about that. You just get your head straight. From what I saw today, I'm going to need you in case another rumble breaks loose. Last I checked, I can't piss hurricanes or fly like a sparrow."

"You find the city, and I'll get my head straight for a fight." Though he never flaunted it, Father was an extremely talented enchanter and veil weaver. His gifts of Autumn Wind were but a smidgeon of what he was capable of. Perhaps it was time to explore what other talents his mantle may have bestowed upon me. "Agreed."

Eamon strained his focus on the road as we drove into downtown Killarney. After looping through the tight streets, we made our way to the front of *The Bleeding Wolf*.

"Eamon," I said as he parked, "thanks."

"No thanks needed. Don't forget young fairy, I'm doing this for me."

"I know, but I still appreciate it. This isn't going to be easy."

"It never is," he shrugged. We listened to his car grumble in silence for a few moments before I finally turned to him and grinned.

"Shit," I said lightheartedly.

Eamon smiled softly. "Shit."

I hopped out of his car, making my way to *The Bleeding Wolf's* entrance. I pushed open the door, allowing the familiar aroma of burning wood and fried food fill my nostrils. It was still very early, and the inn was nearly empty. A flat screen mounted above the rows of bottles behind the bar played some type of loud sports game. Dozens of green clothed men sprinted in matching uniforms, the same uniforms that *The Bleeding Wolf* pinned commemoratively across the pub walls. Then, without warning, a thud from the back of the tavern pounded throughout the building.

Sean trailed Brigid like a desperate beggar as she emerged from the kitchen, a steaming tray of breakfast in her arms. There were mounds of gold mashers, blood sausage, and fried eggs along with a kettle of tea balanced on her platter. Sean sniffed longingly over the food as Brigid served it to Officer Friendly, who I hadn't noticed sitting at the bar. Liam, as he'd been called, was preoccupied with a paperback book titled, *The Space Hurricane*. The novel's cover had a stone-faced man posed in front of a red planet, his tight blue outfit suffocating his bulging arms that were firmly wrapped around a big haired blond woman.

"There you are Adair," said Brigid in relief as she poured a cup of tea for Officer Friendly. "See Liam, I told you he didn't run off." Officer Friendly lazily turned his back to look me over. He gave a quick inspection before nodding. "The only one that sleeps and runs in this town is you ya' horn of Gondor." Officer Friendly groaned. Brigid placed the tray on an empty table and came at me like a pixie in need of nectar. She grabbed at my leather coat, dragging me to the bar and sitting me down next to her cousin.

"Now you just stay right here young man," she said while petting my arm, "and I'll fix you up some breakfast." Sean, who was now floating across from me on the other side of the bar, gave a wry smile as if to say *don't even try getting out of it.*

"That would be lovely," I thanked. Brigid waved a hand at me and smiled before hurrying back into the kitchen.

"Just a heads up," blurted Sean in a forewarning voice, "Liam here is about to grill you. Don't take it personal. He's just protective of Brigid."

"Well then young man," Liam said once Brigid had fully shuffled her way to the kitchen again, "I suppose if you've found your car, you'll be on your way now that you're sober. I can't imagine that Killarney is the final stop for your holiday?"

"Well," I said with a shrug, "I suppose not. It is a lovely place, though."

"Aye," said Officer Friendly as he took a sip of his tea. His eyes beamed over the cup and into mine, narrowing as they did. After a moment, he put the drink back on its saucer, and with a sober face that matched the man on the cover of his book he added, "We'd like to keep it that way." There was a short uncomfortable pause. "Understood?"

I nodded. "Understood."

"Good," he said before scooping a fork full of potatoes and placing it in his mustached mouth. He chomped as if chewing iron, stiff and forceful. Commissioner James Gordon, Captain George Stacy, they were good police officers who for one reason or another despised the hero. I wasn't going to let Officer Friendly's words bother me. I understood quite well that he was just looking out for Bridget. *Why else would he have helped me last night?* He was obviously concerned that I was taking advantage of Brigid's hospitality, which in a way, I sort of was. But it wasn't without appreciation. As soon as I could, I'd pay her back. Still, I needed at least one more night before Eamon and I began our journey. Just one more night of planning and I'd be ready. One more night of exploring what I was capable of. And one more night with Evie, if not to find out where she'd be should I survive this mess.

Then, as if she knew I was thinking about her, Evie showed up. The creak of the top step announced her presence. Together with Lidia, Evie strode down the stairwell, the trace of a smile still lingering from no doubt one of Lidia's amusing quips. The pair made their way to the dining area, unaware that I was more than just some random patron. They sat at a set of open chairs surrounding a small table, Lidia using her arms to describe something epic as they settled in.

I watched in wonderment as Evie continued to brighten up the room. She wasn't doing anything special besides keeping the world in motion. She wore a taught sable jacket over a cotton white shirt, snug blue shorts and a pair of tall hiking boots. Her hair was pinned up, showing off the curves along her neckline. After a short while of perusing the menu, Evie looked up, catching my stare. A pleasant smile spread across her face.

"Adair," she called out. "Where've you been? I knocked on your door, but you didn't answer." My imagination took over, romanticizing over the wonderful possibilities.

"Sorry," I apologized while spinning around in my stool. "I had some things to take care of this morning."

"Hey stud muffin," greeted Lidia in a waggish tone. "How's it hanging?"

"Hey Lidia," I smiled. "It hangs well." Officer Friendly shook his head before returning to his book. Sean beamed with pleasure as he spun around on the stool to face us. I imagined that he hadn't had this much excitement at the inn since his death.

"Come sit with us," Evie demanded, kicking out a chair from her table. I hopped up from my stool and took a seat between the two ladies.

"So," Lidia hummed, "are you coming with us to the fairy fort today? We could use your expertise."

Evie shook her head. "The only reason she wants you to come is because a boy she ran into yesterday would like to meet us there. She doesn't want me to be the third wheel."

"Not true," Lidia protested. "Okay, maybe a little. The guy was cute in a weird way. But cute can also be crazy. I tend to attract those kind. *However*," she said with a guilty grin, "I also want Adair to come because I think the two of you are adorable together."

I tried not to look as awkward as I'd felt, but Lidia was making it difficult. Evie must have felt the same way because she stared down shyly at one of her bracelets. *Time to cut myself from this noose.*

"Of course, I'll go," I tried to say as relaxed as possible, leaning in on the table. "I know my share of fairy lore, too, if you're interested."

Lidia snorted while Sean's eyeballs nearly popped out of his ghostly head. I obviously sounded ridiculous. But to my surprise, Evie stared at me as if I'd offered buried treasure.

"I …" she said slowly while grabbing my hand in excitement. Her skin felt perfect on mine. "Love … fairies." I could see from the hunger in her expression that she was serious.

"Really?" I tried to confirm. "You're not having a laugh at me?"

"Trust me," Lidia protested. "She's not joking. If you saw her room, you'd think you were living in a collectables museum. Fairy figurines everywhere."

"Oh come on," Evie objected, "there's not that many."

"Evie," Lidia laughed, "your dad had to start storing them in your attic."

Evie frowned, turning back to me. "I *may* have a few. Nevertheless, to answer your question, *no*, I'm not joking. Please tell me *everything* you know."

My mind did one of those tugs on the reign that happens when the universe conspires to get you in trouble. I knew damn well that I couldn't actually tell Evie *everything*, but it sure was tempting. *Easy Adair. Easy.*

"Of course," I smiled. "But when do we leave?"

"After breakfast," answered Lidia. "I'm starving."

Brigid came out a short time later with a kettle of tea and lemon water for the table. She gave me the smallest little jocund shove with her elbow before taking Evie and Lidia's orders. Neither seemed to notice. Sean leaned beside Liam at the bar and watched with a grin.

"You're doing just fine," he complimented.

"Adair dear," said Brigid after jotting down Evie and Lidia's orders on a notepad, "I'll just bring your food out along with theirs."

"Thanks," I said appreciatively.

"So, girls," Brigid continued, now focused on Evie and Lidia, "what great adventure do you have planned for today? More ghost hunting?"

"Oh no," Lidia objected after a sip from her teacup. The warmth of the drink must have been a treat, because she paused to savor its flavor. "Today it's fairies. We're headed to the knolls so that Evie can see the fairy fort. Apparently, Evie's family helped keep them preserved. Adair here has been kind enough to act as our guide."

"Good choice," said Liam dryly while continuing to focus on his book. "He's *quite* familiar with the likes of those trees." Brigid shot Liam a look while stomping her boot on the ground.

"That's quite enough out of you," Brigid hissed. Officer Friendly didn't flinch, continuing to flip a page while dabbing his mustached lips with a napkin. Evie and Lidia looked to me for clarification, but I just shrugged. "Well," Brigid picked up again in her soft voice, "you two are in good hands then. Adair is as sweet as he is handsome."

"Isn't that funny," said Lidia while looking over to Evie. "Evie here was just telling me the same thing."

"Oh, is that right?" hooted Brigid. Evie's face turned flush.

"Lidia," Evie hissed angrily, "why would you say that?" I could feel my insides drop to my feet as the two young women engaged in a staring contest.

"What?" Lidia giggled. "You did." Evie scowled. "Isn't it you that's always saying life is too short? Admit it and let's move on."

Move on. That's exactly what I wanted to do now. I didn't feel that this conversation could have a happy ending, so I tried to change the subject.

"Legend has it," I blurted, "that the Fairy Forts inside the Ring of Kerry is a gateway between their world and Earth." Lidia opened her mouth to speak, but only laughed. Brigid, who must have felt sorry for my pathetic attempt to keep things civil, leant a broken grin. But Evie, who had only seconds ago looked ready for war, surrendered her intentions and beamed. "That's what the legend says," I mumbled shyly. "It's ... it's a gate."

"Is that so?" Evie said in wonderment. Lidia studied her best friend's reaction before sipping her tea. Brigid pretended to review the table's order one last time before slowly slipping away. "Please," Evie begged, "go on." I watched as Evie posted her elbows on top of the table, leaning her head on her hands as she waited for me to speak.

"Sure," I said with a little more enthusiasm. "What do you know about the Glen-spinner?"

For the rest of breakfast, I described some of the less macabre history of fairies. Evie seemed drawn like a moth to light, asking questions about the courts, time lapses and *The Rule of Three*. I tried to describe everything as if it were just pretend when in fact it had been my entire life. The more I described it, the more Evie wanted. I began to wonder whether she was just indulging me, but Lidia's bored frown hinted that this was not the first time she'd been dragged into fairy talk.

After our meal, the three of us left downtown Killarney to the Fairy Fort. Lidia, who was eager to escape our conversation, led the way with a brisk pace, following a tourist's map. Meanwhile, Evie and I continued to walk together, taking in the Killarney buildings and shops. After several conversations about sidhe laws and contracts, the two of us tumbled into something far more complicated—our pasts. I tried to avoid anything too entrapping, though Evie pried. Just like any good fairy, I countered in vague technicalities.

I told her that I was born here but didn't grow up in the area. That's because when I was very young, I became sick, and my Father took me away to get better. My Mother didn't come with and was never heard from again. Unfortunately, since my Father didn't like to talk about it, and I was deathly ill at the time, a lot of the details are blurry. Growing up, I was sheltered. My only friend was my Uncle. It went like this for what seemed like hundreds of years until my Father passed away. That's when I traveled here to appease his dying wishes.

All of it seemed to make Evie happy. Eventually, she discussed her own history. She had never met her mother, but according to her father, she was as lovely as she was reckless. Her parents had met in Killarney at a young age, and after a brief tryst, gave birth to Evie. Then, when Evie was just old enough to open her eyes, her mother ran away. Evie and her father lingered in Killarney for a brief time before they moved to a faraway land called Chicago. There, Evie could receive treatments for her own childhood illness. They remain in Chicago to this day, Evie attending the same college that her Father taught at. According to Evie, she only visited Ireland due to a family invitation from a relative.

As upbeat as Evie remained throughout her story, I couldn't help but feel as if our pasts were similarly pitiful. Two children raised by fathers, with no mothers, lost in a world that isn't theirs by birth. Life would go on, but there'd always be a piece of us that felt somewhat slighted. The thought made me recollect last night's dream. *Was my parents' reunion real or merely something my conscience created to help relieve my guilt?* I shook off the thought, focusing on our conversation.

The three of us crossed the threshold between stone path and damp grass, and before long, I was once again slogging up the knoll that Officer Friendly had originally found me on. The sun had helped bake the hilltops since my last visit so that they were dry enough to stand without issue. We stared silently at the twisting Fairy Fort as the trees reached their leafy fingers up to tickle the blue sky. I couldn't help but feel contempt for the rooted pillar. It was the symbol of everything that had betrayed me. I must have looked how I felt because after a quick glance in my direction, Evie tugged at my jacket.

"Everything okay?" She asked.

"Yeah," I replied. "Just thinking about … well, it's nothing."

Evie elbowed my ribs. "Tough guy's gonna hold it all in huh?" she teased. "I see how it is." I gave a half smirk and winked. Evie winked back before returning her eyes to the tree, but not before wrapping her arm around mine.

There were only a few occasions in my life when I could remember everything being so perfect and dismal at the same time. The first instance was when I learned what being a half child *really* meant. While I was overjoyed to live amongst the fairies, free from hunger, disease and destitution, it eventually dawned on me that the same wasn't true for Mother. The second time was when I first laid with another. Fialka and my lips melted together as if they'd been made from the same mold. It was as if she drew something out of me with every taste she took, giving me a gift with a simple press of her body. But even as we took each other in, I knew that my inability to keep myself from indulging in such lascivious desires would cost me my first *true* love, Kalen. He'd never speak to me again. How things change.

And now here I was standing hand-and-hand with a magnificent human woman, whose beauty was only outmatched by her demeanor. Everything she said seemed absolute. Every time she touched me it felt faultless. Yet, as raptured as I was, my Father was still dead, my grandmother was still to blame and a need for retribution still burned inside me. Nothing could fix that, and the fact that it tainted my time with Evie only further fed the fire inside.

Evie tucked her arm deeper along mine as a light wind picked up. The breeze stirred the tree leaves and branches, causing them to clap. It was quite a view to be sure, only to be outdone by Evie's enduring smile. Lidia snuck a peak at the two of us before giving a look that said *I told you so*. But before she could say a word, the distinct sound of a duck quacking cried from her purse. Lidia dug inside, removing the latest in phone technology.

"Hello," she greeted as she pressed the phone to her ear. I could hear the muffled sounds of a man speaking from the earpiece. I didn't feel right trying to focus my ears only to spy. "Of course we're still on. You feel like picking us up?" There was a pause from Lidia as she listened.

Evie leaned into me and whispered, "It's the boy toy."

"Am I a boy toy?" I asked Evie as Lidia went back-and-forth with the person on the line. Evie hesitated before poking me in my chest.

"You should be so lucky," she goaded.

"Yeah," Lidia continued. "Meet us at the Fairy Fort near Ross Castle." There was another pause as the electronically laced voice of the boy toy replied. "Yes, the one that you told us about." The man's voice spoke again. "Well how should I know? I'm not from here." There was another break. "Okay, perfect. I'll see you in ten minutes, tiger." Lidia pressed a button on the phone before placing it back in her purse.

"Well?" Evie asked.

"Well," said Lidia, "he's on his way. He said he wants to take us somewhere special."

"Nice," Evie complimented.

"Mama has her ways," Lidia said in a silly voice while shining her nails on an imaginary lapel.

Just as she'd promised, not but ten Firbolg minutes later a loud and lean red car drove along the fairy knoll path, kicking up gravel as the wheels spun through the road. Settled behind the steering wheel was an untamed young man, his wild eyes darting intensely between Lidia, Evie and me. He had a stripe of green hair rooted like a rooster's comb through the center of his head and a dozen piercings pinned in his ears. He wore a dark dress shirt with a skinny tie speckled with old bloodstains. The man chewed zealously on something, and as the three of us approached, I could smell the rich sting of peppermint through my nostrils. He reached over the passenger seat and opened the door for Lidia.

"Ello' lovely," he greeted in a brazen tone. Lidia smiled and waddled her fingers.

"My mohawk-hero," she replied before blowing a kiss. The man in turn gave a wolfish grin before turning his gaze to Evie and me.

"Evie wasn't it?" He asked.

"Hi Davin," Evie replied.

"Who's the fella'?" he asked.

"That's Evie's squeeze," answered Lidia without any real emotion. "His name is Adair." I nodded hello, to which Davin replied with a nod of his own.

"Good to see you," Davin said to me.

"Yeah," I answered, rubbing the back of my neck. "Nice to meet you."

Lidia cleared her throat. "Now that introductions are over, mind if we get in your car?"

"Right," said Davin while continuing to chomp hard on whatever was in his mouth. "All aboard the Hog-fart Express." Lidia gave a giggle before drawing the passenger seat forward so that Evie and I could enter. We crawled into the back seats, squeezing together so that Evie had to practically sit on my lap. *Victory.*

"So," said Lidia while wrapping her arm around Davin's neck. "Where are you taking us?" Davin pulled on a lever, kicking the car into motion.

"To the ends of the Earth darling," he said while keeping his eyes on the road. Evie and I glanced at each other and quietly laughed.

Davin really did take us to the ends of the Earth. Well, mostly. He drove us to the shores of a distant beach, where after talking to the captain, he arranged a joyride for his car and us on a large rickety ferry. As the ugly old boat floated along the waters, Davin treated us with whiskey and cheese from the trunk of his car. While we ate, he told stories about the century old ferry we were riding on. The S.S. Drunken Hangman was unsinkable, and at one time during a great war, transported cars to the front lines. Despite his interesting appearance, Davin was a pretty interesting guy. He involved everyone in conversation, told a fascinating tale about the time he met Sid Vicious, and took Lidia's feisty jabs with grace. Davin made sure that our cups were always full, ensured that we were always laughing, and later, once the sky began to bruise, showed us a splendid view of the stars.

The hour became late and the moon looked like a tarnished gold piece. Evie and I cozied closer together to keep warm from the ocean's breath. Though the whiskey felt hot on my tongue, it continued to send shivers down my spine. Before long, my legs felt as if they were made of paper and my lips burned with life. *I think I was drunk.* Then again, would a drunken guy be capable of slyly putting his arms around Evie, but not before poking her in the eye on accident? *Or,* would a drunken guy be so bold as to go on-and-on about how the stars were the eyes of dead sidhe before leaning in boldly for a kiss? Okay, *maybe.* But seriously, I was totally fine.

On that note, what was more than fine was the kiss that Evie gave back. There was no hesitation. Her lips, which were a delicious mix of whiskey, honey, and something that drove my insides wild, were smooth to the touch. She curved her tongue along mine, caressing places that made me quiver. The sensation was so wonderful that I'd finally felt as if I'd done something right, and I'd do anything in my power to make it happen again. Even the guilt I felt for blowing off my plans to explore Father's mantle melted away, insignificant at this moment. I don't know how long it lasted, but when the kiss was over, Evie stared into my eyes, her nose and lips pink.

"I want to go back to the inn now," she said.

"Um," I looked around at the water surrounding us. "I don't know how long of a swim it'll be but … sure." I began to remove my jacket.

Evie laughed. "I'll take care of it." She stood up from the back of the car we'd been using as a bench, leaning over to get a view of Lidia and

Davin. "Hey guys," she called out. "It's getting kind of late. Shouldn't we get back?" Lidia, who'd been sitting on the hood of the car with her legs wrapped around Davin, pulled away.

"Um," she hesitated, "okay." She turned to Davin. "What do you say tiger? Want to buy me some beers?"

"*Ales*," Davin corrected. "And yes, I do."

It didn't take long for Davin to persuade the ferryman to get us back to shore. The four of us were soon back in the sleek red car driving towards The Bleeding Wolf. I couldn't tell you how long it took to get back because Evie and I had decided to continue our wordless conversation in the backseat of the car. I didn't know what came over me. This wasn't my usual style. But ever since I'd taken Father's mantle of power, something was becoming more, well … *fairy*. Now add Evie and whiskey into the mix, and suddenly, I was more primal than a starved ogre.

"Don't mean to breakup your fun," Lidia cut in as we parked along the inn, "but we're here."

"Let em' be," said Davin as Evie and I pulled away from each other. "They're fine in here."

"No," Evie called out. "I'm sorry guys. Let's go inside."

"Don't be sorry love," said Davin. "You're just enjoying yourself. You both deserve it."

The four of us walked into the pub, which was now full again. I recognized several faces from last night, but luckily, none of them were Hugh or his henchmen. Brigid hurried from table to table, scribbling orders down onto a pad of paper. Meanwhile, Sean had gathered around a screen with several other patrons who watched a loud televised match. We slipped in, finding a booth with several empty glasses still waiting to be cleaned up. After collecting the assortment of unfilled pints and bringing them to the bar, the four of us sat down and waited for Brigid. Not shortly after she came by, and after recognizing us, exhaled in relief.

"Oh, children, it's just you," Brigid sighed. "Help yourselves to the bar. I'm running a bit behind," she added as she rushed to another table. Lidia hopped up from the booth, and after taking our orders, went to the bar and began pouring drinks. After a short while, she returned with four short glasses of whiskey and four pints of ale. She passed the drinks out in pairs, and after hopping back into her seat, raised a glass.

"To the fairy folk," she said with a proud smile. Evie nudged me.

"To the fairy folk," we said before downing our drinks. The warm and smoky taste of whatever whiskey Lidia had poured was far smoother than Davin's, though I wasn't about to complain about either. After finishing my shot, I clumsily moved to my ale, spilling some on my fingers. Embarrassed, I looked to my table compatriots to see if they'd noticed, but they were all engaged in conversation. I waded that way in a sea of satisfied numbness for some time until Davin broke the silence.

"No way," he called out. "They have a juke box. How did I not see it?" Gavin leaned in over the table, staring wide eyed and hungrily at the music box as if it were prey. "Get ready ladies and gents," he said while slipping out of our booth. He rubbed his palms together. "You're about to learn a lesson in punk rock."

"Oh hell yeah," I hiccuped.

Davin hurried to the box, slipping several coins inside a skinny slot. After a few pushes of some buttons, a loud scream cried from above us. For a moment, I thought it was the wail of Liandan, but vocals, drums, and guitars soon followed. Davin pumped his fist in the air. Several patrons looked over their shoulders, angry at the discord. Lidia, noticing the tension, slipped out from the booth again.

"I'd better make sure he doesn't get killed," she said in a slightly worried tone before disappearing into the crowd.

The whiskey and ales had done their job. All the usual distractions within the inn such as the grumbling patrons, loud sports games, and even louder jukebox music hadn't so much gone away as much as they blended into the background. Somewhere in my stupor, I managed to loosen the tops of the salt and pepper shakers while bobbing my head to the jukebox. *Hey, a prank is a prank.* Evie and I continued to talk, and even though my mouth was moving, I couldn't remember a thing I was saying. I was far too busy fantasizing about tasting her lips again. Evie must have felt the same because somewhere mid-sentence, she stopped talking and grabbed me by the collar, pressing her mouth on mine. We continued that way for who knows how long before finally she pulled back, smiling as she tucked a strand of gold hair behind her ear.

"Did you want to show me your room?" she asked sweetly.

Show her my room? Was she crazy? At the moment all I wanted to stay here and continue—*oh, my room!*

"You'll love the view," I smiled while taking her hand and drawing her out of the booth.

The two of us hurried up the stairs as artfully as two libidinous drunks could, trying to avoid the attention of Brigid or Lidia. We slipped through the lonely second floor hall into 1A, locking the door behind us. It was dark and cold, but that didn't stop me from letting Evie strip off my jacket. Once the coat had fallen, Evie pushed me onto the bed. I crawled backwards to get comfortable before she crawled on top of me, biting at my neck until I gasped for air.

My time in *The Lands of Change* didn't pass without an erotic tale or two. The sidhe were a fickle sort, and from what I'd learned, far more casual about sharing flesh than humans. Being a half-child didn't stop me from having my fair share of experiences, some fantastic, and others frightening. Nevertheless, as wild as those memories may have been, none could prepare me for what came next. Because as Evie stripped my belt from its pant-loop, I realized that we'd both let go, and were riding an avalanche of raw emotions.

I'd been studying her body all day, enamored by the curves and arcs that were absent in most fairy women. Evie frantically pulled me up into a sitting position to strip me of my shirt. She might have been delicate as a daffodil outside of the bedroom, but now she'd become untamed. She peeled off her shirt and brazier all in one fluid motion. Once she'd freed herself from her top, she must have concluded that attire in general was unfit for the occasion, because before long she'd done away with both her and my clothes all together. Her body felt divine. It was beyond me why humans didn't do this more often. I half wondered if we could go about like this forever, but as always, all good things must come to an end.

Worn from another busy day, spiced with whiskey and flooded with the aftershock of eroticism at its finest, I was exhausted. Evie and I lay in bed for some time, her nestled under my arm and resting her head on me. After drawing on the surface of my chest with her nails several times, Evie finally lifted her head and looked up at me. A devious half smirk hooked from the side of her lips as she continued to scratch her fingertips across my skin.

"You're right," she said in a whispered laugh while staring up at me, "I love the view."

Chapter 14

I woke up to cold sheets and a lonely bed. Evie must have slipped away during the night. Dawn's sun had been suffocated by a blotch of gray clouds, making everything in my room look like one of those dated black and white photos that Brigid had hanging on the pub walls. The sheets still smelled like Evie's candied perfume. I cozied up to the blankets, relishing in last night's haze before deciding to roll out of bed. There was a new pair of clothes on my dresser that Brigid must have snuck in while I was out with Evie, Lidia, and Davin yesterday.

Along with fresh undergarments, a pair of denim trousers and a snug short-sleeved shirt awaited. I dressed myself, donning my leatherjacket over the fresh attire. There was a sickening swirling in my head, reminding me of the stars' and moon's ill advice. I decided to head down to the bar in hopes to get my hands on a pitcher of water. Shuffling into the hallway, I headed towards the stairs, but as I did, Brigid and Sean greeted me halfway. They were posted in front of Evie's door, which was open. Brigid carried out a bundle of sheets.

"Good morning love," Brigid greeted. "There's tea on the kettle if you're interested. I just need to finish cleaning your American friend's room and then I'll be down to cook up some breakfast."

"Some friends are closer than others, aye Adair?" Sean snickered. I gave a guilty smile before returning my attention to his wife.

"Brigid," I asked, "do you know where Evie and Lidia went this morning?" Brigid's expression hardened. Sean looked at Brigid's face and then floated through his wife to approach me. There was a short pause. Sean gave me a once over, then stared at me as if I were a rabbit with two heads.

"Darlin'," Brigid said in a disinclined tone, "are you still fluthered? They went back home today, don't you remember?"

There was a moment when gravity grabbed my heart and twisted it apart. Brigid must have been mistaken. Perhaps the girls checked into some other inn, but there was no way that Evie would just pick up and go without saying goodbye. *Would she*? Then again, this was a holiday for her. Maybe I was her disposable boy toy after all. If so, then she'd known this entire time that she'd be leaving, and still led me on. As silly as it sounded, the weight of it all was terribly wounding, even after what I'd been through these last few days.

"She didn't tell you did she lad?" asked Sean. My brows knitted uncontrollably. Brigid's mouth opened into an O.

"Oh, I'm sorry Adair," she said sympathetically, dropping the sheets and embracing me. "You must have known that she was leaving soon though, right?" she asked while patting me on the back. Sean closed in, making it a group hug. "Bit of a draft up here isn't there?" Brigid muttered. Sean's face was inches from mine. His smile faded and drew into a stiff line. "Well I'll tell you what, why don't I go downstairs and get you some warm food for your belly. It'll fix everything." Brigid pulled away, scooping the sheets from the floor before heading downstairs. Sean stayed with me, patting his ethereal hand on my shoulder.

"Plenty of fish in the sea and all that," he mumbled. I walked into Evie's room and examined it. Scattered throughout the confines were a few leftover toiletries and a half dozen discarded wrappers. I went over to Evie's window and looked outside. Pulling in amongst the colorful village buildings was a single clunky car, accented with shades of rust. Eamon put the metal beast into park. He was too busy examining himself in one of the vehicle's cracked mirrors to notice that I was staring down.

"Here you are lad," said Sean in a strained tone behind me. "Something to remember her by." I spun around to find a vein popping from the ghost's neck as he tried levitating a single crimson envelope between his transparent hands. Embroidered in gold was the elegantly written name *Evelyn*. "It looks like her itinerary," Sean said through gritted teeth. I pinched the envelope's end, pulling it from him. Sean let out a sigh of relief as I did. Opening the lip of the envelope, I removed a letter. As I began to read, a nauseating feeling unrelated to last night's libations, filled my stomach.

Dearest Evelyn,

I hope this letter finds you well. You don't know me, but I expect in time that you will. I am writing on behalf of your mother. I am happy to say that she is alive and well. She has asked me to reach out to you to make amends for your many years of grief and uncertainty. While we both understand that a single letter will not heal your many wounds, it's our hope that it will be a start. Please know that your mother's desertion was not by choice. Her disappearance, as harsh as it may have been, was absolutely necessary. Know that not a day goes by that she does not think of you, planning for your future. Unfortunately, even now her circumstances remain too delicate to write. However, it is her intentions to reunite with you shortly.

Enclosed in this envelope are two tickets to the place of your birth, Killarney, as well as local currency for transportation and lodging. Please take anyone you wish. This is a gift from your mother. The start of what needs to be. There you can trace your ancestry, while enjoying the many sites and colorful people. It is your mother's hope that visiting will help you understand why she left so many years ago. Afterwards, she will make arrangements so that the two of you can reunite. You must have many questions, and I promise you that the answers are far more extraordinary than you can imagine.

Sincerely,

Aunt Aveline

Sheer instinct took over. I threw the paper onto the ground as if it were aflame, wiping my hands clean. The memory of Grandmother holding the same crimson envelope while sitting on her throne only a few moons ago in Havgan flashed in my mind's eye. *What could she possibly want with Evie? What profit could Autumn gain from a simple human?* I paced back and forth, retracing what I knew to uncover motive.

"What's wrong Adair?" asked Sean in a concerned voice.

"Everything," I answered. "This is a letter from the fairies."

"Really?" Sean muttered to himself. "I always imagined that they wrote on leaves." He floated over the parchment, which had fallen face up, and read it. "Well this can't be good. Do you think they made this all up for poor Evie?"

"No," I objected. "Fairies can't lie. They can dance around facts or omit truths all day, but this letter," I bit at my thoughts. "It must be true. Somehow, Queen Aveline has access to Evie's mother, and plans on reuniting them."

"Which means Evie is in danger, no doubt?"

"Yes it does," I replied. "I need to save Evie. Revenge can wait."

"Maybe saving Evie would be revenge?" Sean questioned. I didn't respond. "How do you plan on finding Evie?"

"Eamon."

"Eamon the cheat?"

"Eamon, the sure-handed," I corrected as I headed to the stairs.

Eamon was waiting at the bar when I came down, an animated look gleaming through his pale complexion and bloodshot eyes. It looked as if he'd been up all night. Luckily Brigid, who hardly tolerated Eamon's presence, could be heard in the kitchen cooking up breakfast. Sean moaned as he followed me.

"I'm telling you," Sean warned, "this bloke is no good. He cheated my cousin."

"Sean, give him a chance," I objected.

"Oh happy day," greeted Eamon. "Did I hear you say something about Sean?" Eamon's voice became louder. "Good morning to you Sean. I hope all is well in the afterlife." Sean shook his head in disgust.

"Oh piss off," Sean said low while shaking his head.

"Sean has," I paused, *returned your greeting*. Eamon's back stiffened in a proud manner. "Eamon, I have urgent news." Eamon smiled with his pickled lips.

"Me, too." He plucked out a manila folder with several pieces of paper. "Firstly, I need to thank you for suggesting online gambling. I'd have never given it another thought." Eamon drew out the top sheet from the stack. "Here are the earnings after playing fifteen hours of online poker. I am now the proprietor of an account with over seventy-thousand euros worth of winnings." Eamon began to laugh. Sean's wide eyes told me this was a lot. "I could have won more, but the bastards froze my account. The administrator of their website says they're merely investigating to ensure that anyone has tampered with their systems. Good luck finding anything."

"Good job," I complimented. "Now that we have money, I have a change of plans."

"No, not again," Eamon cursed.

"We aren't going to the City of Wind any longer," I informed him.

"We're not?" asked Eamon. "But I did all sorts of research on it.'

"No," I said bluntly. "I just found out that Queen Aveline is responsible for Evie's visit to Ireland."

"She invited your sweetheart?" asked Eamon. "That was nice of her."

"There's nothing nice about Queen Aveline," I replied. "Her invite means that Evie is in serious danger."

"So then," Eamon said as if ready for anything, "where are we going?"

"Evie's home," I answered, "a place called Chicago."

The corners of Eamon's mouth lifted. He began to laugh. I crossed my arms and waited for him to calm down. "Isn't that perfect," he said as he caught his breath. "It appears that we *will* be going to the City of Wind after all."

"Excuse me?" I said with narrowed eyes.

"Because," he said with conviction, "The Windy City is Chicago."

"Shit," I moaned. Eamon began to laugh again.

After gathering himself, Eamon explained that Chicago, a city in a place called *The States*, was an interesting city. It was situated between a great river and massive lake. In *The Lands of Change*, places like that are known as Nexuses, as the energy within the land is amplified by the water. Eamon described Chicago as a place celebrated for its art, attractions, and booming commerce, but also notorious for its dark past. Though the metropolitan's scenery is breathtaking, Eamon informed us that according to a traveler's website, visitors shouldn't lull themselves into a false sense of security, as the streets can be dangerous. It also warned that we shouldn't put ketchup on our hotdogs. *It sounded like a place Grandmother would like.*

Eamon agreed to drive us to a nearby port where we would procure passage to Chicago. Sean helped by checking *The Bleeding Wolf's* ledger, and found the home address Evie provided upon checking in. The plan was to get into Chicago, and then have Eamon use the internet on his cellphone to navigate us to Evie's house. Only then could we warn her about Grandmother. *Well, we could try.* I wasn't quite sure how we'd be able to convince her that a fairy queen was plotting to use Evie for some twisted plot. It was just about this time during our planning when

Brigid came out with a kettle of tea and a plate of steaming rashers, eggs and sausage.

"Adair," she called out, her eyes focused on the dish, "food is ready." She placed the dishes on the bar, looking up once the tray was secure. Her former pleasant face turned sour as her mouth drew into a hard line. "Eamon," she hissed, "What are you doing here? No one wants your damnable phone."

"Serves me right," grumbled Eamon in revulsion, "Here I am trying to help this poor young man, and I get nothin' but threats and warnings for it."

"And how might I ask," argued Brigid, her face turning plum as she slapped my plate in front of me, "do you plan on helping Adair? Are you going to show him how to cheat in cards or how to steal pints from the table?" Eamon took a step back and held his hands up. Reluctantly, I parted my lips to speak, but before I could say anything, I watched as Sean took a deep breath as if preparing to blow out a candle.

"*Brigid*," Sean's whispery voice echoed throughout the tavern. The room went cold. Suddenly, his blue visage colored and became solid. I watched as Brigid and Eamon stared at the ghost. "*Brigid, listen to them please*," Sean pleaded.

Brigid froze in place. "Sh-Sh-Sean?" she called out, but before anything could happen, Sean faded away. Brigid began to shutter, and her eyes fluttered until they drew up into her head.

"This ship is sinking," warned Eamon. "Get her Adair." I hurried over to Brigid, whose knees had buckled, forcing her arm around me and carrying her to a stool. She took several breaths, wiping tears from her cheeks. Sean, who appeared exhausted, leaned his ghostly hand on a table, his blue hue fading in and out. After a moment of gathering her wits, Brigid looked up at me with a child's eyes, scared and confused.

"Am I gone in the head," she asked, "or did I really just see Sean?"

"Brigid," I said both softly and clearly, "I think we're due for a talk."

It took a great deal of clarity, patience, and a few suggestions from Sean to try and explain what was really going on to Brigid. There wasn't a detail I hid, as mad as it all probably sounded. I told her that Sean had been keeping an eye on her in the afterlife, and that I was a half fairy. Though she tried to follow, Brigid was having a tough time with it all.

Finally, after all else failed, I invited a powerful wind into the tavern, flipping stools and taming the hearth within its fireplace. It was only then that Brigid agreed that I might be telling the truth. After a few shots of whiskey, color began to flush through her again.

"Oh no," she sighed, "I haven't been leaving bread and buttermilk for the good people on *All Souls' Day*. I'll be cursed for sure."

"No, no," I objected, "you're fine. It's not like the old days. We aren't supposed to meddle with Firbolg any longer."

"Thank Jesus," she said while signing the cross. She stared at her nearly empty glass for a moment before her jaw went slack. "Oh you poor thing," she said empathetically. "You poor, poor boy. You've had such a tough go at life." Brigid shuffled to me and gave me a hug. Then after pulling away, her eyes flipped to Eamon. "And Eamon, I've been so terrible to you."

Eamon waived his hand. "All is forgiven."

"No," she gasped, "I've been terrible. I need to make things right." Brigid hurried to Eamon and squeezed him. Eamon's cheeks turned flush as he wheezed for air. He fought to raise a pinned arm and patted Brigid on the back.

"There, there," he grunted. "Whew, you're strong." Brigid let him go. He waited for her to turn her back and then doubled over in pain.

"What will you do now?" asked Brigid, her eyes staring at where Sean appeared.

"I'm going to find Evie," I said with as must conviction as I could muster. "I need to protect her. Queen Aveline is wicked and calculating. Whatever masquerade her and Uncle are scheming must be put to an end."

"I'll pray for you love," said Brigid.

"On that note," I added, "I wanted to also thank you for your kindness Brigid. You were there for me when no one else was. For that, I can never repay you."

"Sweet, sweet woman," chimed Eamon.

"However," I cut in, "I'm hoping that half of what Eamon has earned for our trip might help compensate."

"Sweet Jesus," cried Eamon in revulsion. "That's thirty-five thousand euros."

"Thirty-five thousand euros," exclaimed Brigid. Sean, who was still faded in color, smiled weakly.

"Yes Brigid," I confirmed. "It's yours. Eamon, do whatever it takes to send that over."

"Now hold on," Eamon objected.

"Eamon," I said through my clamped teeth, "You can get more. Let's not re-stain your reputation already." Eamon sighed before pulling out his phone and clicking a few buttons. He looked up at Brigid, who was staring at him excitedly.

He fought to lift the corners of his lips, as if they weighed a thousand pounds. "Will a wire transfer do?" he asked in a cheerily fake voice, his smile seemingly holding back his outrage.

Once the issue had been settled, and the money was transferred, I decided that we needed to be off. Time was of the essence. Before we could leave, Brigid packed a backpack filled with some of Sean's old cloths, as well as sack lunches for the car ride. As Eamon packed the last of the bags in his car trunk, Brigid wept while squeezing me like a pillow. Brigid was a working woman, and I could see why Eamon lost his breath.

"So," she said through a snivel, "Sean is here with me then?" Sean, who was looking over her shoulder nodded.

"Always," I answered. "Until you join him." Her nose crinkled and her eyes went glossy.

"Be off then my fairy prince," she said through her pursed lips as she straightened my coat collar. "Go and save your princess."

I leaned in and kissed her on the forehead. "Farewell Lady Brigid,"

We entered the car and road off. The ride to our port was quiet. It was wordlessly agreed that Eamon and I didn't know what came next, which was frightening beyond belief. We were outnumbered, outmatched, and clueless. The only factor keeping us together was our determination to make things right. I wasn't sure what to expect in Chicago, but in the comics, this is where our hero either saved the day or died trying. As we continued to ride down the road, leaving Killarney's streets for clean country hills, I began to wonder if this was all part of Father's plan, or more disturbingly, part of Grandmother's.

Chapter 15

Years ago, when there was less noise and wishes still came true, there lived a boy named Eamon. His mother was a one-eyed sea captain, and his father was the rat-man for a local circus. Such occupations, as anyone might guess, were time consuming, and it was up to Eamon to raise himself the best that he could. While at first the boy born in the backseat of a Volkswagen found it all a challenge, in time he learned the ways of the alley cat. He feasted from silver cans, drank out of golden gutters, and made friends with all the ruffians along the train yards. Before long, he was known throughout the county and had a special place reserved for him at the judge's booth.

But being a fire barrel king isn't all it's cracked up to be. At night under the stars, Eamon wondered what it might be like to be good at something rather than good for nothing. He dreamed of glory, riches, and a straighter path in this crooked old world. So, he set out to use the only skill that he had to make something more of himself. Eamon the Rover handed in his lock picks for a deck of cards to become Eamon the Gambler. Whatever the game, he'd play it. Whatever the stakes, he'd risk it.

While this was all fair and good at first, Eamon soon found himself swimming in a stream of bad luck. He was in debt to the Kerry Gang and Muckross Boys, which was far worse than being poor. It wasn't long before Eamon played with broken fingers, waging bus passes and dentures for a chance to win his fortune. And each time he lost, a little bit of Eamon floated away until he was nothing but skin and bones. Each time he upped another ante, a bitter tear made of crabapples and bee stings ran down his eye until he was all dried up.

Desperate, and surely pressed for danger, Eamon did the only thing he could. He tossed his last farthing into the fountain, begged upon every shooting star and rubbed the luckiest rabbit's foot in the Emerald Isle. When nothing came of it, he trekked to the Ring of Kerry's fairy fort and pleaded for the help of the Good People. Though he'd been warned that asking the Free Folk for their aid was more dangerous than dandy, Eamon called for the sidhe to assist him in his plight. With mud in his hair and rocks in his boots, he waited, hoping that the stories he'd heard as a boy would all come true. Unfortunately for Eamon, they would.

Now to say that a fairy is foul is an understatement. To say that a sidhe is slippery is being kind. And for Eamon, who was vulnerable as a finless fish, he'd just caught the ear of the foulest and most slippery of all Free Folk. Robin Goodfellow, known as Puck to his comrades, was clever, mischievous and the epitome of a wise knafe. No sooner had Mr. Goodfellow heard Eamon's plea, did a scheme begin to form in Mr. Goodfellow's head.

"If this sad old soul wished to have a change of fortune," Mr. Goodfellow thought, "then perhaps we could strike a deal? And in return for borrowing him my luck, I'll gain a servant that can complete my Earthly deeds while I'm away."

And so, Mr. Goodfellow proposed his offer. And Eamon, who was desperate for help, agreed. In return for delivering messages for Mr. Goodfellow or running occasional errands, Eamon was promised a serendipitous return. And wouldn't you know it, Eamon's luck *did* change. He rattled sevens, laid aces, and picked the winning horse at every turn. Eamon's debts were paid, and after a brief time, he was the toast of the town. No one in Killarney, let alone the county, could beat Eamon … ever.

But with success comes suspicion, and it wasn't but shortly after that assumptions became facts. Eamon the Gambler became Eamon the Cheat. No one in Killarney trusted him, and visitors were warned to stay away from his games. Eamon's earnings shrank until they were a few coins jingling in his pocket. He'd been tricked by Mr. Goodfellow, and he knew it. Sure, he was safe from his debtors, but he'd become an outcast, unwanted by anyone. His only choices now were to renegotiate his terms with Mr. Goodfellow or live the life of a stray.

The alley cat who became a gambler soon found himself an exile. He filled the shady corners of pubs, listening to friends chatter, wishing he could join along. And he is there to this day, waiting for the moment when he can reverse his destiny. He is there to this day, pondering how he'll get his revenge on Mr. Robin Goodfellow. He is there waiting for a hero. But *that* is another story.

Chapter 16

Shit. Why did no one tell me that passage to Chicago was by airplane? Who in their right mind would pay money to allow a steel hull that weighs more than a house to fly them thousands of miles through the skies on propulsion alone? *Didn't anyone stop to think that birds are light and covered in feathers?* My first encounter with airplanes had been during Superman's rescue of a jetliner. Even then, as I followed the Man of Steel bravely saving passengers from imminent doom, I thought, "Well if they don't make it, they only have themselves to blame." Yet here I was at some sloppy airport bar, pounding whiskies that Eamon kept feeding me to gather enough courage to board one of these metallic death traps.

"Don't be nervous young fairy," Eamon insisted as he bought me another drink. "You don't know how safe these things are nowadays. These pilots are experts. They're as good at flying those planes as Evel Knievel is riding on a Harley."

I tried to recall what I remembered from the 1974 Evel Knievel comics. "Didn't he break over four hundred bones?" I asked while wincing from the sting of my drink.

Eamon paused. "Well yeah, but he also broke a bunch of records."

"You're not helping."

I brought the glass of whiskey to my numb lips, thinking about how bad it had to be for my insides. The bite from the drink burned, but it didn't stop me from downing it. A portly man sitting across the bar threw some pills in his mouth before chasing them with a shot of something gold. He pounded his fist over his heart as he swallowed.

"Why are humans so careless with their lives?" I said through hot breath.

Eamon chuckled. "It's all well and good my friend. Just have yourself another. We'll be fine."

The loud staticky voice of a woman called out from above. *"Flight 1013A to Chicago O'Hare is now boarding. All passengers report to gate three with their tickets ready."*

"That's us," said Eamon as he held up the two freshly purchased tickets in his hand. He stared at them like playing cards.

"I can't do this Eamon," I argued. "This is folly."

"Look at Prince Charming," Eamon laughed. "Ready to lay down his life for a chance to save his sweetheart, if only he could board an airplane."

"Don't do that," I snapped. "I know what you're up to."

"I'm trying to tell ya' that you sound like a damn coward. Don't you use wind to fly?"

"It's different. It's slower, lower, and I'm not trapped in a metal cage that'll send me spiraling into a fiery explosion."

"What a noodle you are. Now come on. Tighten your bootstraps and let's get going."

"Wait," I begged after choking on the last lick in my glass. "One more please."

"Let's make it two," he said while pulling out his money-card and waiving it at the bartender.

Thank the seasons that I was as ripe as I was, because the details of the flight were mostly a blur. I *do* remember having to use a special bag that a nice uniformed lady provided me to capture my rebellious breakfast. I also remember screaming at the top of my lungs when I looked through the airplane window. Luckily, Eamon had explained to the staff gathered around me that I was on special medication, and that there'd be no more outbursts as he'd upped my dosage. After that, Eamon made sure to feed me enough whiskeys to make a horse legless. Before long, I was unconscious and happy for it.

Ages later I awoke to Eamon tugging me out of my seat to get me off the landed plane. My head was pounding. Together with numb bottoms and strained backs, we shambled through a skinny metallic bridge into a massive building. I'd never seen so many humans as I did when we entered O'Hare Airport. They shoved past each other, exchanging dirty glances. No wonder the courts outlawed us from tampering with the Firbolg. Like Uncle used to say, *Do not downplay the power of humans in large masses.* One ill-advised enchantment could create chaos of immeasurable proportions. Nevertheless, as Eamon and I fought through the groves of funny smelling humans, I couldn't help but feel as if we were on the verge of discovering why Grandmother had chosen to manipulate Evie.

It took some time, but eventually Eamon and I squeezed out of the crowds and into the busy streets. A swarm of yellow cabs rolled along the immense airport like wasps protecting their hive. Eamon called one of the taxis over and the pair of us hopped into its backseat. There was a miniature television playing advertisements along the wall that separated us from the driver.

"Where to?" asked the man behind the steering wheel. He was middle-aged with olive skin, thin gray hair, glasses and most discernibly, a very large belly. He had a headpiece clipped to his ear that flashed electric blue. "No honey," he grumbled, "I'm talking to customers." I looked to Eamon, who was already unfolding the piece of paper with Evie's address.

"Oh, a happy day to you, sir," Eamon greeted. The driver narrowed his eyes while studying my partner in the rearview mirror. Eamon shoved the address through the little slot between the back seat. "Would you be so kind as to take us here?"

The driver shook his head. "Nope," he refused. Eamon frowned. "No honey, I'm talking to the passengers. Would you hold on?" The driver turned around to face us. "Buddy, this is all the way in Naperville."

"What's a Naperville?" Eamon asked.

"Naperville is a suburb about thirty miles west," he complained. "It's a hoity-toity town filled with doctors and soccer moms. Way too far during rush hour."

"Well my friend," said Eamon as he smacked his palms on his lap, "this was a wonderful conversation, but I'm afraid we'll have to try another cab then. Tell your honey I say hello."

"Now hold on there," the driver insisted. "I don't think you understand. None of these cabbies are going to take you there right now buddy. It's not worth the few hours of bumper to bumper traffic." Eamon itched at the shabby hair around his temple. "I'll tell you what, though, how about I drive you to Union Station where you can catch the BNSF train to Naperville?" The driver cleared his throat with a deep heave, spitting a yellow glob of lung butter from out the car window. "There's at least a train an hour."

Eamon hummed before saying, "Deal," while extending his hand through the gap between the seats. The taxi driver scrutinized Eamon's waggling fingers as if they were a dead fish.

"Keep trying to shake hands around here," the driver warned, "and you'll get stabbed brother."

"Noted," said Eamon as he sank in his seat. The cab driver pulled down on a gear, causing the taxi to speed forward. Eamon leaned back with a pleased smile before leaning his head near mine to whisper. "Good news young fairy. I was able to talk this cabby into taking us to a train station. It'll get us to Naperville." I stared at Eamon a second, blinking several times before opening my mouth to speak.

"Eamon," I scolded, my brain throbbing. "I speak the damn language. I don't need you to translate."

"Noted," he said sourly. "To Union Station then."

We drove through the packed highways of Chicago, our taxi baking along with several hundred other cars under the summer sun. We slithered through roads at a snail's pace, giving me time to take in the scenery. I'd never seen anything like Chicago. There were electric signs the size of castles, the smell of exotic foods at every corner, and a skyline so extraordinary that I half believed it to be an illusion. But it wasn't until we crept closer downtown that I had trouble understanding how one city could get so big.

The buildings grew taller than any magical beanstalk, often blocking out the sun with their massive height. They were silver like armor and black like coal. Stuffed between the sky-towers were quaint restaurants, stores and businesses. Art decorated parks and walkways, mostly sculptures with the occasional street performer along its base. People marched in hordes throughout busy avenues, paper bags, and purses in hand. Across the east, a body of water as wide as most oceans in The Lands of Change stretched over the horizon. This must have been Lake Michigan that Eamon had told me about. Boats littered its surface like lilies on a pond. Tiny airplanes, the death machines that they are, flew above the lake with ribbon shaped ads trailing behind them. Crowds of humans in skimpy clothing peppered along the shores, splashing in water or bouncing balls on the gold sands.

Eventually our cab pulled up to a squat, but long downtown building where rows of people were filing in through the doors. Eamon paid the cab driver before the two of us joined the inflow entering inside. We made our way down a deep pair of stairs, and then another, until I realized that we were underground. The tile walls and floors that lead to the ticket booth were an earthy tint of beige with Champaign accents. Eamon volunteered to wait in an enormous line to purchase tickets while I used the nearby washroom. Once I was done with the lavatory and found that Eamon had only moved a few steps in line, I decided to wander a bit. I made my way to a nearby intersection filled with television screens that posted arrival times, gates and delays. Across its walkway, divided by glass doors, was a massive marble lobby. I drifted over and entered, awed by the grandeur of the colossal hall.

The cream stonewalls were polished with royal pillars that reached up towards a curved glass ceiling. Sunlight trickled from the panes onto wood benches covered with bored pedestrians. Statues mounted near the crown of the hall stared down, judging humans with shrewd intolerance. I drifted inside, taking in the brilliance of it all. In The Lands of Change, this would be a place reserved for nobility, but here, it was just a waiting area. I sat on the end of one of the benches, pretending to be a local.

It was nice to take a moment to gather my thoughts. I didn't let my mind wander too far, instead focusing on the issue at hand. Grandmother had contacted Evie about reuniting with her mother. But first, Evie needed to visit Killarney. What connection did Grandmother have with an Irish runaway? Could it be that Evie's mother is one of Queen Aveline's thralls? If so, that would explain abandoning the girl when Evie was just a baby, as no parent would want their child to be part of the cruel sidhe community. Yet it didn't fit with Grandmother's methodology. She wanted Evie to do something else in Killarney. There was something that I was missing. It was about this time, in that place where the present is jilted by contemplation, that a stranger's heated voice cheated me of my thoughts.

"Hey pal," the speaker snapped. I raised my head, breaking free from my trance. Before me stood a group of dark dressed super villains.

Justin Alcala

The lead man, a skinny fellow with midnight hair messily combed to the side, bore through me with his deep-set eyes. He looked about my age with tattoos running down his arms. His shirt, black with a picture of a mountain across it that read *Mordor Fun Run* was tattered with tiny scorch marks. He had gray trousers, chess patterned shoes, and a leather satchel. Inside the bag was a pair of miniature dogs who growled like tigers.

To his right was a pale but beautiful woman with crow colored tresses, a tight top that said *Misfits,* and snug denim slacks. An elegant arrangement of tattoos flowed from her shoulders to her wrists. In her hands were a skeleton wand and ragged book. Huddled closely behind them was a pair of young men who looked far less courageous than their companions. One, a plump boy with curly short locks similar in color to my own, bore a wide face sprinkled with freckles, a beak like nose and ballooned cheeks. He wore a shirt that was a size too small and pants with food stains across the legs. On his back was a duffel bag stuffed with protruding gears and rods. His counterpart, a skinny young man with glasses and a forehead ridden with acne, held a device strewn with switches and buttons.

"Yeah, ginga-ninja," spat the black-haired man, "I'm talking to you." I looked him over. He had all the makings of Winter Court for sure with his light skin and dark features, but none of the personality. His big mouth told me that the guy in front of me was impulsive, an attribute that Winter loathed. "What are you doing in my city?"

"Your city?" I laughed. "I didn't know anyone owned it."

"Well now you know," replied the tattooed man as he stiffened his back. "So why don't you make like a banana and get out of here."

The raven beauty gave her partner a doubtful look. "Not sure that's how the saying goes."

"Babe," moaned the tattooed man, "I'm trying to shake this dude down."

"Oh right," she smiled. "My bad."

"Anyhow, where was I?" the tattooed man continued.

"Me leaving your city," I replied as dryly as possible.

"Oh, yeah," he said as his face relaxed and his tone lightened. It was as if I'd done him a favor. "Thanks man." He took a moment to gather himself, turning his expression back into a fierce grimace while pointing a stiff finger at my face. "I know you're not human ginger-boy, and I want you out of Chicago or else."

"Okay," I said simply while shrugging. "Actually, I'm leaving for Naperville, so I'll be out of your hair momentarily."

"Really?" he inquired. There was a short pause. "Well, hey, that fixes everything." He turned to his comrades and puffed out his chest. "You see guys, I am like ...the ultimate protector of Chicago. No *spookies* linger without my consent." The girl next to him rolled her eyes while the pair of sheepish young men snickered. Not but a bat of the eye later, Eamon stepped through the glass doors into the Great Hall with a pair of tickets in his hand.

"Adair," he called out after spotting me. "I have tickets. Let's go."

"Well my dark and mysterious friends," I said while standing up, "as welcoming as you all are, it looks like it's time for me to leave."

"Okay, Adair," said the tattooed man, "I hope you enjoyed Chicago."

"You have no idea," I uttered while beginning to walk away.

"Hey, real quick," the tattooed man requested as he grabbed my jacket. "What exactly are you?"

"What do you mean?" I asked with my limited patience.

"Well, you're not a mortal," he said as if it were obvious. "And my Spidey-senses are telling me that you're not evil either. Are you like undead or something?"

"Spidey-senses huh?" I asked. "Well, wobble my webs and call me shaky." I paused. "Amazing Spider-Man, November of 1966 I believe." The skinny guy with glasses smiled.

"Awesome," said the chubby young man.

"I'm sidhe," I said frankly. The tattooed man looked confused.

"He's a fairy, babe," the dark beauty cut in. The tattooed man cocked his head back. His eyes squinted and his foot tapped along the hard surface.

"No shit?" He said in amazement.

"No shit," I replied.

"Well hell man," he dug in his pocket and then extended his hand. There was a business card pinched between his fingers. "I've never met one of your kind before. I'll tell you what Adair," he continued while grabbing my hand and forcing the card in it, "I'm Ned. I'm the guardian of Chicago. Think Superman's strength with Batman's style."

"I thought you were a Marvel guy?" Asked the pudgy guy in the background.

"Billy, we talked about this," said Ned with a stone face and resolute tone. The exchange seemed serious, as if they were talking about politics or religion. "You can enjoy both publishers equally. This isn't the White Sox and Cubs." *The first part was true.* Ned turned his attention back to me. "Anyhow, if you ever come back to the Windy City, come visit the bookstore on this card. It's called *The Prologue.* I'd love to ask you a couple of questions about your people."

"I thought you wanted me out of your city?" I challenged.

"Dude, you're a fairy who knows comic books," Ned complimented. "You get a temporary pass. Don't abuse it."

"Right," I responded. "Will do." Eamon, who had been waiting patiently, politely slipped to my side and waived hello to the Guardians of Chicago.

"Oh, happy day," Eamon greeted. "I hate to break up new friendships, but Adair, we only have five minutes to board."

"Well, thanks again Ned and friends," I said as I slung my backpack over my shoulder, "but it's time for me to head out."

"You know where to find me," said Ned and then winked.

"Sure do," I replied. I refrained from using a rude hand gesture. Just because Ned and I agreed on some trivial comic book stances, didn't make us friends. I didn't know who he thought he was, but unless he was the right hand of God, he had some nerve trying to intimidate me. He had no idea what I was capable of.

We boarded a silver steeled rampart on wheels shortly after leaving The Great Hall. Although the grinding of iron below was fearsome, traveling on the ground was far less terrifying than the best airplane ride would ever be. Passengers inside the metallic quarters were hush. Most gazed at the seat in front of them or thumbed at their phone. A few travelers joined me in gazing through the windows, enjoying the sites as we sped past. There were small towns, patches of forest and most discernibly, a collection of castle towers that stood amongst the urban buildings along each stop. While initially it was all very captivating, before long, all that I thought about was Evie.

I understand that the two of us had only shared a few days together, but that's not what this was about. *I think.* I was concerned for her. Humans had no idea how viperous sidhe could be. If Grandmother was up to her usual schemes, then Evie was in real danger. Unlike Father, Grandmother had no love for Firbolg. I'm sure she'd wipe them all out if given the chance. Maybe thwarting Grandmother's plans wouldn't just keep Evie safe. Maybe, much as Eamon had said, rescuing Evie would also spearhead my campaign of revenge while doing some good for Earth. *Hey, a fairy-boy could dream.*

It took longer than expected to arrive at our destination. Granted, time can move slow when Eamon wants to talk to you about old girlfriends, his glory days at the poker table, and where he'd be now if he'd become a movie star. I imagine living as a social exile could get pretty lonely, so I mostly endured. But just about the time when Eamon began sharing his secret recipe for the perfect whiskey sour, a loud announcement called out from the speaker above.

"Now approaching Naperville," said a stodgy man's voice.

"Well class," Eamon announced, "that concludes booze-enomics for today," The train began to briskly slow down. "Make sure to do your homework as often as possible," he added with a half-pie grin.

"All right Eamon," I said while staring out the train window into the station's parking lot. "It's time to get serious. I'm sure Queen Aveline has one of her many spies watching Evie, so we'll need to tread lightly. They can be very dangerous."

"Can't be worse than that troll with boobies and pink hair."

"You haven't met Liadan yet. It can be far worse."

"Right. What's the plan then?"

"Let's first get to her house. Did you look up her address?"

Eamon lifted the map glowing on his phone screen. "All taken care of young fairy."

"Good. We'll need to do a little scouting to gather some information. I don't want us falling into a trap."

"Understood. First work on not getting killed by fairies before saving your Bonny lass."

Justin Alcala

"Wait, one last thing."

"Yes?" Eamon said as the woman on the phone told him to turn right at Fourth Avenue.

"Let me talk to Evie about why we're here."

"Copy. I'll let you tell Evie that you're a stalker."

"I'm not a stalker," I objected.

"I'm just jerking your chain. Now, shall we follow the phone-lasses voice to our destiny?" I nodded.

The two of us navigated through the perfectly paved streets of Naperville by using Eamon's latest in phone technology. At first the homes seemed dated, but as we continued to walk, I was amazed by the size of some of the houses that we passed along the way. They were three or sometimes four floors high with manicured lawns, opulent gardens, and massive swimming ponds. I wondered how many people each house could hold, even though many seemed vacant from the windows. As we continued our trek, it occurred to me that I hadn't really come up with a plan as to how I was going to tell Evie that she was part of Grandmother's evil plot. I didn't think that I was clever enough to pitch the truth in a positive light, yet I felt compelled not to lie. This was going to be more difficult than trading a redcap for his hat.

The buildings became humbler with every block until finally we made it to a small home that's address matched the one we'd been given. Evie's home was quaint, located at the end of the street next to a thicket of wildwood. It was unkempt, constructed of peeling white wood adorned in ivy. Birds chirped from the trees and flowery perfume from a patch of roses sweetened the air. Hanging from a side window was the glass ornament of a woman with insect wings. I assumed the decoration was trying to depict a fairy, though it's childish outfit and cheerful disposition were fairly inaccurate.

"Hate to break it to you young fairy," said Eamon as he stiffened his collar in order to hide his face, "but I don't know how we can look natural at the end of a block leading to nowhere. Shall we perhaps leave before any of Queen Aveline's spies see us?"

"Trust me Eamon, if sidhe spies are around here, there's nothing we can do now."

"Suggestions?"

"Yeah," I said while walking up the stairs of the front porch. "Let's knock."

Eamon's face went pale, but before he could say a word, I was already wrapping on the door. It took a moment, but eventually shuffling and lumbered footsteps came from inside. A clicking of entrance lock followed by a tug at the door gave way to a human silhouette. Squeezing between the entrance was a man of average height with sandy hair, thin gold framed glasses and a manicured gray goatee. He wore a collared shirt that was suffocated by an olive vest and tan trousers. In his hand was a red leather book.

"Hello. Can I help you?" He asked with an accent similar to Eamon's.

"Good afternoon, sir," blurted Eamon before I could get in a word. "And a happy day to you." The man raised his bushy brow. "My name is Eamon, and this here is my, uh, nephew Adair."

"Good afternoon gentlemen," the man at the door greeted.

"Sir, we hate to be bothering you," said Eamon as he slowly crept up the porch steps, "but we're mates of Evie."

"Oh?" said the man at the door.

"That's correct, sir," replied Eamon. "We met the young lass during her recent visit to Ireland." The man at the door nodded, tucking his book closely to his chest. "I don't wish to take up too much of your time, sir, but long story short, Evie made us promise her that if we ever in town, we'd come say hello. Well, as luck would have it, we were in need of coming to the States for a family affair. So, here we are." *Eamon, you slippery scoundrel.*

The man removed his glasses and bit at their end. "That sounds like Evie. I'm her father by the way. The name is Tom. Please," he begged, opening the door for Eamon, who had crept directly in front of it, "come in."

"Oh, happy day," Eamon replied as he lifted his luggage and walked inside.

The two of us were guided to a room crowded with brown dusty bookshelves. Tom escorted us to a pair of patchy chairs that stood across from a work desk. There was a half-eaten sandwich resting near a pair of framed photos. One of the pictures was set in a wild garden. A very young Evie sat in a pearl dress along her father's lap. There were clear colored tubes in her nose with a chord that led out of the shot. While Evie's face was beaming, Tom's expression was sterile. The second photograph was taken from afar, amongst a sea of young men and women in a classroom. Tom stood at the front of the crowd, apparently giving a lecture. I could tell that he'd aged a lot between photos, as his hair was now grey, and bags hung under his eyes.

"I'm guessing Evie made a lot of friends in Ireland then?" Asked Tom as he slipped into the chair across from us.

"Oh yes, sir," said Eamon with a high pitch voice. "She seemed to be quite in her element back on the Isle. What a sweet girl." Tom stared at the bookshelves behind us, tapping his finger on his desk as he did.

"Yes," he said after a moment. "I always knew she'd take well there." Tom pushed his sandwich to the side, studying it with a weak frown before looking up at me. "Adair was it?" he asked.

"Yes," I answered.

"Are you close to Evie as well?" He inquired.

I hesitated. "Yes."

"So you know her friend Lidia as well then?" asked Tom.

"Yes," I said simply.

"He's the talkative one in our family," Eamon spouted with a gummy smile.

"Well, I hate to disappoint you both, but it appears she's out at the moment," said Tom as he leaned back in his chair. "And I'm not quite sure where She disappears a lot. Maybe she's with Lidia. Anyhow, I would love to talk more about the Isle, but I do have a work deadline to meet. You're both welcome to stay until she returns."

"Oh, no," Eamon protested. "Sir, I wouldn't have it. It's not even an option."

"Are you sure?" Tom checked. "I have some beers in the fridge if you'd like?"

"Sir," Eamon said with a frown, "not all Irish drink you know?"

"I'm sorry," Tom apologized. "I hate that stereotype as well. The beers are there though if you'd like."

"Well, traveling has been exhausting," Eamon grinned as he hopped up from his seat. "I suppose an ale or two couldn't hurt."

Tom snickered as he stood from his chair. "Adair, would you like one as well"

"No thank you," I said, my head still hurting from the drinks I'd had at the airport.

"Not a problem," said Tom while heading to the back of the house. "Eamon, why don't I show you where the fridge is while Adair goes and makes himself comfortable in the front room?"

"Happy day," said Eamon while following Tom towards the kitchen.

I wandered towards the unexplored half of the house in search of the front room. Evie's home was simple, but pleasant. It had large windows that bathed the house with sunlight, feeding the dozen potted plants along the wood floor. There was a handful of tarnished copper sculptures nailed to the canary walls. The roughly cut art was shaped like birds and elk. In Evie's front room was a beige couch sandwiched between two tall cedar lamps. The air felt stale and the outdated newspapers strewn across the coffee table told me that the area wasn't used much.

I could hear Tom and Eamon conversing in the kitchen, so I decided to explore a bit more. I followed a short hall connected to the living area, which lead to a pair of bedrooms. One was clean but dreary. Its drawn drapes shaded the furniture with shadow. It was filled with wood dressers and tattered books, but little more. The second room, however, was anything but simple.

The white bedroom swirled with green and yellow light from a glass fairy hanging in the window. It was the same fairy I'd seen from outside, strung with twine and pinned by a skinny nail. Evie's bed was small, with grass green sheets. I could smell her honey scent from the fabric as I moved in closer. She had several shelves polluted with dusty elf and unicorn figurines. In the corner was an easel with a half-painted canvas. The picture was a rendering of the Fairy Fort. I smiled.

I'm not going to lie. I liked Evie a lot. But I had to remind myself that I wasn't doing this because of how I felt. No, I was trying to save Evie because that's what Father would do. I was trying to save Evie because I wanted to thwart Grandmother's plans. I was trying to save Evie because I didn't know what else to do with myself. So, as I sat there in her room staring at one of her paintings like some obsessed ex-boyfriend, it occurred to me that no matter what Evie felt about me, I was obligated to protect her.

"Adair?" A voice called from the doorway, causing me to leap from my skin. I spun around to find Evie. *How the hell didn't I hear her?* She had her hair up in a bun and was wearing a snug olive jacket over a white shirt. She had light denim pants, brown riding boots and a backpack with dozens of cartoon patches. I noticed that she wasn't wearing any of charms or bracelets, which might explain how she crept up on me.

"Adair," she reiterated. "What are you doing here?"

What was I doing here? Wait, what was I doing here? In the history of loaded questions, Evie's might have been the most dangerous. If I were to be honest with her, I was doomed. If I lied, I was despicable. Uncle had trained me to always have a plan, yet here I was with no idea what to do. I was starting to act like a real fairy, all passion, no guile.

"Now that's a funny story," was all that I could muster. *Bravo Romeo.* "I was, hmm, you see Evie … I." My mind went blank and panic set in. "I'm worried about you."

"Uh, okay," she said while crossing her arms tightly. "But it still begs the question, what are you doing here?"

"Evie, do you believe in destiny?"

"Whoa," Evie objected. "Hey Adair, I don't know how to break this to you. I had a great time, but I thought we were just having a little fun."

"Oh," I said with a frown. "Wait, oh. No, no. Evie I think you're great, but that's not why I'm here."

"Okay," she said with wide eyes. "Then why?"

"Evie," I said while scratching the top of my head. "I'd like to tell you, but I don't know how."

"Adair, you're starting to creep me out. Why don't you just be honest and tell me what's going on."

"I'm worried for your safety. Evie, there's someone from my past who wants to hurt you, and I think I'm the only one that can protect you from them."

"Someone wants to hurt me?" she asked slowly as if questioning my logic. I nodded. "And you say that you're the only one who can protect me?"

"Yes."

"And why is that exactly?"

"Because, well," I hesitated, "I'm just going to say it." My heart pounded as if it were trying to break from its cage. What was the likelihood that Evie, the girl obsessed with fairies, would indulge the idea that sidhe were real? *There had to be a chance, right?* "Evie ... I'm a fairy."

Evie gave a groan before massaging her earlobes. My answer must have disgusted her. I couldn't blame her. Here I was, a graceless ghost from her past, traveling hundreds of miles to haunt her with farfetched declarations. She looked past me, staring at a pixie figurine on her shelf. After a pause so grievous that it brought new meaning to the phrase *silent as the grave*, she cleared her throat.

"You're worried for my safety," she reiterated, "because someone from your past wants to hurt me, and you're the only one who can protect me because you're a fairy."

"That pretty much sums it up," I said with a weak smile.

"Damn it, Adair," Evie bit back. "I asked for honesty."

"Evie wait," I objected, "think about the last few days. The letter from your mother's friend." Evie's grimace washed away, replaced by a blank stare. "Why do you think this stranger wants to reunite you with your mother? It's a ploy to get back at me."

"She wants to reunite me with my mother because the woman abandoned me you jerk."

"Damn," I said while pulling at my hair, "I'm sorry. That's not how I wanted that to come out."

"How do you know about that anyway?"

"I found the letter in your inn room."

"What? You went into my inn room?"

"Brigid let me in after you checked out. I was looking for you. You didn't exactly say goodbye you know."

"I'm sorry for that," she sighed. "But it doesn't give you the right to get all weird on me."

"Evie," I said with a heavy throat, "This *honestly* isn't about that. You must believe me. You're in danger. I'm here to protect you."

"Because you're a fairy," she suggested with scorn.

"Technically a half-fairy, but yes."

Evie continued to massage her ears, her eyes fixed on the carpet. "Adair," she said as she peered back up at me, "it was good to see you. We had a magical time in Ireland, but you need to leave."

I lowered my head, giving myself a second to gather my thoughts. At one time in my life I'd have been more tactful about what I said to get what I wanted. After all, I'd learned from the best, Uncle. But things were different with Evie. I didn't feel right about bending the truth with her. It was devious and hurtful, something I never wanted to be with the woman as long as I lived. So, when she asked me to leave, even though I was telling the truth, I didn't hesitate.

"Sure," I said while tucking my hands in my jean pockets. "Whatever you want."

I turned towards the door and started to walk out. I could hear Evie's breathing pick up. I stopped at the bedroom's threshold to give one last look. As I glanced back, I noticed that Evie's eyes were glistening. Our stares met one last time before—

Wam! A heavy crash came from the kitchen. The noise sounded as if a door had been kicked open.

"Who are you?" I heard Tom bark, his words slightly trembling.

"Silence you ass," said a strange, but familiar voice.

"Gah," shouted Tom as if in pain.

Evie and I continued to stare at each other, frozen. Then, in unison, better judgment kicked in, and we rushed to the other side of the building. Evie and I raced one another through the canary halls until finally reaching the kitchen. Neither of us were ready for what we found.

Standing near the fridge was the body of Tom, now adorned with the head of an opened maw donkey. His head brayed boorishly before his human hands sheathed his lips. Beside him, near a pea green stove, was Eamon. He crossed his fingers like a crucifix, directing the symbol towards a third human figure across the room.

"Back," spat Eamon, "back I say."

The stranger, who wasn't a stranger at all, ignored Eamon, instead admiring his work with Tom. He looked the donkey-man over several times while balancing two half-guzzled bottles of beer in his hands. He was pale with a bright green mohawk, finger cut gloves and ragged clothes. His curled grin was malicious.

"Davin?" Evie called out.

Davin twirled around with both beers plugged to his lips, spilling suds across his Anarchy t-shirt. "Hello," he said after nearly finishing the bottles. "Just who I was looking for."

I leapt in front of Evie, shielding her with my arms. "You'll have to get through me first you bastard."

"I was talking about you," Davin said coldly.

"Oh," I replied, slackening my posture. Eamon, his fingers still crossed over one another, sidestepped behind me.

"You'll still have to get through him," Eamon hissed, "to get to me."

"Gavin," yelled Evie. "Fix my father right now."

"Hee-haw," squealed Tom.

"You heard her," I ordered, taking a deep breath in case I needed to blast Gavin out the window. "Fix Tom or I'm going to show you the meaning of being long winded."

"I don't have time for this," Gavin bellowed. He dropped the bottles. The glass shattered, and beer spread throughout the linoleum floor. I tensed up, ready for him to attack, but instead Gavin snapped his fingers, causing Tom's head to return to normal. Tom palmed his face, checking for all his parts. Then, like a wet dog, Gavin shook his entire body back and forth, shedding his clothes into pieces of twigs and dry soil that fell to the floor. Underneath his old outfit was a peculiar frockcoat, striped long socks and neck cravat. Gavin brought his hands to his cheeks. He plucked his skin off like a mask, revealing the beaming visage of none other than Uncle.

"Uncle?" I gasped.

"Robin Goodfellow?" Eamon screamed.

"Gavin?" asked Evie.

"*Puck*," seethed Tom.

Chapter 17

Once upon a time, in a place beyond distance and measure, there was a fairy named Puck. Now Puck was not his true name, as it is with all sidhe, but rather the one he borrowed out. Those who knew it, cursed it, and those who didn't, prayed they never had to. For Puck was only good at two things—being mischievous and being puckish. He reveled in horseplay like artists do poetry and hard workers do rest.

His father, King Ruari, was a lily-livered fairy who often forced himself upon his lowly servants. When one of the maids he'd dishonored birthed him a son, the King ordered the baby's murder. But even as an infant, Puck was clever. Before his mother's capture, Puck traded himself out for an alder log. When the King's guards unbound the swaddling, they found only a piece of wood in the elven servant's arms. For Puck had escaped to Earth, where he grew for many moons, letting out his childhood frustrations on the Firbolg through pranks and nonsense.

Not shortly after, the King achieved what would be his only accomplishment. He married a beautiful noble who was as devious as she was crafty. She would be called Queen Aveline, and together they bore one son, Prince Oran. Much to their dismay, the Prince was neither lily-livered nor devious. Instead, he was curious and kind, and after learning that he had a brother, the Prince set out to find Puck. He searched high and low, turning every stone and picking every bone until finally finding his deserted half-brother Puck within the wilds of Earth.

Though opposite in every sense of the word, the two grew quite fond of one another. They capered amongst the Firbolg, Oran fond of the Firbolg's innocence, Puck their gullibility. And even though the Prince negotiated a contract that safely returned Puck to his rightful home, the brothers often celebrated each other's company amongst the humans. When Prince Oran studied mortals for the sake of understanding, Puck adventured in the name of mischief. Puck made himself popular amongst painters and poets, feeding their heads with absurd ideas and outlandish expressions. This was the brothers' routine for many whirls of the Earth.

Then, on a week that ended in two Sundays, the brothers were ordered by the King and Queen to return to The Lands of Change. A new decree forced sidhe

to stay amongst their own kind, never crossing the threshold between realms again. This decree was another fairy absurdity for Puck, and he quickly thought of a way to outwit it. He proposed to the King and Queen that he should mediate between worlds, reporting valuable information directly back to his majesties' ears. And because Puck was so talented that he could spin curse words into poetry, and because the King and Queen were greedier than a wolf in a sheep den, they agreed.

Although Puck was delighted, still The Lands of Change anchored him to them. For his brother Oran, to whom Puck had helped marry to a mortal, was forced to return home to aid his ill son. And because Puck was the ailing child's godfather, he was sworn to protect the young one. Puck found himself busy, hopping between worlds to safeguard his godson from the many fairy dangers. Puck's time in The Lands of Change were spent teaching his nephew the ways of the Free Folk. During his tutelage, the pair became very close, and before long, they were partners in pranks.

But nothing in The Lands of Change is safe for long. Aware of this, Puck began to teach his godson everything he could about the Firbolg, knowing that the child may one day need to return. And much as Puck expected, the day came when the devious Queen and lily-livered King devised a plan to attain more power. Though their plot was swathed in mystery, Puck recognized that the well thought out scheme involved his precious nephew. Powerless to even speak of it because of the fairy hierarchy, Puck attempted to thwart it instead. Together with his brother they tried to find flaws in their parents' flawless plans. And although they were never able to say a word, the brothers devised what they hoped would be the answer to their problem. For Puck was only good at two things—being mischievous and being puckish, and he hoped it would be enough to stop the King and Queen.

Chapter 18

There was a moment when all went hush. Eamon stooped behind me while Evie hurried to Tom, squeezing his arm. An old pain rolled through me. Judging from Tom's clenched fists, he had it, too. The pair of us glared at Uncle, ready to pounce. Uncle dusted his shoulders off, ogling us from the corner of his eye. It was a classic comic book standoff, like Batman and Robin against The Joker or Cloak and Dagger versus Silvermane.

"I wouldn't do anything silly if I were you," Uncle said slowly in his grimy voice to Tom and I.

"You mean like beat your face in?" I bit back. Tom nodded to me.

"Yes Nephew," Uncle confirmed. "Like *beat* my face in."

"What are you doing here Puck?" Tom growled. "Your kind isn't welcome here."

"Oh really?" asked Uncle as he fabricated a false frown while he pressed his hands over his heart. "Then why have you let Adair in?" Tom gave me a suspect look, furrowing his brow. "That's right Tom. Meet my nephew Adair, the white stag of Autumn Court."

Evie's jaw dropped. Tom pushed her behind him. I gave Evie a fleeting glance, but she was locked on Uncle.

"No fairies in my home," Tom demanded. "Now get out. All of you."

"Tommy," Uncle said while wiping an imaginary tear, "I'm hurt. After all I've done for you?"

"All that you've done for me?" Tom seethed. "You've ruined my life."

"Second that," squeaked Eamon from behind me. "But in hindsight, I think I can deal with it."

"Silence Eamon," Uncle hissed. "I'll handle you later. And Tom," Uncle resumed, a wolfish grin rising, "if you're really that upset, I'd be happy to undo all that I've done for you? That is, if you don't mind me taking back your daughter." Evie gasped. I charged forward, but Uncle spit down at the ground, causing the linoleum floor to swallow my feet up as if I were standing in quicksand. My blood boiled. "Nephew, you reckless boy. Have I taught you nothing?"

"You betrayed us," I shouted while struggling to free my legs. "Father is dead because of you."

Uncle frowned. "No you boob. My brother died so that he could save his *son*. And I helped." I cocked my head back. *What was he up to?* "Now," Uncle said between deep breaths, "if you'd be kind enough to stop your chirping, I'll explain."

Tom must not have cared for Uncle's explanation. He looked around the kitchen before digging into his sink and arming himself with a large knife smattered with dried tomato sauce. "You'll die before I let you say another word," he hollered, lifting the blade over his head and hurling it at Uncle. The knife spun several times before changing into bright confetti.

"Tisk, tisk, Tom," Uncle condoned as he shook confetti from his wing shaped hair. "Keeping secrets from your daughter."

"What is he talking about, Dad?" Evie whimpered.

"Your father has been lying to you Evelyn," said Uncle cooly, pointing his long clawed finger.

"No," Tom yelled, "don't." Uncle smiled. A thousand words passed between their stares before Uncle cleared his throat.

"In particular," Uncle switched his attention to Evie. "I find it comical that Tom doesn't welcome fairies in his home, when in fact, you are one my dear."

Evie staggered backwards, leaning on the dishwasher for support. Tom turned to her pleadingly. "Don't listen to him," he insisted. Evie looked to her Father with glassy eyes.

"Daddy," she called out in a trembling voice. "Is this true?"

My mind was blown. Uncle couldn't lie. In some way or form, Evie was a fairy like me. I was sad to see her so confused, but things were starting to make sense. Her personality, our attraction, and most importantly, Grandmother's interest in her. It was all because she had sidhe blood.

"Oh, it's true," Uncle confirmed, folding his hands together. Tom pressed his eyes shut. "You see, Evelyn, many moons ago your father met a beautiful young fairy who he fell madly in love with. Before long, the two were expecting. After you were born, your mother tried to take you home with her, but Tom insisted you stay. That's where I came in. He and I struck a bargain, you see. I helped barter a fairy pact that kept you on Earth while your mother returned to the Lands of Change, as all queens must rule their kingdoms."

"Are you saying," Evie trembled, "that I'm ..."

"Yes my Lady," Uncle said with a theatrical bow, though his face was expressionless. "You are the daughter of Queen Orla. That makes you the fairy princess of Summer Court. Very storybook, eh?"

Evie's face went blank. Tom turned to her, trying to put his arm around her, but Evie pushed away. "No," she objected, "don't touch me."

"Evie," Tom pleaded, "you must understand. Telling the truth was impossible. Puck knew that, but he didn't warn me." Evie buried her head in her hands. Everything went quiet. "Sweetheart, anyone I tried to mention it to thought I was crazy. They'd tear us apart if I allowed you to believe it as well." Evie lifted her head. Her eyes were pooling.

"Crazy," she considered, wiping a tear from her cheek. "Yes." She shifted her gaze to me and sniffled. "This," she paused, "explains a lot."

Maybe it explained a lot for Evie, but not for me. As much as I wanted to help her, I had questions of my own.

"And what about Father?" I demanded.

"Adair," Uncle glowered. "You offend me. I adored your father."

"Then why did you back Queen Aveline's accusations?"

"Because that's what the Queen ordered me to do," Uncle protested. "And that's what your Father *wanted* me to do."

"What?" I asked while wiggling in linoleum.

"If you haven't already caught on, Queen Aveline and Queen Orla are up to no good. While your Father was powerless to tell me the details, our centuries together helped me put some of the pieces together. The Queens are in league with mortals and have hatched a plan that will help them gain control over the court."

"But alliances are illegal," I objected.

"Thank you for your astute awareness," Uncle said plainly. "I'm still working on all of the facts, but I know Evelyn and yourself are pawns to be manipulated. And for that reason, I've vowed to protect you."

"But why did Father sacrifice himself?" I blurted without any real guile or composure.

Uncle sighed. "Oh, come now Adair. You know damn well that your father doesn't look at the world like most of us. He saw an opportunity to thwart your Grandmother while keeping you safe, so he took it. Besides," he persisted with a hint of disappointment in his voice, "he's back with your mother now."

"How?" I asked with a frog in my throat.

"Come boy. You couldn't tell that he hitchhiked inside of you?" Uncle asked wearily. "He had to so his spirit wouldn't be trapped in the Lands of Change. I tried to talk him out of it, but he's as stubborn as," Uncle looked me over, "*you.*"

The sapphire light I shed when I'd first arrived, the dream of our old cabin—it was real. Father was with Mother. A part of me felt relieved, while yet another part felt naked.

"Don't trust him young fairy," Eamon squeaked.

"Eamon," Uncle whined, "Come off it. Don't act like you haven't made out on our little deal. You now have fairy luck *and* friends. You humans are very ungrateful."

"Your face is ungrateful," I heard Eamon say under his breath.

"So what now then?" I inquired.

"For starters," Uncle said as he grabbed both Evie and my hand. Tom reached out to stop his daughter, but Evie followed. "I need to get you both out of here. Your old babysitter, Liadan, is in town."

"How?" I challenged.

"Oh, I don't know," said Uncle dryly, "fights in sidhe pubs, a scream fest on an airplane. Shall I go on?"

I lowered my head.

"What do you propose then Mr. Puck?" asked Evie. Her words were no longer shaky, and her chin was held high.

"Evelyn, no," begged Tom.

"Dad," Evie said slowly, "this has nothing to do with what you've done. I get it. Well," she shrugged, "mostly. But you need to admit that I've been different for a long time."

"Honey, Puck is not to be trusted," Tom pleaded. Uncle shook his head.

"Daddy," Evie said sweetly, "I don't trust Mr. Puck." She paused. "I trust Adair." My heart beat hard. Tom wiped a tear from his eye as Evie moved closer to me.

"Sir," I cut in, "I know Uncle has a reputation. Heck, I don't trust him either, and he raised me."

"Ouch," said Uncle without signs of agitation.

"But my Father was one of the noblest sidhe in our lands. If this is all part of his plan, then I trust it. I'll do everything in my power to keep Evie safe until she can return to you."

Tom pursed his quivering lips. He studied me for another moment, his jaw clenched. "You'd better," he finally uttered.

"I will," I guaranteed. "Now Uncle, what's the plan?"

"Finally," Uncle sighed. He snapped his fingers, and the linoleum burped my feet out from its depths before returning to a normal. "Adair, do you still have your Father's cloak?"

"I do," I said while unslinging my pack.

"Good," he smiled. "Let me see it."

I flipped my backpack from off my shoulders and opened it. Digging inside, I plucked out the old cloak and handed it over.

"Okay," I said with resolve, "what now?"

"I have no idea," answered Uncle.

"Well," Eamon mocked, "talk about fairy ingenuity."

"Your father broke the barrier in order to prearrange some countermeasures here on Earth. I'm hoping his old cloak is loaded it with some more tricks." Uncle dug through the lining as if trying to find a secret pocket. He began to growl as his efforts proved fruitless. I peeked at Evie. Her body was stiff, and her arms were crossed. "Come on Brother," Uncle cursed. He squeezed every wrinkle, crease and flap, but came up empty. Then, as he slipped his fingers along the edge of the hood, a crooked smile leapt on his face.

"Got it," he shouted as he pulled out a handful of trinkets from a hidden pouch. There was a twig diadem, Father's crystal dragon tear and a stack of vouchers with intricate writing. Uncle plucked out the papers and examined them. There were four tickets. Uncle read the inscription before nodding. "Right then," he said as he passed them out, afterwards handing me back the various items and the cloak. I looked at my ticket.

The Museum of Science and Industry presents Colleen Moore's Miniature Fairy Castle. Admit One.

"Oh happy day," Eamon said while staring at his ticket. "We're going to avoid being murdered from fairies by going sightseeing. Why don't we just take an architectural tour while we're at it."

"I do enjoy tours," Uncle said matter-of-factly.

"I was joking," Eamon sizzled.

"Easy," I warned. "There has to be more than meets the eyes." I turned to Uncle. "Right?"

"Of course there is," Uncle hesitated. I frowned. There was a short pause and then his voice hardened. "Your Father was a great enchanter. He could turn night into day, transform himself into forests or rivers, and he even once compelled a dragon to donate some of its treasure. I'm sure we'll understand more of his plan once we go to this," Uncle inspected his ticket, "Colleen Moore's Miniature Fairy Castle."

"Well," I conceded, "what do we have to lose?"

"Oh," Eamon spit back, "just our lives."

Evie stepped between us and lifted the cloak. "Easy Mr. Optimistic," she said to Eamon as she caressed the leaves covering the cape. "I'm the one who should be terrified here. Now, before we do anything, let's think of how we'll deal with any bad fairies should they arrive."

"Sidhe," corrected Uncle.

"Sure," Evie shrugged.

Just then, a shimmering echo of chimes called throughout the house. The ring was light and ghostly. Tom and Uncle locked eyes.

"Is that what I think it is?" asked Uncle.

"Yes," Tom said grimly. "The fairy charm. It's in Evie's room."

"Then there's no time," Uncle announced. "They're here."

"Who's here?" Eamon asked with a quaking voice.

I focused my ears on the sounds around me, magnifying my perception. Beyond the chimes, I could hear whispers in streets.

"Someone's in the front yard," I warned.

"Very good," Uncle complimented. "Now, I still have my car."

"What about Father?" asked Evie.

"I'm safe honey," said Tom. "Right Puck?"

"Wait," Eamon mumbled. "What?"

"Oh yes," answered Puck. "That charm's ward is good for centuries." I didn't understand what they meant but listed it on the low end of our priorities. We needed to get Evie out of here.

"Wait, charm?" Eamon begged.

"Can we escape through the back?" I inquired.

"Yes," answered Tom.

"Would someone please tell me," hollered Eamon, "what the shit is going on?" Everyone went mute. Uncle walked up to Eamon and slapped him across the cheek. "Ow," Eamon cried. "What was that for?"

"I told you I'd deal with you later."

"Christ," hissed Eamon as he rubbed his reddened cheek.

"Listen up young ones," Uncle whispered, "Liadan and some of her goons are outside waiting for us to leave the safety of the house's enchantments, so we'll need to slip out back. If we can hurry into my car, I'll race us to the museum."

"Did you park out back?" asked Evie.

"No," said Uncle as he dug into his patchy coat. "I parked in my pocket." He plucked out a miniature toy car similar in color to Davin's Irish hotrod.

"Magic?" asked Evie.

"No my dear," Uncle chuckled. "Magic is what mortals use to cheat. This is the real deal. It's enchanted." Evie looked confused. "I'll explain later."

I was nervous but tried to shake it off. I needed to invoke whatever part of Father was in me to get through this ordeal. He'd be levelheaded and calculated. It was crucial that I did the same.

"All right," I called out. "Uncle, I'm assuming you're the only one of us who can cover himself in the veil. Why don't you sneak out first and get the car ready in the alleyway."

"Can do," Uncle said as he tossed the toy car in the air and caught it.

"The what?" asked Eamon.

"You'll see," said Uncle.

"Perfect," I complimented. "Evie, you know the layout of your backyard, so you guide Eamon and myself once we get outside."

"Right," she replied.

"I'm going to cover our backs," I broadcasted. "If they catch us slipping out, I'll try to buy us some time."

"Thank you," Tom said as he stared at his daughter. Evie hurried over and hugged him. Tom kissed her on top of her head. "I love you so much," he gasped. "I'm sorry about all this." Evie squeezed harder.

"What about me?" Eamon asked. "What should I do?"

"Right," I said. "Eamon, you follow Evie to the car. If something bad happens, do what you usually do."

"And what's that?" asked Eamon.

"Panic, scream, and run." I said with a grin, trying to defuse some tension.

"I'm feeling creative today," Eamon retorted without missing a beat. "I might add some flailing of my arms into the mix."

We all smiled.

"Okay team," I said after taking a deep breath. "Let's go over this one more time."

After ironing out a few more details, the group decided to hatch our plan. Those of us who were escaping gathered around Evie's sliding backdoor. Meanwhile, Tom peaked out through the front window. Once he felt the coast was clear, Tom gave the signal, a fake sneeze followed by two coughs. Upon hearing it, the team spun into action. Uncle swirled like a ballerina, disappearing into the veil. Evie gently dragged the backdoor open, allowing a now invisible Uncle to slip through. We collectively counted to thirteen, and then tiptoed out into the yard. Evie took Eamon's hand and guided him to the side of the garage. I let them hurry ahead, scanning the yard. I could still hear Evie's glass fairy chiming, and as I glanced at it through the window, I saw that it glowed in its frame. There were birds singing, crickets chirping, a car motor lightly rumbling from the alley, but no whispers near the front yard any longer. That scared me.

Evie and Eamon made their way to a tall wood gate that separated the backyard from the alley and carefully lifted its clasp. Eamon held the handle as he walked forward towards the back road. Evie, meanwhile, waived me over. I nodded. It would take little more than stepping on a disobliging twig to gain the attention of our visitors. I shut my eyes, taking a deep breath. I needed to summon my inner Batman. I opened them again. To my horror, Liadan's beady red irises had begun to materialize between Evie and I. Evie locked in place. The banshee scowled as she continued to form. She lifted her fingers and untied the ribbon around her head with one hand while removing her cheek dagger and throwing it on the ground with the other. My ears twitched. I could make out a set of footsteps clamoring behind me. I was surrounded.

On instinct, I opened my mouth and blurted, "Evie, banshee. Cover your ears," before lifting my palms toward Liadan. This was going to get ugly.

Luckily, Evie knew what the hell I was talking about. She cupped the sides of her head to block out any sound, and then, sticking to the plan, darted out into the alley. *And that's why she's awesome.* Liadan ignored Evie's exit, instead focusing on me as she continued to take shape. I'd already heard the banshee's scream two times, well, technically, two-and-half times. Once more and I was a goner. But I had nothing going for me when it came to fighting malevolent spirits. So, after a quick leap to scoop up Liadan's dagger, I spun around in order to meet the goons sneaking up behind me. At least I'd go out fighting.

Three sidhe approached. It was obvious that they had no understanding of the Firbolg. They tried to disguise themselves but botched horribly. One, a summer warrior with dark hair and skin, wore a fedora with a jade kimono and bellbottoms. The other two, pale autumn soldiers, sported cheap cowboy and musketeer Halloween costumes. There was no way I was going to let these doofuses beat me. I focused on the lawn between us, urging the air around me to hurl up loose earth. As instructed, a gust of wind blew down onto the backyard and then curved upwards, spraying them with blinding soil and grass. The three fairies grabbed at their eyes.

"I am the vengeance," I spat as I rushed the summer warrior and kicked him in the privates. "I am the night," I continued as I used wind to smash the two autumn soldiers heads together. All three dropped to the ground. "I am Batman."

"Hey Batman, watch out behind you," shouted Uncle from the alley. I spun around to find Liadan within hands reach, her arms extended, and her body fully formed. The open gate behind her gave me a framed view of Uncle hanging out of driver's seat window. He signaled for me to hurry. Out of pure instinct, I sprung up into the air, allowing a current of wind to push me skyward. Like a grasshopper, I leapt over Liadan, landing in the alley. Eamon pushed open the backseat door, and I quickly dove inside.

"Go, go, go," I ordered. The tires screeched in protest. We kicked forward at blinding speeds. I jabbed my index fingers into both ears before peeking out of the back window. Liadan pursued me into the alley and was now watching as we drove away. She didn't scream or give chase. She just stared at us with her drawn jaw.

"Can we go any faster?" I hollered. I'd nearly forgotten that I had my fingers in my ears. I watched as Evie, who sat in the passenger seat, pointed left and then right along the suburban roads, helping Uncle navigate to the highway. The freeway's lanes along Interstate 88 were full but moving fluidly. We blended in with the other cars, matching their speed. We were safe, but for how long was anyone's guess.

"How far until Chicago?" I asked, unplugging my ears. Evie turned around in her seat, eying the dagger I kept between two fingers.

"At this time of day?" she hummed. "An hour or so."

"I could go faster," Uncle suggested with a guttural laugh that sounded more like a death rattle.

"Good God no," Eamon moaned.

"An hour is good Uncle," I objected. From my angle, I could see the slightest smirk from Uncle's face. He was enjoying this.

"How do you know my dad will be safe?" asked Evie.

"My dear Princess," Uncle said while swerving in and out of traffic, "I've been making charms since men and woman called themselves Romans. If not for my enchanted plume, Shakespeare would just have been a washed-up actor."

Evie stared at Uncle from the tops of her eyes. "You're saying you gave Shakespeare a magic pen for his plays?"

Uncle gave a hoarse hum. "Hmm, yes."

Evie shook her head. "Yeah right."

"No legacy is so rich as honesty," quoted Uncle while unfurling the frills on his driving hand's sleeve. "You may believe what you want my dear. But to answer your question, your father will be fine so long as takes that charm along with him wherever he goes. He and I have already discussed the details."

"Thanks Puck," Evie nodded before staring out of her window.

We drove down the twisting highways of Illinois for quite some time. Once we'd merged onto to I-290, shock and uncertainty hitched a ride, stifling conversation. I never paid much attention to road systems in any of my comics, but as I leaned my head on the car's glass as sleek sedans and immense vans rode by, it occurred to me how interesting Earth was. Car after car zoomed along an immense stone road, carelessly guiding vehicles powered by fire and harnessed through steel. Children nestled in back seats watched televisions from carpeted ceilings while their parents steered merrily along. I looked at Evie, who was combing her fingernails through her hair, and wondered.

My mind idled with unproductive thoughts and impractical whims until finally, the gaping skyline of Chicago emerged. We drove deeper into its arms until we were immersed in the beeping horns and parades of pedestrians alongside the skyscrapers' feet. The city was still as beautiful as I'd remembered it this morning, but an ominous shadow from the late afternoon sun casted along it. We steered our way through the heart of the downtown area, emerging near a park with a colossal wedding cake shaped fountain. Sculpted seahorses swimming in the pool sprayed water from their yawning muzzles while a stream of blue jetted up into the sky.

"That's Buckingham Fountain," said Evie as we stared out our windows.

Eamon's jaw dropped. "Oh happy day," he mumbled. "I read about it in a tourist's guide."

"Maybe we should take the architectural tour after all," Uncle tossed in. Eamon frowned, crossed his arms and leaned back in his seat.

We hugged the shores of the Lake until arriving at the Museum of Science and Industry's parking lot. Uncle parked between two large trucks. Once we'd withdrawn, he checked to make sure there weren't any spectators before tapping the car's hood. The sports car shrunk until it was a red toy sitting along black cement. He scooped up the model and handed it to me.

"Here," he whispered as he shoved the car in my hand, "take it. You never know."

"I couldn't," I refused. "Besides I don't know how to drive."

"True," he said as he tucked the car in his pocket. "Oh, and I release you from your Rule of Three." I felt a tension in my neck and shoulders release. "You no longer have to conduct any pranks, though I highly advice that you keep your sense of humor." Even after all I'd accused him of, Uncle was still looking out for me. He placed his hand on my shoulder. "I never was able to tell you how sorry I am about Oran."

I began to choke up. "Me, too," I said while slapping my arm on his.

"Um," Evie said as she stopped ahead of us, "I hate to be the burster of bubbles Puck, but I'm not sure security will let you in dressed like that."

Uncle stared down at his wardrobe. He looked like a cast member from an offshoot pirate movie. He snarled before waving his hands over his face. Within the blink of an eye, he'd changed back into Davin.

"Honestly," he griped as we moved towards the museum stairs, "I don't think kids know what fashion is today."

"Are we sure," said Eamon as we walked towards the entrance, "that they'll let him inside?" No one answered.

There was a short line that we waded through, and after showing our tickets, the four of us made our way in. The museum's interior was enormous with sky lofty ceilings and stretched halls. A steam locomotive greeted visitors near the entrance and full-scale planes hung from ceiling. We pushed passed the crowds towards directional signs for the Fairy Castle. After passing through a farm exhibit and several architectural displays, we made our way into the presentation chamber where lo and behold, Colleen Moore's Miniature Fairy Castle awaited.

The model castle looked nothing like Havgan or the Crystal Tower. It was a Firbolg interpretation the size of a small car with medieval towers and gardens, encased in a glass display case. As I circled the model looking for clues, I found that the other side of the building's walls was exposed so that runny nosed children and fanny pack sightseers could gawk at its finely crafted interior. Inside were dozens of rooms, from an intricate dining area with a replica round table from King Arthur's court to a drawing hall with a crystal chandelier and elaborate mural. It was all very beautiful to be sure, but none of it told us what to do next. I took a few deep breaths, waiting for other visitors to leave. Once it was clear, I let loose and slapped on the glass surface.

"Great," I gasped while pacing. "There's nothing freaking here."

Uncle stared at me very hard for a moment, frowning.

Evie patted me on the chest. "Easy white stag," she said while reading the inscriptions along each room. "There has to be something."

I cocked my head at her. "Does there?"

"Look," Evie said in a calm voice, "I didn't know your father, but unless you were lying back at my house, he sounds like a good man. Or, err, fairy." Evie shrugged. "Fairy-man."

"Nailed it," Eamon mocked. Evie stuck out her tongue.

"Fairies don't lie," Uncle said indignantly while scanning every corner of the castle and display room. "And Brother wouldn't do that. There's something here. We just need to think outside the box."

"This is one time," Evie said while looking at the small-scale magic garden encased in glass, "that I literally think we should think inside the box. Now, does this furniture have any significance for your kind?"

"Our kind," I smiled.

"Right," she said while looking down at her shoes. "I'm still getting use to the idea. I meant our kind."

I passed on the chance to poke at Evie, instead searching the model kitchen and Prince's bathroom. "No," I sighed. "I wish there was."

"Well, that's just great," said Eamon while shaking his head. "What'll we do now?"

"Eamon," I said bluntly, giving him a deadpan stare, "you don't have to stay here. Last time I checked; you were only in it for revenge. Well," I said while pointing at Uncle. "There he is."

"Even if I could kill the bastard," Eamon shouted while glaring at Uncle, "there's still a bloodthirsty banshee out in the streets searching for us. So," he caught his breath, "although I'd love to walk away, I'm just as trapped as I was when I first met you."

"Okay," Evie called out, "easy everyone. We're all a bit stressed. Let's just take a minute."

Eamon's face turned radish red. He flailed his arms in the air. "Or else what? Is Mr. Goodfellow going to slap me again?"

"No," I objected.

Uncle smiled. "Never say never."

"Shut it," I hissed in Uncle's direction.

"You see," Eamon bellowed. "He's not to be trusted, Adair. Now, unless you want to spend the rest of our days staring outside Barbie's dream home, I suggest we ditch your Uncle and go."

Uncle, Eamon, Evie and I exchanged looks. After a moment, Uncle opened his smirking mouth to speak, but Evie shushed him before he could get out a word.

"Wait," she said steadily. "Maybe we aren't supposed to be outside Barbie's dream home. Maybe we're supposed to be inside it."

"Huh?" I said, dumbfounded.

"Everyone take out your tickets?" Evie requested. We all dug in our pockets and fished out the passes. The once white paper with generic designs was now glowing gold. "Look," Evie exclaimed, "something's happening to them."

"They'll need something to trigger the enchantment," said Uncle. He stared at the paper pinched between his fingers before looking up at me. "Adair, what was the last thing your father said to you again? When we were all," he paused with a frown, "at the Crystal Tower."

I took a moment to recall those last moments with Father. I was so afraid, but I could still remember everything. I'd called out to him after he'd addressed the sidhe crowd. He'd fought to get close to me, looking into my eyes before telling me, "When the time comes," I said out loud, "use what I've given you."

Suddenly, a sizzling resonated within the room and the four of us disappeared. I hadn't noticed that I closed my eyes, but when I'd opened them, I found that I was standing in a life size great hall with the others. The four of us took in our surroundings. There were elegant statues, polished armor and masterful paintings strewn along the blonde marble walls. A floating staircase twisted to a second floor, and a gold-framed archway led outside. There were smells of cooked meat and the sweet sounds of violins. Four strange looking humans bearing exaggerated features—long chins and cartoonish noses—stood in attention just in front of the fireplace, their white suits flawless.

"What the shit?" I said as I spun in poised circles, ready for anything.

"Very good, Oran," Uncle complimented to the ceiling.

"It's amazing," Evie cued, grasping my hand and tugging it so that I stopped in place.

"I need a drink," Eamon respired wistfully.

"Ah, sir," called a longhaired man in a white frockcoat. His snow hair was pulled tightly to his scalp and his cheeks were shaper than a dagger. He had a silver platter in his hand with a single letter. "Welcome home." He bowed before lifting the tray. "A message from your father if you would."

"Um," I said while taking the letter. "Hey buddy, I don't mean to be rude, but where the heck are we?"

"Not at all," said the man as he dipped his head. "You're home, sir." He lifted an arm and gestured to a dozen other men and women as they entered from the gold archway as if to present themselves. "We are your humble servants, and we are here to see to yours and Lady Evie's every need. You will want for nothing."

"Think inside the box," I said while looking at Evie.

She jabbed me in my ribs. "Easy white stag. Now, what does your dad have to say?"

I peeled open the lip of the envelope and read the parchment inside.

My dearest Adair,

Long, long ago when stones were still soft, there was a fool who left home to find his brother. He was Autumn Court, so naturally he assumed that he had nothing to gain from his trip besides finding his sibling. Well, after many days of searching, the fool not only found his brother, but a reason to never come home. Because during his time amongst the Firbolg, the fool learned that the endearing humans were unblemished by the fairy ways. So he stayed amongst them to find someone worthy enough to keep him happy. But, as all good stories go, it would be the fool who found himself questioning his worth to make another happy. And from it, you were born.

I met your mother in a time before roads and cities. It was a time when the Firbolg were still made of clans, and they referred to us as the Tuatha Dé Danann. Son, I tell you now, and I tell you honest, your mother was lovelier than a grave flower, and the mystery of her exquisiteness was something I wanted to spend every day trying to solve. Soon, we were wed, and for one meager decade, the two of us spent everyday side by side until you were born. That's when we learned that we could love something more than we did each other.

You were such a good boy, and watching you grow was our favorite pastime. But then, in a week that had three Sundays, you were struck with fever. We had to make a choice. All it would take was passing you through the Green Rift to cleanse you of your mortal illness, but in turn, we could never return. Worse yet, while the courts were forced to honor our marriage contract, they refused to let your mother set foot in our world. After much deliberation and heartache, I took you into the Lands of Change, and shortly after, the borders were closed. Your mother and I never saw each other again.

Now, this isn't a tale to make you feel guilty. I know that your mother and I would give a thousand lives to protect you. This is a lesson about a fool. There is danger in The Lands of Change. I never realized it until I left, but it is a terrible place. Earth is unsafe for you and the half child of Summer, as our kind will surely be searching for you both. I wish I could have done more since learning your grandmother's plans, but this is what I can offer.

Please, do what I only wished I could. Enjoy this secret home that I've enchanted for you and the half child of Summer. Anyone inside will be safe for the remainder of their days. There is nothing good for you beyond your new home. Only heartache. Enjoy your paradise and be as happy as your mother and I are now.

I love you Adair. Take care of Evelyn.
Oran.

Chapter 19

Some things are just meant to be together. Vodka and tonic. Green eggs and ham. *My parents.* Father's plan was clear. He'd exposed Autumn and Summer's wicked plot but was burdened by The Rule of Three to keep quiet. In a last-ditch effort to protect Evie and myself, he crossed the Green Rift, leaving a trail of breadcrumbs for us to follow. *His end game?* Hide us in a clandestine paradise, a place that he no doubt had been waiting centuries to share with Mother.

This told a hundred tales. It explained Father's exhaustion on that day in his study. It would take a great amount of himself to create our sanctuary. He'd be exhausted for days. It also explained the expedited summit of the courts, undoubtedly directed by the Queens to launch their scheme before father could thwart it. Most importantly though, it explained how wicked Grandmother really was. I imagined even now after the death of her only son, her eyes were dry, her smile was sly, and her soul was cold. Her mind raced ahead to the day when her schemes would surface.

Regardless, if I were to honor the dying wishes of a great sidhe, I'd keep away from it all. It wasn't too difficult. Weeks had gone by since our arrival. While we pretended we could still leave at any time, there was never a dire need to think about it. Every comfort one could ask for was in our new home. We held great feasts in the dining hall, attended concerts in the garden, and at night, Evie, Uncle, Eamon and I visited the roof of the main tower to watch the stars dance their glittered ballet. Naturally, it took some getting used to. It's gauche to be waited on hand and foot by an army of servants when you know that there are people who want you dead. It was especially hard for Evie, who constantly worried for her Father. But through the insistence of Uncle that his wards would hold, and the persistence of our servants' hospitality, those fears sank to the bottom of an ethical ocean.

We lived in dreamland after all, alongside some of the finest company one could ask for. After meals, Eamon shared some of his hand-me-down stories by the hearth, while in the afternoon, Uncle conjured illusionary games to tutor Evie and me on our hidden talents.

Evie was eager to learn wild form, a gift of Summer, while I began to unlock the secrets of wielding the Veil. But as wonderful as Eamon and Uncle were, the best company was always Evie.

Admittedly, things were awkward between us at first. True, we enjoyed some magical days in Killarney together, but since then, it had been all danger and peril. We didn't want to force anything. But as moons past, eventually jokes became whispers, whispers became kisses, and nights stretched out up until dawn. It was simple for me. I adored her, and our new home only nurtured such sentiments. For her, though, I couldn't be certain. She was withdrawn by nature, so I never knew if the feeling was mutual. Then one day, she addressed it.

We were in the library, her reading Andrew Smith by the light of a candelabrum while I dove into my favorite Morbius comic. I watched from my peripherals as she slapped her book shut, as if something profound had come to her.

"What's up?" I asked from my seashell shaped reading chair. Evie, who was curled up in pillows, leaned her chin into her fingers, staring at me with a smile. She inspected me from top to bottom. "What?" I insisted.

"You're in love with me aren't you?" she asked through an enduring grin.

I whistled. "Wow."

"Answer the question. Yes or no?"

"Evie," I chuckled, "what the hell was in that book?"

"Just answer the question."

I paused. "Fine. Guilty as charged."

"I knew it," she smiled. She rolled over so that her body was facing me but remained silent. The tick tock of the library's grandfather clock was the only sound in the room. I stared back, waiting for more, but Evie didn't budge.

"Well?" I said loudly.

"Well what?"

"Well damn it, how do you feel?"

"Are those the words you want to use at a moment like this?"

"Fine," I said while plopping my comic book down. "How the *heck* do you feel?"

Evie laughed. "I don't know," she said while combing her fingers through her hair. "I mean," she hesitated. "Yeah, I think so."

"Yeah, you think what?"

"Yes," she said seriously. "I love you."

I didn't know until this moment, but I'd been waiting a very long time to hear those words. A weight lifted from my shoulder, and all at once I felt complete.

I stared at her as the orange from the candlelight flickered off her face. "Okay great," I said confidentially, my chin held high. "When do you want to tie the knot?"

Evie picked up one of her pillows and threw it at me. "You're impossible."

"Wait," I said while blocking the pillow. "Why not?"

Evie stammered. "You're serious? How would we?"

"Evie, there's a damn chapel in our house."

"Who'd look over the ceremony?"

"Uncle married my parents. He could do it for us, too."

"Puck?" she complained.

"Why not?" I asked while sitting up from my cozy chair. "Come on, he's not that bad. I mean the guy did save our lives. Not to mention that he taught you how to turn into a freaking falcon. I'm sure there are a lot of women out there who would marry me if they could turn into a falcon." Evie rolled her eyes. "Seriously, though, he could conduct the entire thing."

"I don't know," she said through a beaming grin while shaking her head. "Can you really see yourself being stuck with me for the rest of your life?"

"Can you?"

Evie put a finger to her lips. The girl was a flip of a coin. I'd seen her as stubborn as a weed on some days, and impulsive as the weather on others. I crossed my fingers that unpredicted storms were in my future.

"Okay," she said bluntly. "But I'll need Father and Lidia to be here. Oh, and Brigid, too."

"Trust me, we're going to need witnesses. Otherwise no one will believe that you agreed to this."

"That's it," Evie hooted, throwing another pillow. "The wedding is off."

I stood up and tottered over to her. "No going back now," I insisted before leaning in and kissing her.

***

The next few moons consisted of preparations. Uncle spent his time learning how to pass through Father's enchantment in order to gather our attendees, as well as composing our marriage contract. The document had to be flawless in case we ever needed to present it to the courts. Meanwhile, the servants were in an uproar to arrange the castle for guests and a wedding ceremony. Eamon, who was in his usual state of panic, needlessly stressed over what he'd say during his speech.

"This may be my only opportunity to do something like this," he pleaded. "What would my granddad think if I couldn't even get a proper speech right?"

As for Evie and me, we didn't much let the flow of this wedding thing slow us down. Then again, we had it easy. All we needed to do was show up. Everyone else seemed to want to do the rest. So, while the castle was in turmoil, we just sat back and watched as everyone fell to pieces. Every morning we ate breakfast while the servants dashed to rearrange furniture, and every night we went to bed while listening to Eamon practice his speech in the neighboring room.

Then one day, shortly after learning how to return to Earth, Uncle returned with our guests. We were baptized with relief to see Tom in one piece, and it was an added bonus to have Lidia and Brigid. For the next few days before the wedding, we savored the company. It was a delight to hear Brigid was adjusting to being married to a ghost. She also firmly requested that she help hem Evie's dress while Lidia aided with moral support. As for Tom and me, we spent the next few moons getting to know each other better. After all, I was marrying his daughter.

He was quiet, but in a sage like way. He reminded me of Father. We spent a lot of time over drinks talking about The Lands of Change and Tom's history. He once explained to me that from his perspective, he'd fallen for a girl in his youth, who just so happened to be a fairy. And even though she'd abandoned him, the gift she left behind was all worth it. Since then, he'd just been trying to make things as right as possible. It was simple, but respectable. I was happy to have him.

Finally, though, the night of our wedding had come. The servants prepared my clothing. It was a bit outdated for my tastes, but then again, the help were mere shadows of Father's creativity, no doubt behind the times when it came to human fashion. The tailored coat clung tightly to my frame. It was sable with white vines that striped elegantly down its fabric. Beneath it, I wore a black vest with matching trousers over a white puffy shirt and a pair of tall dark riding boots. I looked like a damn vampire romance cover, but everyone insisted that it would complement Evie.

When I arrived in the main hall, I noticed that the servants were adorned in black-and-whites like my own. Harps played in the background and the aroma of rose petals emanated throughout the castle. I could hear mumbled voices whispering past the chapel doors. Eamon waited just at the entrance, his available hair slicked back and tied with a bow. He sported a white tuxedo that already had a light trace of cigarette ash near his sleeve. I wanted to tell him not to be nervous, but the same jitters crept up my leg and bit me.

With servants and friends handling everything, I barely had time to ponder what was about to happen. Today, Evie and I were binding ourselves to one another. We'd be together forever. I couldn't foresee any better fate for myself than waking up to her every morning, wasting our days talking about nothing as we grew fat and old. But then again, would I be enough to keep her happy? *Uh oh.* The wedding hadn't even started yet, and I'd already had too much to think. But before I could completely fall apart, the servants ushered me into reality.

"For you, Sir," said one of the pages as he held a glass of water to my lips. I took a sip and thanked him. "It's time, Sir," he said after patting my face with a handkerchief. The great doors opened, and I was ushered inside. Lit candles scattered throughout the quarters like stars in the sky, brilliantly shimmering off the gold pillars, sculptures and other accents that colored the room. In the flower covered pews were dozens of servants. Brigid sat at a front pew with a large puffy dress, and Uncle waited at the altar in a suit of gold, his hair still bird-like and spread. A long scroll floated at waste height, scribbled with tiny lettering.

Eamon and I were brought to the front near Uncle, who nodded to me with his mischievous grin. I smiled back. I'd been wrong about him this entire time. He was my very good friend, as wild as he could sometimes be. He wanted nothing but the best for me. We waited there for a moment before the chapel doors opened once more. The light harp that was playing throughout the castle silenced, replaced by the heavy call of the violin. The candles dimmed and whispers went mute. Everyone stood up. Two shadows waited near the threshold of the doors. I could hear Tom murmur.

"Ready?" he asked quietly. There was no answer. I couldn't see if Evie nodded or smiled. Suddenly, the two began to walk forward. As Evie walked into the chapel's light, I took glimpse of my future. *It looked amazing*.

The white gown flowed off her like champagne. Her hair was elegantly curled and bound with small decorative vines. Her skin seemed to glisten like lake water and her eyes shined like diamonds. She looked up at me as she approached, a delighted smile stretched across her face. The same smile I'd seen the first time we'd met in *The Bleeding Wolf*. As we met at the altar, Tom handed her off, and together our hands united. I stared at her, dumbstruck and hypnotized by her beauty.

"Let the ceremony of marriage begin," Uncle called out as everyone took their seats.

Apparently, blacking out is my thing when I'm nervous. I don't remember much of the service, just the dizzy highlights. I remember Uncle reading the terms of the contract, and me stuttering through my vows. I remember Evie pledging herself to me. I remember the sting of the knife as Uncle pricked my finger, the coolness of the quill as it soaked my blood, and the scratching noise crooned as I signed my name to the contract. I remember laying Mother's diadem on Evie's lovely blond hair, a ring being placed on my finger, and the kiss that would echo a thousand centuries.

"By the authority endowed to me by the courts," Uncle announced at the end, "I announce this contract sanctioned by The Lands of

Change." And with that, the contract devoured itself, shrinking into a blue flame that all at once disappeared. I felt a warm heat in my chest as if I'd had a shot of whiskey, and as I looked to Evie, I could tell from her sudden gasp and squeeze of her hand, that she'd felt it, too. "Go now and be together."

We left the chapel to a storm of music and the thunder of clapping and made our way to the gardens. Lamps lit up the green fields and newly installed marble ballet platform. As we took in all the sights, from our grand cake to the crystal fountain, our attendees poured in behind us. The rest of the night was spent dancing and celebrating until finally the moon began to fall. Exhausted, we thanked our guests before making our exit, entering our chambers as man and wife. I'll leave the rest to your imagination, but let's just say that it took several weeks to regain my strength.

This is the part where I say, *and we lived happily ever after*. It's the part where anyone being told the fairytale becomes overjoyed because everything worked out perfectly for our happy couple. But that wasn't the case. Because although we resided in paradise, happily married with some of the best company one could ask for, fate has a way of turning life upside-down. Yes, much like bad milk in fresh tea, it wasn't long before it all spoiled.

At first being newlyweds was exciting. Not but three months after our wedding, Evie came to me with a gift. It was a neatly wrapped box. When I opened it, I found a miniature glass fairy like the one Evie had kept in her room wrapped in tissue paper. Since I'm as thick as wood, it took me a second to understand. I just stood there with the glass figurine in my hand, staring at it as if it were a puzzle. Then it hit me. *We were expecting.*

From there, it all happened so fast. Everyone was so excited for Evie and me, that they didn't give us time to think. We picked out the baby's room and children's names until our faces turned blue. The castle's help stitched miniature garments and constructed wood toys. Eamon painted the nursery and Uncle made veiled visits to Earth to get Evie anything she might need. Once news made it to The Bleeding Wolf, Bridget promised to help with anything Evie might need. But, as the days passed and quiet anxiety grew into full fledge fear, an idea crept into our minds.

At first, I thought it was just me. Like a common cold, I waited for it to pass. Only it didn't pass. It festered. The reality was that while we were happy in Father's paradise, it wouldn't be long before this sanctuary felt more like a prison. Evie was rightfully nervous about her inability to see doctors or specialists. Plus, even if the birth process went well, how could we punish our child by trapping them in a single household with only illusionary servants, Eamon and Uncle as companions? How could we force this child into the seclusion that Evie and I suffered in our own childhoods? It wasn't right. We needed to go back to Earth. But the only way to do that meant putting an end to Grandmother's plot.

I knew that Uncle wouldn't agree to it, so we had no choice. We planned against him. Not shortly after Evie and I collectively agreed to return to Chicago did we ask Uncle to teach us how to return to the other side in case there was ever an emergency. He was reluctant at first, but because he trusted me, and because he wanted the baby to remain safe, he eventually agreed. Shortly after, he taught us how to surpass Father's world. And with that, all Evie and I needed to do was hatch our plan. We had elected to give up paradise to have a sense of freedom. We'd risk it all for peace of mind. If it went as planned, there'd be nothing to worry about. But if we failed, we'd be marked as fools.

Chapter 20

Long, long ago, when powerful dragons still lived on land and sea, there was a sidhe woman who went by the name of Aveline. Born of nobility, and branded by beauty, she learned early on that what one desires must be taken. Aveline did not acquire such practices from her pompous parents, nor from her unfriendly friends. No. She learned it through the blood and pain of her own experience.

Her elder sister Mara, to whom her parents arranged to take the Autumn throne once she became of age, was just as lovely and twice as cruel as Aveline. Each sunrise, Mara gloated about her future queendom. Each moonrise, Mara tormented Aveline with promises to make her head of the housemaids. Though Aveline would never let her enemy see her grief, her loathing for her sister twisted into a frightening fury. Soon, Aveline's seed of hate grew into an untamable thorn bush.

Time passed, and Mara's marriage to the Autumn Prince drew near. Though the future Queen grew ever more wicked, her sister Aveline bent to her sister's will. She waited on Mara hand and foot, seemingly ready for her future as a housemaid. And every time Mara made a snide remark, Aveline made note. Every time Mara struck her sister, Aveline tallied the count. She lay it wait like a serpent in a shrub or crocodile in shallow waters, ready and waiting to strike.

That time came on the day of her sister's wedding. Every maid in the Autumn lands had assembled to dress their future queen, and after the gown had been draped, the help began to adorn their highness in jewelry. Each of Mara's fingers were graced by silver rings from far Spring. Mara's neck was decorated in ornate necklaces from northern Summer. She wore rare bracelets from Winter and master crafted anklets from Autumn. By the end, Mara bore one-thousand-three-hundred-and-thirteen pieces of jewelry.

But upon walking to the alter, Mara was unable to carry the weight of her attire. The audience watched in horror as Mara collapsed. Inch by inch, Mara crawled her way to her groom before dying. No one ever knew how a fairy born free of age and illness could pass in such a way, but rumor surfaced that her black heart poisoned the rest of her flesh.

And because Mara's parents had promised a bride for marriage, they offered their second daughter Aveline as recompense. By the following season, Aveline had become Queen of Autumn.

Later, when her sister's mishap had all but been forgotten, Queen Aveline took the one-thousand-three-hundred-and-thirteen pieces of jewelry, the same number of wrongs that Mara had committed against her little sister and melted them down. She requested that the master smith take all the cold-iron she'd laced in each piece and fashion it into a dagger that she later gifted it to Liadan, her banshee Lady-in-Waiting. She named the dagger "The Queen's Reprisal," and for years it helped keep Liadan's jaw shut.

Chapter 21

It was the day of our great escape. Uncle had left for Killarney to ward *The Bleeding Wolf*, and Eamon was off flirting with one of the maids in the gardens. We'd told him a hundred times that they weren't real people, but it never stopped him. Evie and I had packed our bags the night before, arming ourselves with an arsenal fit for *The Punisher*. Along with an array of silverware, tools and other things that go "stabby" in the night, we brought Liadan's cold-iron dagger, Father's dragon pendant, and Evie's miniature fairy ward. The two of us dressed in our Firbolg clothes. I didn't tell Evie, but I secretly wore my Autumn tunic underneath. Using what Uncle had taught us, we held hands and concentrated on the Museum of Science and Industry.

You given I've what use," we repeated three times, "comes times the when."

A familiar sizzling sound fizzed in the room and then suddenly we were back at the museum. The air was chilled, and the fresh smell of lemon floor cleaner tickled my nose. The building must have been closed because all lights were dim. I stared at our model house, imagining how many children wished it were real. I slipped through the veil, disappearing from human eyes. Evie meanwhile shifted into a flaxen mouse and was already darting through the museum halls before I took my first step. Together we followed the path back out to the main doors, where we waited for a patrolling security guard to depart. Once the patrol woman used her keys to open the alarm-doors, we hurried behind her to make our exit. *Black Cat, eat your heart out.*

The Stygian sky wore a shroud of dark clouds that suffocated the moon. The air was no longer hot like it was when we'd entered the museum. Evie transformed back into her human self, and the two of us scurried through the museum lawn towards the main street. As we did, a soft popping noise cracked behind us. I spun around, surprised to find a speeding bat charge me.

"There you are," cried the bat's rider. It was Fergal. He wore the same ceremonial attire I'd last seen him in but was now filthy with frizzy hair and a worn expression. "I've been searching high and low for you Adair."

Alarmed, Evie quick-drew the miniature fairy ward and held it at Fergal. Tess slowed down in front of Evie.

"Well that's a pretty ornament," complimented Fergal. Evie frowned. She took in the miniature sidhe, drawing her eyes to Fergal's penis gourd.

"Um Evie," I spoke quietly, extending my arm. "This is Fergal. He's a friend."

Evie dropped her guard. Fergal pulled Tess's reigns, and the bat landed on my hand.

"How do you do my Lady?" Fergal greeted with a bow.

"It's Evie," she said simply. Fergal ignored her, clearing his throat.

"Sir," he shouted directly into my ear. I winced. "There is great danger about."

"I know," I replied. "That's why we're here. We need to stop Grandmother."

"It's too late," Fergal warned. "Queen Aveline and Orla have united the Autumn and Summer armies, taking the kings and queens of Spring and Winter prisoner. They claim that they have the legal right to create their alliance and have usurped the courts."

I frowned. "And nothing from the court's book of contracts stopped them?"

"I'm afraid not, Sir," Fergal glowered. "They must have found some minor loophole in the Court's pact. They're amassing all the armies now. And when I say all the armies, I mean Summer, Autumn, Spring and Winter. It appears that they look to pass through the Green Rift."

"That's bad isn't it?" Evie cut in.

"Yes, darling," I answered. "Real bad." I closed my eyes and took a deep breath before returning to the conversation. "Fergal, how could this happen? The court's contracts are designed by the best and brightest sidhe."

"How indeed my Lord," said Fergal as he scratched his frizzy hair. "I'm not sure to be honest," he confessed. "Truthfully, I've been living in the wilds since your escape. I've had little chance to gather any real facts." *Fergal's words kicked me between my legs.* The poor guy had been living like a refugee because he'd helped me flee from the courts. "Once I found out, though, I immediately snuck off to find you. It wasn't easy," he said as he waived his finger at me, "but I knew the son of Oran would be able to come up with some type of plan."

"Well," I said while straightening our back. "your right." I looked to Evie. "Our mission doesn't change. We need to get to the Fairy Fort in Killarney so we can stop Grandmother. Evie, I was very drunk last time. How long does it take to get back to Ireland?"

"Oh my God," Evie said while slapping her forehead. "You didn't tell me we needed to head back to Ireland. We don't have the time or money for that."

"What are you talking about?" I asked.

"Adair," Evie said while shaking her head. "That trip is a ten hour flight and a few thousand dollars. What were you thinking?"

Apparently, I hadn't been thinking. I was feeling really stupid that I'd let such a major detail slip through the cracks. The plan was already crashing and burning.

"Sir," Fergal said while stomping on my shoulder. "No need to fear. We can use the nearby rift that your Grandmother opened. It's how I made it here. Any sidhe that crosses its waters will be transported through the Green Rift."

"Where is it?" I asked.

"The seahorse sprout," Fergal said, pointing north.

"Are you talking about the Buckingham Fountain?" Evie asked.

"Is it big with seahorses?" Fergal countered.

"It is," Evie replied.

"Then yes," Fergal said while patting Tess behind her oversized ears.

"I knew it," Evie said while shaking her head. "I'd always been drawn to that damn fountain."

Fergal looked confused. "Why?"

"Don't worry about it Fergal," I interjected, not wanting to risk him knowing who Evie *really* was. I'd sworn to keep her and our unborn child safe, and I wasn't going to risk it all now. Telling anyone, even sweet loyal Fergal, could go poorly. "She's just a fountain enthusiast."

I looked to Evie and shook my head. Evie nodded. Fergal grimaced as he pulled Tess's reigns, taking back to the air.

"All right then," I called out, puffing out my chest. "If what Fergal says is true, then there's no time to waste. We must get to the Autumn lands. Darling," I said while ripping open my jacket, revealing the red tunic with an autumn leaf on its chest. "Are you ready?"

Evie tried to contain her laugh, covering her mouth with her hands.

"Come on," I begged. "I've been waiting a long time to do that."

Evie doubled over in hysterics. "No, no," she said with watery eyes after catching a breath. "It was cute."

"Cute?" I objected.

"I mean," she stopped herself. "Very epic. Please," she gasped, "put on the cape."

"I will," I said as I dug Father's cloak out from my pack. Defiantly, I clasped the cloak around my neck. Evie covered her mouth with her hand. "Now, shall we?"

"Sure, Leaf Man," Evie said as she calmed herself, "let's go." Russet feathers sprouted from her head and her eyes turned gold. "Follow me," she instructed, her voice going hard. All at once she'd transformed into a falcon and took to the air. Fergal bobbed his head.

"Impressive," Fergal complimented. "Now I understand why you're being so mysterious." He slapped Tess's reigns and quickly followed behind Evie skyward. The three of them skimmed the belly of the grim clouds. Already behind, I called forth for a heavy wind, and sped into the night sky.

The trip was brief. The three of us followed the lakeshore, hidden along the rim of slate clouds. Once we'd reached Buckingham Fountain, Fergal took the lead, diving down until he splashed into the water's surface. Evie's silhouette fluttered after him, descending through the pool. I held my hands out and quickly followed, praying that the portal would accept me. *Here goes nothing.* As I plunged in, the familiar sensation of a dreamlike vacuum filled my mind. Random memories and arbitrary emotions flashed before me, as they had when I'd first crossed the Green Rift. I waded in lifelessness until finally my senses returned.

When they had, I found that we were back in Summer's courtyard, spit out from the Weeping Pond onto the nearby grass. Columns of armed Summer, Autumn, Winter and Spring warriors surrounded the pool at the ready, staring over the four of us as we lay prone. On top of the royal platform, elevated above the massive army, stood Grandmother and Queen Orla, both dressed in grandiose robes and surrounded by their many servants. A loud set of trumpets called out into the gardens.

"Loyal subjects," Grandmother announced proudly in her brown leather robes that had been fashioned to mirror the texture of tree bark, "I give you the heroes of our lands, Prince Adair of Autumn, and Princess Evelyn of Summer. It is their marriage contract that has created the strongest alliance that ever graced our realm." Grandmother's cold eyes thinned as she bore a hole through me, her deadpan expression masking the jester smile underneath. Liadan, who I hadn't noticed before, peaked her translucent head from behind Grandmother's shoulder, her jaw once again bound by ribbon, but no longer clasped by a dagger.

It all made sense now. Grandmother and Queen Orla weren't angry that I'd escaped through the Green Rift. They were counting on it. Liadan wasn't chasing me this entire time. She was shepherding me. The Queens wanted me to meet Evie. They needed us to get married on Earth. By doing so, our contract bypassed the laws of the courts, but still bound an alliance between Summer and Autumn. *What had I done?*

Queen Orla, who wore a revealing top that looked more like a tangled scarf wrapped around her chest, gazed down at Evie. "Hello Daughter," she greeted in her heavy, demure voice. Evie took my hand. "You are as beautiful as I'd expected." Queen Orla looked down at her other daughter, Ailsa, who embraced Orla's lower legs. "Ailsa, don't you think that Evelyn is beautiful?" Ailsa sneered. "Oh yes," Orla said under her breath, "very beautiful."

General Stroxson and a small number of his guards crowded the area that Evie, Fergal, Tess, and me anchored down at.

"Grandmother," I shouted while reaching for Liadan's cold iron dagger sheathed in my pack's side pouch. *Wap!* A dull, but hard slap hit me in the back of the head. Evie screamed. I put my hand towards the spot where I'd been struck and felt blood.

"You will address her as Queen Aveline," said General Stroxson, the blunt side of his cold-iron spear now red.

"Be calm General," Grandmother called out through a false tone of sympathy. "Clearly, Earth has rubbed off on young Adair's manners."

"Grandmother, how could you?" I shouted, glaring at her as I held the back of my bleeding head.

"How could I?" asked Grandmother innocently, placing her hand on her heart. "How could I what? Prince Adair, I haven't done anything. It's *you* that went ahead and fell in love." Queen Aveline stared down at Evie. "But how could you not? She's so lovely." Queen Orla and Grandmother exchanged pleased looks.

Suddenly, Fergal took to the air. "You killed my master you red handed fiend." He guided Tess over the army's heads towards the platform. Liadan materialized into a solid figure, catching Fergal with her hand. I watched as the pint-sized champion recoiled, his fingers curling in agony as both he and Tess went limp.

"No," I hollered as I jutted forward. Evie grabbed me by my cape and yanked me back.

"Adair," she said in a hushed tone, "stop or you're going to get us killed."

"Killed?" said Grandmother in a low tone from her spot on the platform. I strained to listen. "Never." She bowed her head to Stroxson. The General nodded to a pair of guards standing on each side of me. The pair grabbed me by my arms and lifted me up. A third guard clamped a pair of silver handcuffs with sharpened barb interiors onto my wrists. An acidic burn throbbed from where metal met flesh, causing me to shriek. I fell to my knees as the pain road up my arms and into my chest.

"Don't you understand?" Grandmother asked rhetorically. "We need you both alive in order to keep our alliance in order. Well," she said with a shrug, "at least until the child is born."

I tried to convert pain into fury to fuel a hurricane at Grandmother, but the scorching sensation inside me was too overwhelming. Evie leaned in to try and help, but several guards tussled with her before shoving her away.

"Daughter," said Queen Orla as she watched Evie being hauled to the platform. "Worry not. Your husband will be kept safe. Liadan and your sister, Ailsa, will be caring for him." Ailsa stood up and glared at me. She wore a metallic armored corset that reminded me of an offshoot Wonder Women costume. Meanwhile, the guards held Evie in front of her mother. Queen Orla put her face close to Evie's. "In the meantime, you and I have some catching up to do. Perhaps you can escort Queen Aveline, myself, and our army to Earth? We'll need a guide who knows Chicago as well as you do."

Evie sobbed. "Why are you doing this?"

Queen Orla shook her head. "Child, be still." Orla stroked Evie's face. I watched in anguish as Evie's eyes fluttered before she collapsed into the guards' arms.

"Bring her with us," Grandmother ordered in her usual cold voice. "We march."

A second roar of trumpets signaled, and the columns of soldiers began to trudge towards the Weeping Pond. Row after row filed into the water's surface. Autumn soldiers armed with spears and shields, Summer sentinels adorned in emerald chainmail, Spring champions with silks and swords, and Winter warriors hidden in their frosted black cloaks. The columns marched into the portal, submerging as if they'd stepped into a sinkhole, headed directly to Chicago. There numbers seemed limitless, like sand on a shore. Finally, Queen Orla, Grandmother, and a limp Evie reached the edge of the Weeping Pond.

I watched hopelessly, shivering in torment. Grandmother turned around, eyeing me one last time. *How long had she been planning this day? Was it moons or centuries?* I didn't know. And yet in that moment, perhaps because of our history, I recognized through her seemingly empty stare that Grandmother was finally savoring the fruits of her labor.

Queen Orla, Evie, and Grandmother took one step forward and disappeared. The entire army, apart from a smattering of palace guards, Liadan and Ailsa were gone. Ailsa sauntered over to me, squatting so that we were eye to eye.

"Oh, I know what you're thinking," said Ailsa. "They've left us all alone. Time to make my big escape." I winced from the burning in my ribcage before meeting her glare. Her black look was thirsty, with clenched teeth and flailing nostrils. "Let me assure you that none of that will be happening." The diamonds pinned in her face shined in my eyes. "Don't worry. You and I are going to have a lot of fun." She smiled with her perfect teeth. "Remember, when the cat's away, the mice will play."

I didn't have any breath in me to spit in her face, but if I did, it would only be a nibble of what was sizzling on my plate. They'd taken my freedom, my Father, my wife, and were laughing about it. I couldn't stomach it much longer. Luckily, the physical pain was so severe that flouting my grief was simple. Ailsa took her hot finger and traced my open lips.

"Hmm, yes," she moaned in pleasure as she shut her fluttering eyes while stroking her neck. "We're going to have lots of fun."

A set of hands grabbed me by my cape's collar and lifted me up. The sentries who'd been left behind were towing me towards the crystal palace. Ailsa stood up and was greeted by Liadan. The banshee pointed at me and then wagged a finger.

"Oh, I won't kill him," Ailsa hissed, as if she understood Liadan's mute complaint. "Well, not until we get word anyway." Ailsa cleared her throat. "Guards, take him to my room and bind him next to the others."

The pain from the cold-iron manacles made paying attention to the many twists and turns of the white halls nearly impossible. Sweat and tears rolled off me as I agonized through my tour. At last we reached a set of grand marble doors with lilacs etched into the threshold. I could smell lavender flooding from the room. I tried to use what little focus I had to listen. The sounds of the summer birds from nearby windows were tainted by something far less sweetly, sobs and whimpers from behind the doors. One of the guards turned a key inside the lock and pushed the heavy barriers forward.

I was towed into a high ceiling bedroom that had been converted into something from people's nightmares. There were paintings along the walls of old crones skinning child flesh and headless women walking down fields of fire. A writing desk made from teeth and a leather chair tanned with sidhe faces decorated the front portion of the room. Near the grand ruby sheeted bed were four wooden torture racks, victims stretched across them. The fragrance of decay spoiled my senses, and all at once, I understood that the scent of lavender had been used to drown out the sickly odor. The guards hauled me to one of the racks, and while one stripped me of my belt, backpack and other equipment, throwing them onto the bed, the second unbound a corpse lying on top and tossed it to the floor. I watched as the stiff dandelion skinned carcass fell. It wore a crown of rotten elderberries and was dressed in a blood-stained marigold robe. The two sentries forced me along the wood's hard surface and stretched me out. Although I was frightened beyond belief, a sudden surge of relief came over me once they removed my manacles in order to tie me to the wrack.

"The Princess has commanded all of the prisoners elevated," one guard with a framed face and steel eyes said to another.

"As she wishes," the other with her green eyebrows and pink skin responded.

I could hear gears cranking from under my cradle, but my body was too worn to investigate. Slowly, the slab I rested on rose until it was upright, allowing me to once again take in the room. I watched as the guards went to the three other wracks haloed around the bed and rotated them until they were vertical. Tied to the wrack across from me was the half-dissected cadaver of a large man with a pointed crown wrought like sun rays and decorated with eyes. It was King Branwen of Summer Court. Next to him was a pallid sidhe with pale hair drawn tightly in a high braid. His eyes were painted over with a stripe of black, and an orange line colored the bridge of his nose. There were cold-iron nails driven into his arms, staining his limbs in blood. He had been stripped of his clothing, though the white-feather symbols enveloping his right shoulder told me this was the haggard, and barely recognizable Prince Carrick, Knight of the Swan.

On the fourth wrack directly across from Prince Carrick was the hideously maimed body of King Ryland of Spring Court. His basil eyes were wide and bulging, and his mouth was frozen into a hideous smile. The rest of his body was covered in patches of green mold and funguses that seemed to have devoured parts of him. Gaping wounds were filled with spores that created craters along his flesh. Prince Carrick, whose eyes fluttered open, shuddered upon seeing his father.

"You may leave us now," Ailsa instructed as she came into sight. The palace guards bowed before taking their leave. Ailsa walked between the four torture wracks, stopping at mine. "How do you like my work?" she asked while rubbing the leaf symbol on my chest. "It's beautiful isn't it?"

I conjured up the energy to speak. "I'd love to see things from your point of view," I gasped out, "but I don't think I can get my head that far up my ass."

Ailsa smiled. "Oh, I like you. You're much more entertaining than your Father." I clenched my teeth together as she leaned in and licked the inside of my ear. "Tragic isn't it? He sacrificed himself to keep you safe. But it was all part of Queen Aveline's design to begin with?"

"Can we just cut to the chase," I said tiredly. "You want to torture answers out of me. Let's get it over with."

"Oh my," she hummed. "It appears my reputation proceeds me. Yes, it's true. I will be torturing you," she said bluntly. "But you're wrong about one thing. I don't want any answers from you. We already have everything we need to know. I'm going to hurt you because I want to."

"You wretched monster," Prince Carrick bellowed from behind her.

"Hold your tongue," Ailsa snapped. She took a deep breath and then smiled at me. "You'll upset our guest." Ailsa took a step back, studying me as if I were a puzzle. Her fingers waved to unheard music as she chewed on her lip. "Oh yes. Quite delicious," she said to herself. "I know what I want to do with you."

Ailsa spun into a pirouette, dancing her imaginary ballet until she was out of sight. I focused my ears. I could make out a rustling sound across the room, followed by the opening of a drawer. A moment later, there was the friction of cloth along skin, and then tiptoed footsteps dancing back in our direction.

"A novice torturer," Ailsa called out from behind my torture wrack, "will go straight to inflicting terrible pain upon their subjects." I could hear her footsteps tap to my side, and soon her diamond pierced face was nearly pressed along mine. She wore a see-through silk robe that tightly wrapped around her bare body. In her hand was a metallic rose. "But a good torturer knows that inducing pleasure first further enhances the agony later applied. The summer sun is twice as scorching for the frog that sits in the pond."

I watched as she continued to dance, her swaying now more provocative. Though her frame was exquisite, my stomach churned in disgust. She closed her eyes, caressing her own neck as her hips tried beckoning my desire. I wanted nothing to do with her, and as she peaked an eye open, a snarl of her lips gave evidence that she knew. She twirled her way to me and brandished the metal rose under my nose. My head kicked back, but I'd inadvertently taken a breath. The fresh floral smell tickled down my airway, slithering into the lower half of my body. My breathing sped up as throes of pleasure gushed inside me. Ailsa pressed her body onto mine, digging into my waistline and grabbing at parts of my body.

"Don't resist," she moaned. "You'll ruin it for both of us."

"Stop," I screamed, trying to combat against the flower's enchantment. But it was too late. Everything in my body tightened, then released. Ailsa laughed like a jackal, watching me as I tried to catch my breath. She walked backwards and dived blindly onto her bed. My watery eyes watched as she took notice of my effects along her sheets.

"Oh," she smiled while picking up Liadan's dagger, "what have we here?" She carefully picked the knife up by its handle, examining it. "I can definitely work this into part two of your torture. Let's see," she smiled, digging into my pack, "what else do we have here." Ailsa rifled through the pack, throwing silverware along her floor. Finally, she removed the dragon tear. "Well, well. Isn't this pretty?" She placed her finger on the sharp point of the jewel. "Oh, it's sharp, too."

She stood up and walked over to me. "Now," she grinned, "let's get to the fun part of our act." Ailsa put her hands along my waste, and then unbuckling my wet pants, pushed the dragon tear downward. Terror struck as I felt the point of the tear on my flesh. There would be a tremendous amount of pain in my future. Then it hit me. Though Ailsa's intentions were laced with sadistic amusement, her actions were in err.

I opened my mouth and called out the autumn dragon's name. "Faro."

A cool gust of wind called into the room and suddenly the seam of my pants burst open, ripping the front of my jeans to shreds. Flying to the ceiling, and growing at an exponential rate, was an ivory dragon. Its bullet shaped head was covered in rigid scales. It had four sharply clawed talons, a long whip like tail, and a pair of bat wings springing from its spine. The monster flew up to the ceiling, gawking down at everyone below. I could hear the cracking of muscles as it continued to grow until it all but took up the entirety of the ceiling.

Ailsa took a step back, her mouth gaping open. "No," she screamed in genuine terror, "it can't be."

Chapter 22

In the waning days of the old gods, when the lands were blighted, a banshee named Liadan was made to haunt the lands. Although much of her origin is speculation, it's said that she was taken from her Firbolg parents at birth and replaced by a changeling. For years she served her master in the Lands of Change, a cruel sidhe that went by the name Leechfinger. Liadan obeyed her master hand-and-foot, until her knees were bruised and her fingers stiff. But it didn't stop Leachfinger from hating Liadan. Anytime the mood fit her, Leachfinger would take her favorite cudgel to Liadan's back until the girl was bloody.

Now in the days before the Green Rift closed, a sidhe could wander back-and-forth between the fairy realm and Earth, so long as they presented any findings to the rulers of their court. Leachfinger, who'd stolen another human infant, had no choice but to present her findings to the Autumn court, dragging poor Liadan along with her. However, Leachfinger and The Lady of the Autumn Court, Queen Aveline, were far from friends. It's whispered that the two came to be enemies on account of Leachfinger once holding title as the harpist for Aveline's sister Mara. Once Mara died, Leachfinger lost her chance to be part of the royal court. And since the lead culprit of Mara's demise was none other than Queen Aveline herself, Leachfinger swore to expose her.

So, it's no surprise that when Queen Aveline lay her eyes on the downtrodden Liadan during Leachfinger's presentation, the Queen jumped at the chance to sabotage her accuser. Queen Aveline permitted Leachfinger to keep the newly kidnapped infant so long as Liadan could be borrowed out to scrub the Autumn Castle of Havgan for a week and a day. The greedy Leachfinger agreed and set off for home with her new child in hand. It was during this time of service that Queen Aveline warmed herself to Liadan. She spoke comforts to Leachfinger's mortal servant, offering food, fine clothes, and a warm bed fit for royalty. Soon the young girl opened up to Queen Aveline and confessed the cruelties of her master. That's when Queen Aveline offered Liadan a way out of her service from Leachfinger.

Queen Aveline informed Liadan of an enchantment that could transform mortals into fairies. With such power, Liadan would be an equal in status to Leachfinger, and could strike back at her sadistic master. So filled with anguish was Liadan, that she hurried to Leachfinger's home immediately to exact her revenge. As instructed, Liadan snuck to the cradle of Leachfinger's newly stolen infant as it slept. She used a feathered quill that Queen Aveline had given her and pierced the baby's heart. Then with the child's blood, Liadan scribed the fairy name that Queen Aveline had chosen for her into her own flesh.

Leachfinger, who was nearby, heard the commotion and hurried to check on her new child. Upon seeing what Liadan had done, Liadan hastily went to punish her servant. She beat Liadan with her cudgel until the girl's body was broken. Lying in a heap of splintered bones, Liadan cried in confusion until her tears turned to blood. But Leachfinger didn't put her servant out of her misery. Instead, she allowed Liadan to suffer, berating the girl as she convulsed on the floor. With her last breaths, Liadan wailed until her body gave way.

But every so often, those who die in The Lands of Change rise again as malevolent specters. And of all the dark specters one can be, there's none more terrible than the banshee. With help from Queen Aveline's enchantment, Liadan rose again, now more fairy than Firbolg. She crept to Leechfinger at night, waiting just outside the sidhe's cottage. Leechfinger, who was inside harping her instrument, heard a scream so terrible that it plucked the strings from her tuning pins. The wail was an orchestra made from a woman's moan, animals shriek and a dead man's rattle. It tore into Leechfinger's heart and made her body tremble.

Terrified, Leechfinger took her cudgel and ran outside to find the source of such an enchantment. But no sooner than she'd made it to the threshold of her door, did she hear the scream a second time. The howl was even more intense than before, nearly dropping Leachfinger to her knees. And as she limped to the forest line to find her attacker, Liadan appeared. Her figure was now ghostly and monstrous. Her hair had grown long, white and ragged. Her eyes bled crimson. Her jaw stretched tenfold.

Leachfinger begged for her life, but before she could finish her *please* and *sorry*, Liadan screamed a third time. The last baying was far too much for Leachfinger's body. With her cudgel in hand, Leechfinger doubled over in pain before her heart stopped. Liadan watched as her former master breathed her last breath. The murder satisfied the banshee and created a fire that could only be calmed by more death.

Though the story of Leachfinger was over, the legend of Liadan had just begun. For the human-fairy hybrid swore to serve a new master, Queen Aveline, loyally for the rest of her days. After all, it was Queen Aveline who had instructed the girl on how to exact her revenge, as misconstrued as her instructions might be. And from that day on, any enemies Queen Aveline made headed their actions. For it only took three wails from her Lady in Waiting before they joined Leachfinger in the ranks of Liadan's victims.

Chapter 23

The dragon opened its crocodile shaped jaw, displaying a pair of silver fangs. Emerald mist fumed from its maw. Ailsa pulled her hand out from the tangle in my belt and shredded pants to flee. The dragon's emerald eyes followed her like a cat ready to pounce as she ran to the exit. Once she'd reached the threshold, the dragon unleashed its breath. A fountain of green acid rained down onto Ailsa. I watched as she flailed, letting out a gurgled scream. Her figure steamed and withered until falling over. *Death by sperm dragon.* The dragon then spun its head to me, crashing down next to the bed. I looked up at the giant and hoped I wasn't next. It lifted its claw and swooped down, slashing my bindings with its clawed finger.

"Thank you," I said while massaging my tender wrists. The dragon tilted its head. I wasn't sure if it understood me. Then, after taking a deep breath, the creature dissolved into a cloud of mist that rose to the ceiling before dissipating. I unbound the straps from my legs, collected the dragon tear now tangled in my ripped jeans. It was cracked and no longer had any shine to it. I took note, then hurried to Prince Carrick. The Knight of the Swan was barely conscious. I slapped him on the cheek several times. His head bobbed slowly, but I could tell that he wasn't fully conscious. I used a part of my ruffled cape to cover the head of a cold spike sticking out of his arm and pulled it out.

"Gah," he screamed. A vein in his head pulsed as he drew his mouth open. "Why would you do that?" He looked me over. "And," he paused, looking down, "why don't you have proper trousers?"

"Listen, it's a long story. Do you want out or not?"

There was a short hiatus. "Free my hand, and I'll handle the rest. Meanwhile, if you have any decency, please find a pair of pants."

"Copy," I said while untying his hand. "And, I'm sorry about your Father."

Carrick frowned as he looked down at his Father's corpse. After a moment, his face straightened. "As I am about yours."

I nodded. After releasing Carrick's hand, I hurried to a pack where my leather slacks were waiting. I removed my shoes and jacket before redressing. I was now in full Autumn-ware.

Carick's orange painted nose rose into the air. "I find it strange you sure you wish to wear those colors any longer?" Carrick asked through gritted teeth as he pulled the last of the nails out of his arm.

"Of course," I nodded. "I am the last of the true Autumn court after all."

"That's very," Carrick took a break from his sentence, "poetic of you."

"Okay buddy, tease all you want, but not right now. You and I are not out of the fire yet. There's a number of well-armed guards downstairs."

"And what, pray tell, is your plan?"

"We sneak past them, jump into the fountain, and save Earth from the Queens' army marching their way."

"And why would I have any interest in helping Firbolg?"

Sidhe, selfish to the last drop. I'd assumed that because Carrick was a knight, he was noble. But that was something only true in legends. Carrick, whose Father was now dead, inherited the Spring throne. He was technically ruler. *Oh, how I hated dealing with fairies.*

"Listen, I hate to be a downer," I said while retrieving Liadan's dagger from my pack and placing it in my belt, "but unless you help me put down Queen Aveline and Orla, you won't have a spot on the Spring court."

"No season lasts forever," he said with his chin held high. "Spring will always have its turn."

"Are you that delusional?" I asked while digging into a large chest near the foot of the bed. There were armors, robes and a single sword with a swan's head along the hilt inside. "The system is broken pal. You can either make a move while there's still time, or Summer and Autumn will hold control of this realms forever."

"Ridiculous," he said while taking the blade I'd offered. "Mother has escaped, and is most likely arranging a counter alliance with Winter as we speak. There shall be a great battle soon."

I laughed. "Even if that's true, and you get the greediest of seasons to help you, what makes you think that you can fight the current army with two queens, two kings and perhaps a smattering of rebels at best? Face it, your reign is at an end unless you do something quick."

"And you would have me throw myself into the human lands in order to attempt a two-man revolt?"

"I'm saying we get one shot," I growled as I clapped my hands. "Let's use the element of surprise and aim for the heart."

Carrick, who was now donning his armor, stopped in his tracks. "What is it you truly wish to accomplish? This rebellion you seek seems like the motives of an individual fueled by something more than revenge."

I sighed. "They took my wife."

"Ah," cooed Carrick as he strapped his chest plate across his torso. "The truth comes to the surface."

"Damn it Carrick, everyone in the realm knows that you're a great champion. Help me get things here back in order. We can return the balance."

"I will get you to the gardens," Carrick said arrogantly as he looked at his own reflection in his blade, "no more."

"Shit," I swore at the ceiling. "Fine, then let's hurry. Apparently, I have to do this alone."

Just then a distant rumble, followed by a trumpet called from the gardens. I ran to the window. Stomping onto the grounds was a shabby female giant with patchy hair and a swollen belly. The creature's clumsy armor, made of bark and roof shingles, was littered with arrows. The behemoth tossed a palace sentinel across the yard with a roar from her crooked mouth. She was nearly the height of a castle tower and used her advantage to pick defenders from guard posts like berries from a tree. A pair of shadowy figures rested on the creature's shoulder. I could see the shadows pointing towards parts of the Crystal Tower. The titan hurried through the gardens, hurling nearby boulders and broken crystal pillars at guards trying to assemble.

I looked to Carrick. "Well, no time like the present."

"Agreed," he said while twirling his blade. I rolled my eyes as we made it to the door.

Luckily, Carrick was familiar with the tower, and after a few stairwells and halls, we made it outside. The giant was now just a stone's throw away, smashing gates with her massive fists. I looked up to see who was on its shoulders. Uncle and Eamon balanced on what appeared to be a former boat-dock-made-shoulder-stand by thin rope. Uncle seemed to be directing the giant towards her next target while Eamon was holding onto a thick strand of the giant's neck hair for dear life. Uncle looked to me, and then tapping the giant on the ear, pointed in my direction.

"Bazdus," Uncle hollered, "there they are."

Bazdus the giant ignored the several arrows bouncing off the back of her head and plodded over.

I cupped my hands over my mouth and hollered. "Room for two more?"

"Yes, yes," Eamon whined. "Just get up here."

I opened my palms, calling for a surge of wind to take Carrick and myself up. My request was met, and a gush of air lifted us onto the giant's shoulder.

"Welcome aboard," Eamon wearily welcomed as he squeezed Bazdus's body hair, his knuckles white. "Oh, whose the pretty warrior woman?"

"I am no woman," Carrick bellowed.

Eamon paused. "My apologies. Who's the very lovely man?"

Just then a massive cold-iron bolt from a ballista whizzed past us. I looked down to see several guards arming siege weapons. "Quick introduction," I hurried. "Carrick, you already know Uncle." Carrick narrowed his eyes. "My shaky friend here is Eamon. He's a coward."

Eamon gave a thumbs up and smile. "I also go by weakling, milksop and namby-pamby."

"Eamon," I continued, "this is Carrick, Knight of the Swan."

"Charmed," Eamon greeted.

"Now," I said as I a guard below loaded a catapult with a cold-iron boulder, "can we get the heck out of here?"

"Bazdus," Uncle yelled, "to the fountain please."

Bazdus nodded and hummed like a whale, trampling through bushes and decorative walls to get to the stone fountain. Arrows, bolts and catapult ammunition bounced off Bazdus as we marched across the yard. Not shortly after, we reached the Weeping Fountain. Uncle patted Bazdus on the neck.

"Thank you old friend," he said while petting her neck. "Remember, go to the hidden briar patch and don't come out until you hear from me." Bazdus bobbed her head. "Well all, this is where the train stops. Everyone off." And with that, Uncle put his hands together as if he were praying and dived off Bazdus's shoulder into the fountain's pool. Eamon took a moment to examine the approaching squad of guards below.

"See you back in Chicago," Eamon squealed before cannonballing down and splashing into the fountain.

I cleared my throat. "Carrick, I know you're a talented warrior, but that's a lot of guards. My offer still stands. Come to Chicago."

I didn't give him any time to answer. I used my cape like wings to glide down into the waters like a diving bird. The familiar uncomfortable wading of the Green Rift took over as I splashed into the pool, massaging a surreal sensation through my mind. Dreamlike visions and vague emotions passed through me. All bizarre. All forgettable.

When my senses returned, the air was brisk, and the sky was dreary. I could tell from the naked Chicago trees that time had passed since we were last at Buckingham Fountain. Gold, red and russet foliage littered the gravel. Lake Michigan, which lay in the background, changed her gown from a royal blue to graveyard grey. *Autumn was here.*

"Where, pray tell, is this?" asked Carrick with a sour expression from behind me. I was relieved to see he'd come to his senses. His eyes drew to the skyline, and his hand drew to his blade hilt. I looked around for civilians. The chill had warded most humans off except for a lonely vagrant resting on a park bench. He had a puffy beard, raggedy beige long coat, White Sox baseball hat, and sunglasses. However, the constant flow of cars along the nearby freeway just a few hundred gallops away still posed a lack of privacy. We were exposed.

"Guys," I announced, "we need to get someplace where no one can see us. Somewhere that's safe to talk."

"Oh, but it is safe to talk nephew," Uncle objected. "I shrouded us in the veil." Uncle followed the vagrant as he ate leftovers from a to-go box. He waved his hand in front of the homeless man's face. There was no reaction. "I assure you, no one can see us."

"Uncle," I said sincerely, "I'm not quite sure why you rescued us, but I owe you."

"I *rescued* you," Uncle said as he walked over to me, his hand clenched on the lapel of his olive coat, "so I could do this."

Uncle raised his hand and slapped me across the face. The force was far more than I'd anticipated. I fell hard to the ground. A savage fury boiled inside me. I spun around and leapt up, but Uncle was too quick. He grabbed me by the hair with his long-clawed hand, drawing me backwards so that it appeared as if he were dipping me during a dance.

"You thoughtless fool," he said coolly, staring me down. "You've ruined everything. Was your Father's paradise just not enough for you?"

"It was a cage," I spat through my clenched teeth. "And Queen Aveline knew it. She planned on every move we made."

"No," Uncle replied, his voice still calm. "Not every." My back screamed in pain from the way it was bent. "Had you and your reckless wife just listened, had you just stayed where Queen Aveline couldn't find you, none of this would have happened."

"That castle was no place to raise a child," I pleaded.

"Well congratulations," Uncle applauded. "That child will now be raised by the two most wicked Queens in history."

Uncle let go, pushing me onto the ground. I fell with a thump. Eamon hurried over and patted me on the back. Uncle was right. Had I just listened, none of this would have ever happened. Both Evie and my unborn child would be safe. Worse still, I'd squandered all of Father's efforts, including his sacrifice. The entire future of both realms was in shambles and it was all my fault.

"This squabbling is not why I agreed to come," Carrick declared as he watched the cars zoom by. "I wish to stop the Queens."

"Agreed," Eamon seconded. "Adair, I know ya' might be feeling awful, but if we're going to save the day, you'll need to tighten your bootstraps. Times a wasting."

Evie must have been terrified. I thought about how overwhelming all of this had to be for her, wherever she was. My throat felt itchy and my eyes began to blur. If I were going to make this right, if I were going to follow in the footsteps of every superhero that I'd ever adored, including Father, it was time to stop feeling sorry for myself. I'd need everything inside me to mend my blunders.

I took to my feet. Uncle stood tall with his hand still clasping his long coat's lapel. I gave him a look while massaging my jaw.

"Good hit," I confessed. The edge of Uncle's mouth curled. "Now that I've ruined everything, anyone have any idea as to how we can fix it?" Everyone went quiet.

"I have an idea," Uncle announced. I gave him a curious look. "Never play a trick that you can't get out of," he directed to me.

"Go on," Carrick insisted.

"It was never my intention to have you captured ,Adair," he said as he folded his hands behind his back, "but if we are searching for the Queens, we're now at an advantage."

"Oh happy day," Eamon mumbled. "This should be rich."

"And how are we at an advantage?" Carrick demanded.

"Because any minute now," Uncle collectedly replied, "Liadan will be charging through this fountain in order to report Adair's escape. Trust me," he said while placing his open hand on my chest and pushing me backwards until we were behind a large porta potty marked *Park District*. The blue container smelled ripe. Carrick and Eamon followed us, creeping behind the portable toilet for shelter.

"And why would Liadan care," Carrick whispered, "when Queen Aveline is invading an entire realm?"

"Oh Carrick," Uncle said in a hushed tone while picking up a discarded apple core from the ground and crunching into it, "you clearly don't know anything about the Autumn court. The banshee-servant will do anything to please her master, and her master is only pleased when her servants are properly serving." There was a short pause. Eamon's eyes went around the group and Carrick's nostrils flared as his mouth set in a hard line. I squinted as I digested the idea. "Yes," Uncle hummed, "I'm quite certain that she'll be arriving any moment now."

Chapter 24

Once, on the far side of yesterday, a hero was born. Like most heroes, his story began in tragedy, and was consecrated by villainy, power, motive, and conflict. Ravaged by illness as a child, the hero's only cure involved being torn from his mother and taken into a world without reality. While the boy's new home mended his body, it also exposed his mind. His Father, one of the few honorable sidhe, mentored his son to be kind, just and wise. As fortune would have it, the boy's sly fairy godfather would further aid in the hero's mentorship. He taught the hero to also be cunning, clever and resourceful.

As time passed, the hero became a man. His wanderlust heart bled out its youth and yearned for devotion. His father, who recognized the signs, sought to give the hero what he desired. However, the hero's father knew that pledging oneself to a sidhe could only end in misery, as fairies made for harrowing companions. So, he searched the lands of the Firbolg in hopes to find someone who could make his son as happy as the hero's mother did for him. Unfortunately, the hero's father would not be alone in his search.

For every hero needs a villain, and the greatest villains are those who know the hero best. The hero's grandmother, the ambitious Queen of the Autumn Kingdom, recognized her grandson's yearning and took advantage. Being one of four fairy queens, she used her leverage within the court to ally with the Summer Queen—a wicked ruler whose Earth-bound daughter could be promised, if only the young lovers were united. Before long the two queens plotted a course that would cast the hero down to Earth like a falling meteor. There he would certainly fall in love with the Summer Queen's daughter. The queens measured every detail with extraordinary precision until all that was left was to hatch their plan.

But the hero's father, who'd found the Summer Queen's daughter during his search for his son's bride, uncovered the plot. Furious, he confronted the queens. He promised to put an end to their plans and expose the truth to the ruling court. But the Autumn Queen silenced her son through enchantments. And although she knew that he would no longer be able to reveal her scheme, she also knew that such fairy powers were faulty. Her son was now a great risk. Time was of the essence, and the queens, as well as the hero's father, rushed their plans. In the end, the two courses collided. For the hero's father, it would cost him his life. But in his sacrifice, he allowed the hero to inherit new fantastic powers to become a superhero. As for the Queen, it set her plans off course. For the hero's Uncle, who loved his brother beyond measure, joined the conflict.

But the story was not over yet. For the hero stick lacked a champion's identity. He would find that in the Summer Queen's daughter. Though the half-sidhe was the offspring of the cruel Summer Queen, her time on Earth made her sweet like the hero's mother, virtuous like the hero's father, and clever like the hero's Uncle. She drove the hero's heart into the heavens and his body down into the ground. Before long, the two were wed, and the hero had everything that a he would need ... or so he thought.

For a trap can only snap if prey takes the bate. And while the hero and his bride were safe so long as they dare not come out from their fortress, the queens knew that such was not the nature of fairies. Before long, the hero surfaced once more, luring himself and his bride into the snare of the queens. In the end, the hero was outwitted, and the payment was more than he could bear. The queens took his bride and unborn child, using them for gain. Outmatched, the hero was forced to make a decision. He could give it all up as a bad job, dying a coward's death, or do what all heroes do in such bleak times. He would fight. So, along with his comrades, the hero prepared for his daring ending. He would go against all odds and take back his bride, no matter what the cost. *But that is another story.*

Chapter 25

The four of us hid behind the blue porta potty near the fountain. I took the time to look over the inappropriate art and large lettering that spelled, *Biff shits here.* It was a bit avant-garde, but I respected the statement the artist was trying to make. We peaked our heads out from the blue plastic and watched the fountain in hopes that Uncle was right. While we were concealed by the veil, it occurred to me that if anyone could see us, we'd look like a pack of fat deer hiding behind a skinny sapling. My eyes darted between Lake Michigan's horizon and Buckingham Fountain. It was getting late, and I hoped that something would occur before the moon peaked. Confronting a banshee at midnight can be really bad for your health.

But just as my knees began to sting and the scent of porta potty turned my stomach inside out, activity stirred in the monument. The color changing lights that shined on Buckingham twitched. The streams being spat and by the fountain's seahorse statues sputtered. A harsh slurping sound gargled from the pool, followed by an ashen figure spitting out from the water's surface. Liadan had arrived.

Unlike the four of us, the translucent figure of Liadan didn't clumsily get spit out of the fountain. Instead, she glided up over the pond and above the walking gravel. Around her collar was a necklace I'd never seen before. It was a simple rope that fell at her chest, decorated by small bones, and to my horror, a set of bat wings with Fergal's head. Urge took over. I leapt forward, ready to strike. Without looking, Uncle held out his hand, restraining me by my shoulder.

"That is what Liadan was occupied with," Uncle uttered, "during your great escape. Feral's death is the only reason you were able to get away at all Nephew." Carrick grabbed me by my other shoulder as I tried to charge. "There will be a time for revenge Adair," Uncle insisted, "but it is not this moment. Now, if you would stay still, I may still be able to hold the veil."

I took a breath and then hung my head. *Poor Fergal.* My father's noble servant had been butchered for his loyalty, while I, imprudent and cowardly Adair, hid behind a freaking porta potty. I picked my head back up and followed the banshee. She seemed to be searching the skies in an attempt to map it out. Once the gray clouds rejected her attempts, Liadan looked to the towering skyline. She stared at the massive horned tower huddled behind its sisters and took to it. The homeless man who'd been scarfing down on a half-eaten burger dropped his meal and sprinted towards Michigan Avenue. Liadan didn't seem to care. Instead, she glided westward until she was all but swallowed up by Chicago's rising darkness.

"Shall we?" asked Uncle in a slapdash tone, as if we weren't trying to trail a murderous banshee.

"I insist," answered Carrick. "The smell here is revolting."

"Are you sure you're not a princess?" Eamon inquired. Carrick gave Eamon a blank stare.

"Uncle," I asked, "are you certain that the veil will hide us?"

"So long as the three of you stay near me," Uncle said while moving forward, "maybe."

"We're doomed," moaned Eamon.

"Team, listen up," I instructed in my best leader guy voice. It was no Captain America or Mr. Fantastic, but it would have to do. I placed my hand on Uncle's shoulder. "Group-hug around Uncle. Don't stray, and if Liadan does see us, plug your ears before attacking. Let's move."

The four of us trailed Liadan's path through the park, our arms reached out onto Uncle's back. It wasn't long before we could see the banshee's gray spectral outline sail over Michigan Avenue and into a distant alley. We tiptoed behind, giving enough space to react. We covered far more distance than I'd expected, passing above a river and out of downtown, carefully dodging pedestrians along the way. We then crossed a bridge arched above a highway into an area filled with small businesses, parking garages and apartment complexes. The streetlights grew sparse and the sidewalks were all cracked. Before long, we were in a baron part of Chicago where only ruddy storage facilities, gravel lots, and far off train tracks remained. Whatever few streetlights we came across were intentionally broken. We were in total darkness.

Eamon used his phone's weak light to keep an eye on both our target and where we were stepping while Carick used his heightened sense of sniff out danger. Meanwhile, Uncle's eyes had turned bright yellow with a thin red slit. His sight must have now been that of some wild creature. *Ninja-mutant.* Liadan stopped in front of a warehouse with a single twitching light that flickered. It was a graffiti covered building with red eroded brick, smoky arched windows, and gargoyles along the corners. The massive horned creatures stared over their stone beaks towards the main doors of the building. Liadan's ghostly figure materialized, becoming solid. Her hair and gown no longer drifted as if she were wading in water, and her bare feet pressed to the ground. She gave the door three hard knocks.

The rusted doors were large enough to drive a truck into. There was a moment of silence when all that could be heard were crickets. But the hush was cut into by the screech of the corroded door as they slid open. It was dark inside, but I watched as several shadows came out to greet Liadan. They wore long coats with baseball caps and workman's boots. It was more poorly disguised fairies. After patting Liadan down, the figures guided her inside.

"Shit," I swore under my breath.

"I should have never taught you that word," Eamon whispered.

"Focus you fools," hissed Carrick as he huddled closer to Eamon and I. "We must strategize if we wish to infiltrate this fortress."

"It's more of an abandoned warehouse," Eamon said quietly, "but who am I to split hairs?" Carrick narrowed his eyes at Eamon.

Uncle, who'd been checking his pocket watch, cut through our clustered argument by slapping shut the clock's cover and clicking the latch with his thumb. I focused my ears to hear the dial ticking as he tucked it in his breast pocket. It was fast, too fast to be timing anything natural. He stepped between the group and the warehouse, inspected the building. He kept his hand clasped on his lapel while humming like a wolf. His caterpillar eyebrows furrowed, before one shot up.

"What is it Uncle?" I asked.

"Intriguing," he said collectedly. "There are no defenders."

I shook my head. "I'm not sure an immortal army of fairies needs to worry about security."

Uncle seemed to disagree, shriveling his lips while groaning. "Very intriguing," he repeated.

"Well," I sighed, "regardless, my wife is in there, so we need to make a move."

"Just know," warned Uncle, "that this may be another trap. Queen Aveline tends not to take risks."

"I get that," I said with balled fists, "but this may be the only shot we get. I have to try."

"Very well nephew," Uncle said while clapping his long fingernails together. "Though I must request that you allow me to separate from you in order to gain a better advantage. Timing is everything."

I opened my mouth to ask what he meant, but Uncle vanished into a cloud of dust, acorns and twigs before I could say a word. Eamon and Carrick grimaced while raising their hands as if pleading for an explanation. I had none to give. Uncle had abandoned us. We were now on our own.

"Now what?" asked Eamon.

"I guess we try the door," I shrugged.

"You're joking right?" Eamon questioned. I didn't say a word. "Oh happy day," he mumbled.

Carrick shook his head in disgust before raising his blade and clanking towards the door. "We are wasting time. Come, let us meet these murders in battle."

I tried stopping Carrick, but only managed to fumble with the scabbard dangling from his leather belt before letting go. He had already charged out of my reach. I watched as he trampled over the cracked cement pathway towards the door. Eamon and I stumbled to chase after. We caught up just in time for Carrick to knock three times on the iron door. There was only silence.

"Damn it Carrick," I hissed, "you've put us in a terrible position."

"That's a matter of perspective," he replied. "In my opinion, I'm one open-door shy of exacting vengeance." Carrick closed his gauntlet, beating on the door with the bottom of his palm. Still no one answered.

"Carrick," I said through my gritted teeth, "I know what you're going through." Carrick grunted. "Really, I do. But charging into enemy territory because you're angry doesn't help. It's how I ended up here in the first place. Now, if you wouldn't mind, let's run back before anyone spots us. We can think of a better plan."

"Agreed," Eamon whispered, backing up.

"I am the Knight of the Swan," he belted, his chin lifted. "I never retreat."

Just then, a bloated orange balloon came tumbling down onto Carrick, popping and splattering a colorless liquid. Carrick was covered in a pungent fluid. The Knight of the Swan puffed snot out his nose before gaping down at his wet armor. He growled. *Splat.* A second balloon, bulging and blue, slapped onto Carrick's shoulder guard, bursting into a fountain of foul fluid. I looked up to the source. A stream of the same biting liquid sprayed me in the face. My eyes gripped closed before impact, but the odor stripped my nostrils of sensation. After wiping my brow, I opened my eyes and spotted two gargoyles with bright yellow super soakers and water balloons in hand. A third, who crept up behind them, held a burning roll of newspaper. Now I recognized the smell.

"Gasoline," Eamon shouted as he sped to the crumbling street. Carrick froze. I took a gulp of air and blew a spiraling torrent towards the gargoyle's newspaper torch, blowing out the flame. The monster inspected the charred reel, tilting its head. I didn't waste any time. I lifted my hands and pushed forth a massive wind wall at the roof, blowing the streams of gasoline back at the creature armed with a super soaker. The gargoyles spread their wings in the torrent, trying to fly forward. Though my wind was strong, their weight bore through my efforts. Before long, three hulking stone monsters flew down and surrounded me.

"This is bad," I muttered as they circled around Carrick and I. But as one reached out to grab me, a sudden flash of silver cut through the gargoyle's hand, dropping the granite limb onto the cement we stood on. The act was so quick that I hardly registered that it came from Carrick.

"For justice," Carrick challenged as he swung again, slicing off one of the creature's horns. The beast roared before flying back up onto the rooftop. Carrick reeled his blade in a half moon pattern, cutting the stomach of a second gargoyle. The creature inspected its chipped torso as gravel poured out. The monster groaned before withdrawing, beating its wings towards its retreating sister. The third gargoyle, whose head darted between Carrick and I, raised its hands in surrender.

"Open the door," I commanded. I called a light breeze to flap my cape behind me. *Hey, why try to intimidate someone if you're not going to do it right?* The creature guarded itself with an arm, but slowly stepped backwards until it was at the door. Up above, the two wounded gargoyles squealed and shook their heads at their sibling. The cornered gargoyle looked up and shook its fist.

"Screw you guys," the gargoyle hollered in an unusually ordinary male voice without moving its mouth. "They don't pay us enough for this crap."

Then cautiously, it turned around and guided its fingers towards a specific point of the door. After running the tips of its claws over the seam, the same spot that Liadan had knocked on, the creature banged three times. The screeching of the door's joints cried like Liadan's song, heightening my already nervous state. As the door slowly crept open, the winged beasts on the roof flew away, shaking their heads. Their brother sighed below.

"So much for trivia night," it muttered. Once the door was halfway open, the gargoyle crept backwards, its arms still held up in surrender. Carrick raised his blade as if to strike.

"No," I protested. "Let it go."

Carrick shook his head but lowered his blade. The monster wasted no time. It took flight into the night sky. Once it had reached a safe height, the gargoyle flew in the opposite direction of its siblings towards the city.

"There are no prisoners in war," Carrick said as the door jolted to a sudden stop.

"This isn't war," I said as we stared inside. "This is a rescue operation."

A wall of green stared back. I narrowed my eyes to understand what I was seeing. From floor to ceiling and wall to wall stood a massive shrubbery blocking all other view. I tried to focus my hearing but could only catch the rustling of hedge leaves. Carrick sniffed at the air. His mouth twisted into a sneer. Eamon caught back up with us, hiding behind me as I looked for an opening between the bush's branches.

"Now, I'll take the lead," I said firmly as I pierced the leafy veil. "If anything kills me, kill it back."

Carrick said nothing. He took his blade and chopped a makeshift hole in the shrubbery. "Everything is war you fool."

I groaned but followed as Carrick cut through the prickly branches until reaching the other side. To my surprise, waiting past the safeguard was the massive complex in its entirety. It was an amalgamation of forgotten mechanical parts and freshly grown garden. A graveyard of broken cars was coated with fresh grass. Autumn trees with fire colored leaves stood between corroded vehicle lifts. Rusted chains and vines tangled together over tarnished tool bins. The three of us skulked forward through the vehicle warehouse, searching for anything that moved. Nothing did. A bead of sweat dripped down my forehead and a lump swelled in my throat. *This couldn't be right.*

"Where is everyone?" whispered Eamon.

"Your Uncle was right," Carrick muttered as we reached the center of the massive storeroom. "This must be a ruse."

"Of course it is a ruse," called out a loud female voice. A harmony of crackling flames and a wave of heat filled the room. The warehouse lit up with the laughing faces of hundreds of hanging Jack O'Lanterns. I scanned the shimmering building with its new tiger design. Grandmother sat at the back of the warehouse, perched on a leather car seat raised by a nest of pepper tree pillars. Her cheeks were rosy, and her complexion was bright. A pair of orange moons lit up her irises and a shade of blood colored her lips. She wore a ginger gown with black bows, bracers, boots, and a crown made of crow feathers. "Now, tell me how my only Grandson managed to escape The Lands of Change this time?"

"Cut the shit," I snapped.

"You really do use that word a lot," Eamon nudged in.

"Sorry," I apologized.

"Queen Aveline," Carrick yelled over us, pointing his metallic fist in her direction. "You are unfit of any crown. I shall have vengeance for what you did to my Father."

"Ah, Prince Carrick," she said with a plane face and bored tone. "Of course you will." She blinked several times, her gaze unwavering. "Well then," she said in an undisturbed voice, "come have it."

Carrick pressed ahead, readying his blade. I knew this wouldn't go well but didn't have the time to stop him. As he paced down the bumpy cement towards Grandmother, a figure rose up beneath him. It was Liadan. She glided her way behind the Knight of the Swan, extending her palm as she solidified. Carrick was blind to her presence. Liadan rested her now corporal hand onto the Knight's scalp. His body locked up as he fell over in a heap of clanging armor. I watched as he slumped onto his back, his jaw clenched, and his steel fingers coiled. Liadan, whose hair now hung over her face, shifted back to her ethereal form. Her ghostly figure swayed again as if in water. I eyed Carrick's cold-iron sword on the ground, wondering how quickly I'd suffer the same fate if I tried to wield the weapon myself.

"Bravo," Grandmother said flatly. "What an exciting reunion."

I took a few steps forward, Eamon gripping my cloak behind me. "Where are the others?" I demanded.

"Yes," Grandmother answered. "You mean, where is your wife?"

I squinted. I was here on a desperate attempt to get back Evie, but truth be told, Grandmother held all the cards now. I crossed my fingers and toes that she'd open negotiations. Now that we were exposed, it would be the best chance of getting out of this alive. I was also perfectly content with the *smash-and-grab* technique if it presented itself.

Grandmother looked to her right. Evie and Queen Orla promptly appeared. Evie's eyes grew wide. She looked to be more concerned for me than herself. Even in a time like this, her beauty took me by surprise. She'd been dressed in an emerald gown with a tree branch design and matching crown. Her cheeks were painted with a light kiss of glitter and her lips shined glossy pink.

Queen Orla stood behind Evie. The Summer Queen wore green silk that bore her shoulders and upper chest. The dress had a swaying skirt with tree designs that matched Evie's. Queen Orla, for as enchanting as she might be, appeared tired and worn with bags beneath her eyes. She clung her trembling laced-glove hand onto Evie's shoulders, glaring down at me.

"There she is," Grandmother said simply. "Now, what foolish acts will you take in order to try and retrieve her?" Liadan, who'd been halfway between Grandmother and me, squared up. I was now face-to-face with the two most powerful fairy queens and the deadliest banshee in existence. On my side were an unconscious knight and a man who made cowards look gutsy. The only way I was getting out of this one was to stick with my plan.

"Queen Aveline," I begged as if walking on verbal ice, "I don't want any trouble. All I want is my wife."

"I'm afraid that's not possible," Grandmother replied. Queen Orla combed Evie's hair with her fingers, studying me from the tops of her eyes.

"Why not?" I asked gently.

"You see," Grandmother explained while crossing her legs, "without your marriage being looked after, our treaty with Summer is illegal. We need to protect our assets."

"And what if Evie and I decided we wanted to break our vows?" I challenged.

"You are quite predictable Adair," Grandmother said in a tone that was neither mocking or expressive. "As long as that child of Autumn and Summer grows inside Evelyn's belly, you're threats are hollow. I only need the child."

And there you have it. Evie and I weren't important figures in Grandmother's scheme. We were animals to be bred. I looked to Evie as she shielded her flat belly with her hand. Her eyes went glassy. I tried not to let my emotions get the better of me. It had betrayed me so many times, and I wanted to stay levelheaded. I needed to get us out of here. Bigger things were afoot.

"What if Evie and I joined you in your campaign?" I asked.

"No young fairy," Eamon begged behind me.

The Queen's chin raised as she pressed her fingers together. I'd complimented her. Her ruminative gaze was the closest she'd ever get to a smile. There was a short pause, and then after looking at Queen Orla, she turned to me and spoke.

"I'm afraid that's not possible," Grandmother answered. "Everything is going according to plan. Your allegiance is a factor that strains my aspirations, though I do appreciate the request."

"Queen Aveline," Orla called out, "take this boy prisoner and be done with him. Our visitors will be here soon."

"Visitors?" I inquired, readying to make a desperate escape if my attempt to buy time didn't work.

"Yes, you stupid boy," Queen Orla cursed. "Did you think our plan was to merely take over The Lands of Change?"

"You want to take over Earth, too?" I retorted.

Queen Orla laughed a sickly sound like a seagull. In the history of top creepy laughs, it was as follows. In third place, the Joker after one of his bizarre one-liners. In second place, Vincent Price at the end of that Thriller song. And taking home the gold was Queen Olra after I asked if she wanted to take over Earth.

"Earth is not enough," Queen Olra said through her grizzly smile.

"Silence," Grandmother cut in. "You share too much." Grandmother waived her hand, and suddenly the entire building filled with sidhe at the ready. Rows of Autumn, Summer, Spring, and Winter soldiers crowded into the warehouse. General Stroxson stood at the front, his goat beard braided with gold twine. Along a nearby rusted van were several shackled prisoners including mortals and a blue skinned man with the top hat.

"Adair," Evie gasped. Eamon and I spun around, taking in the surrounding army. We were trapped.

"Do you think your Uncle is the only master of the veil?" Grandmother announced. She flipped her wrist again, and suddenly the legion of warriors held their weapons at the ready. I was in deep trouble.

"I don't want to die," Eamon cried while shaking my arm. "Do something Adair. I want to see my kids."

"You don't have kids," I said while dragging him closer to Carrick's paralyzed body.

"And I never will unless you do something," he pleaded.

"Eamon," I whispered while eyeing the swan shaped hilt of Carrick's sword, "when I give the signal, you go for Evie. I'll get you two out of this." Eamon moaned.

"Please don't make me test my bravery," he begged. "I started with very little, and it's nearly all used up."

"Be strong," I said aloud, though it was mostly for myself. "All right Queen Aveline," I shouted. "You made your point. I'll go quietly so you can torture me or whatever it is you want to do."

"Acceptance of one's circumstances," Grandmother declared, "is not very fitting of you Adair." It was out of character for Grandmother to say something so suggestive. I didn't know what her end game was, but even now it felt like she was poking me with a stick again. "Queen Orla," she announced, "would you be so kind as to claim your daughter's husband?"

Queen Orla's face went blank. "Me?" she gasped. Grandmother nodded. "Why not your hideous ghost woman?"

"Because," Grandmother insisted, "they have a heated past that I do not wish to surface before our visitors arrive."

"Then why not one of our warriors?" Orla disputed.

"We must lead by example," Grandmother warned. "If we are not willing to get our hands dirty, why should they?"

The troops glanced at one another from the corner of their eyes. Queen Orla balled her fists. "How dare you? This is unacceptable," she blurted while stomping her way to me. "We shall talk about this later Aveline." Grandmother's eyes narrowed.

Meanwhile, the plan I had smelled of *stupid*, but it wasn't going to stop me from *giving-it-a-go*. First, I'd let Queen Orla drag me away. Once I was close enough to Evie, I'd call forth a gust of wind to jut her towards the exit. From there, I hoped that I still had my head attached to my neck so I could stir a whirlwind under Carrick's blade and use it as a distraction while Evie and Eamon escaped. But just as Queen Orla went to grab my wrists, she gave a barbed grin and wild eyes. I could see the shine of cold-iron claws capped over her fingertips. Orla jabbed the metallic fingernails into my bicep, dragging me towards her face.

"You killed my favorite daughter," she growled, spitting on me as she did, "and raped my other. I'll kill you myself once that pig-child of yours is born." The pain in my arm was excruciating. I could feel each nerve and muscle throbbing. Every instinct wanted it to stop it. Without thinking twice, I begged for the wind to come to my aid. A tide of air drew from behind me, pushing Queen Orla backwards. In that moment everything slowed down. I watched as Queen Orla plummeted. At the same time, I saw Grandmother in the background subtly waive her hand. Carrick's blade sped under Queen Orla on its own and pointed upwards. The sharp tip of the cold-iron sword pierced through Queen Orla's back and protruded out of her chest. Orla's eyes widened, and then in an instant, they were cold. She lay on the ground, motionless. Evie screamed. Liadan, who'd only been a stone's throw away, flew behind me and solidified. I spun around as she lifted her arm to strike. I tried to dodge her hand as it came down once, twice, three times.

"Cease your attack Liadan," cried Grandmother. "I need him to be able to speak."

Liadan hesitated, her paralyzing palms held outward. I tried to catch my breath. Grandmother looked to Queen Orla, studying the dead sidhe without any signs of remorse. I was still in shock, yet my mind raced to figure a way out of my very compromising circumstances. Evie's eyes darted between her mother and I, her hands covered over her mouth. Eamon swore under his breath.

"Sons and daughters," Grandmother announced as she stared at Orla's corpse, "Queen Orla has been murdered. We are in danger of losing our great alliance. Protect Princess Evelyn with your lives." An Autumn soldier in a front column blew into a gourd-horn, trumpeting a signal. The rows of sidhe began to move like a tidal wave until they were lined up in a bow shape around Evie. "Liadan," Grandmother continued, "bring him to me. I have questions about his Uncle's whereabouts."

Liadan's eyes flashed red. Her hair, long and white, coiled into several tentacle-like chords that reared upwards.

"Medusa," Eamon screamed. "Run for your lives."

Eamon sprinted towards the door. I wanted to save Evie, but as I tried to move forward, a strand of Liadan's hair threw itself at my foot, wrapping around my ankle. The white tresses swept me onto my back. Stunned, I stared up at the metallic ceiling, bearing an intense pain along my spine. Near the entrance, I could hear Eamon rattling the main door, while on the opposite side of the warehouse near Grandmother, I heard the fierce hiss of a large cat. I picked my head up, looking past Liadan, who lingered over me. A massive gold puma, where Evie had been, stood with its mouth hinged open. It clawed at guards who attempted to subdue her. Last I checked, Evie had difficulty transforming into a hawk. Nothing like eminent doom to bring the best out in people.

We were outnumbered and surrounded. Maybe this story didn't have a fairytale ending after all. *Shit.* In mere moments, the guards would most likely murder Eamon and Carrick, drag me somewhere for torture, and imprison Evie until she gave birth to our child. Ultimately, we were all goners. So, as Liadan wrapped my wrists and legs with her hair, stretching me out like skinned hide, I began to understand that Grandmother was so brilliantly calculated that I never stood a chance. She'd thought everything out, from Father's sacrifice to Evie and I falling in love. It was all part of her preconceived scheme to make her more than just the Queen of the fairies, but Queen of the realms.

Chapter 26

Liadan lifted me higher off the ground, suspending me over her. She forced me to watch as puma-Evie pounced on a Summer warrior, only to be grappled by several others. Liadan then spun me around to witness a column of spear-bearing soldiers corner a screaming Eamon near the locked entrance. I shouted in anger only to find that it excited her. Her bleeding eyes were a pair of full moons and a heavy grinding heaved from her flared nostrils. She tried to smile, causing her old dagger scars in her face to rip open. Wine colored droplet trickled down to her chin. My eyes filled with tears.

But just as all seemed lost, my ears picked up on the roar of engines and the rumble of a heavy throttle outside the warehouse. I wasn't the only one. Grandmother, Liadan, and several other Autumn soldiers shot their heads to the front door, curious as to the source of the cacophony. Unexpectedly, the gargantuan entry doors withered into a shade of amber. I watched as the solid metal entrance collapsed into a shower of rusty sand. Eamon, whose back had been pressed along it, fell outside. The blinding headlights of a hotrod and motorcycle silhouette poured into the building. I squinted and tried to make out the drivers.

The engines thundered once more before both vehicles charged in. As light from the Jack O'Lanterns hit the hotrod, I spotted Uncle with a wide grin behind the wheel. I could hear the *Dead Kennedy's* song, *Holiday in Cambodia* blaring from his radio. He turned the steering wheel with force, entering a controlled skid that spun the car completely around, ramming several guards like bowling pins. The now clear lane allowed the motorcyclist behind him to race his hog in my direction. I watched as the brawny green barkeep with a foliate head pointed an axe with one hand at Liadan.

Liadan swayed back-and-forth before shifting into her ethereal form. Her now insubstantial strands of hair released me from their grip. The Green Man rode through Liadan's ghostly visage, using a knee to steer the handlebars while scooping me up in his free hand. Everything was moving too fast for me to process. One moment I was in the grips of Liadan, and the next, I was on the back of a colossal motorcycle racing towards Evie. I looked back to see Liadan giving chase. Behind her, Uncle mowed over another group of soldiers to make room for Eamon. Eamon pulled himself from the mound of rust flakes and hurried into the passenger seat, screaming in a high pitch tone all the way. *One down. One to go.*

I held onto the Green Man's leather vest, which reeked of bourbon. His axe smashed through shields, and as we continued to ride, I could hear his laughter. Several guards tried to stop our path by forming a lethal wall of spears, but just before we reached them, I begged for the winds. A strong current took the soldiers skyward, allowing us to drive beneath them before they hit the ground. I looked ahead and saw Evie. Her eyes went wide and a smile rose from her face. Hope bubbled to the surface of my mind. It was like every comic book I'd ever read. We were moments from saving the day. *Lois Lane, eat your heart out.* Then I saw her.

Grandmother had managed to slip behind Evie and leaned over my wife's shoulder to whisper something. I was too late to let my keen ears make out the words. Black veins webbed throughout Evie's flesh, causing her to collapse to the ground. Grandmother hooked her arms under Evie's, allowing her limp body to stay upright. A special kind of heartache reserved only for the worst tortured souls devoured me. We were a stone's throw away, yet seconds too late. Grandmother's gaze crept upwards to meet mine. Her pupils went wide and her lips narrowed. Then, in a flash, both her and Evie disappeared.

"No," I shouted. The Green Man turned the bike abruptly, using his anchor of a leg to guide the motorcycle completely around. As he did, Liadan, who was directly behind us, turned solid to palm the Green Man's leafy face. The Green Man tumbled over, forcing the motorcycle to fall sideways and pin my leg. My cape tore and the effects on my equipment belt spilled all over. A torrent of pain crawled its way from my ankle to the rest of my body. I pushed at the bike's hot gears crushing my leg. Liadan, now solid, stepped on top of the sideways bike seat, adding weight. She grimaced, removing the ribbon from her head. She was going rogue.

I did the math. With Evie secure, and the child of Autumn and Summer safely in her belly, there was really no need for me. I'd done my part by killing Queen Orla. I was now expendable. One last shriek from Liadan and I'd be back with Father.

Liadan freed the ribbon and let it float to the floor. Her jaw went loose, dropping to her collarbone. I cowered in fear, readying for her song. As I clung to the ground, the effects that had spilled from my equipment belt lay in front of me. They were all pieces of memories, from Father to Evie. There was the cracked Dragon's tear, silverware from the fairy castle, and Liadan's dagger. *Wait, Liadan's dagger.*

I spun my upper body to face Liadan and raised my hands in surrender. Liadan was sucking up a large gulp of air. She stopped and let out a cackle that sounded like the hissing static of an old record. I hurled the dagger at Liadan's head, begging the winds to guide the weapon true. A current of air whooshed from behind me, forcing the knife to dart hard into Liadan's forehead. A plunging sound plopped from her skull. Liadan cocked her head back, then, looking up at the hilt of the dagger, cringed before slumping forward onto the floor. Her body fizzed into mist, arising into the air. I had just slain Liadan, the most terrifying banshee in the realm.

I didn't much feel like celebrating, nor was there time to. General Shit Head had somehow coordinated a massive row of soldiers through the chaos. Hundreds of sidhe rallied, pointing their cold-iron weapons onward in an even row. I tried again to lift the bike, summoning wind to my aid. My efforts were futile. The mammoth motorcycle was too much for any force I could muster. Slowly, but thoroughly, the lines of soldiers marched in unison towards me. I didn't think they'd honor my unconditional surrender. In fact, I was damn sure that after killing Liadan, I was about to be poked like a pig and bled out.

"Slay them all," General Stroxson confirmed. The soldiers closed the distance until they were hovering over me. A squad of Summer fighters raised their curved blades, ready to strike the Green Man and myself. I shielded my head and readied for the blow. But as I did, I could feel a release of pressure from my pinned leg. I opened my eyes and saw that the motorcycle had turned into a mound of rust grains. Uncle, who was now out of the car and in front of me, focused on the column of troops.

He extended his hands in front of his one eye, squaring his fingers so that he was staring through the hole between them. It looked like he was assessing art more than trying to rescue me. But before my doubts could set in, a large white hair leapt on my chest from where the soldiers were coming from. I turned around to find that Uncle had somehow transformed the first few rows of executioners into jackrabbits. The tall eared animals scurried away from Uncle as he grabbed the Green Man by the collar. Meanwhile the hotrod beeped as it skid clumsily so that its front bumper was facing the entrance. Eamon squeezed at the steering wheel.

"I don't know how to drive this thing?" he hollered.

"Come, come Nephew," Uncle instructed in his calm raspy voice. "I'll need your help with this one."

I grabbed the Not-so-Jolly Green Giant by his arm and with Uncle's helped dragged the bartender away from the next row of warriors. The hotrod's back door opened by itself, allowing Uncle and I to struggle to get both the giant and ourselves into the backseat.

"Eamon," Uncle said coolly. "If you would be so kind."

The car burst towards the entrance. I could hear metal clanking behind us as the guards stabbed into the car's trunk before it roared outside and onto the street. Eamon hit a curb and two trashcans before gaining control.

"Eamon," Uncle growled.

"I'm doing the best I can Captain," he yelled back.

I turned to look out the back as we sped away, watching as the warehouse shrank. It was calm. No one raced out of the building. It took me a second to understand why, but then I recalled the queen's discussion. They were, after all, waiting for guests, whoever they are. As I continued to stare, the warehouse suddenly vanished. Queen Aveline had used the veil to ensure there were no more unwanted guests.

I didn't know what to think. The woman I will now, and forever more only refer to as Queen Aveline, had murdered my Father, used me to kill her business partner, and kidnapped my wife and child. Uncle, Eamon and I were now *kill* on sight. She'd taken everything from me, and yet, despite my anger, I was powerless. Queen Aveline was smarter than me, stronger than me, and had years of schemes at her disposal. All I had was my mad Uncle, cowardly cohort, and a lot of bad choices.

"We'll not be able to face that army alone," Uncle confessed as he gazed out of the backseat window with me. I stared at him as he leaned his head on the glass, his eyes following the passing lights. For the first time since I'd known him, he sounded desperate. "I've," he hummed in his raspy voice, "failed your Father."

No one said anything. Eamon pretended to be focusing on the road, though I caught him trying to get a glimpse of us from the rearview mirror. I pressed my hand onto my face, peaking out through my fingers.

"You didn't exactly have the odds in your favor," I apologized, "once I was involved. I tend to do that." Uncle shrugged.

"How were you to know?" he buzzed. I pursed my lips, to which Uncle placed a hand on my shoulder. "Besides, it's not fun unless it's dangerous, remember?"

"For what it's worth," I said as I leaned my head on his shoulder, "thanks for saving my life." Uncle wrapped his arm around me. An image of Evie crossed my mind, making my eyes water. "Not that it's much for living."

"Never play a trick that you can't get out of," Uncle said through a solemn smile. I tucked in my lips to hide my grimace. Uncle looked me over. "We'll get her back."

"How?"

"Not sure yet, but we will," Uncle insisted. "After all, we're heroes aren't we?"

I smiled.

The three of us drove for some time, not really going anywhere. I think we all needed a moment. We'd failed. Queen Aveline still lived and Evie was gone. I'd come into this magnificent woman's life and turned it upside down. She went from traveling student to political prisoner, as well as wife to a loser in a matter of months. Once she'd had our child, she'd most likely be disposed of. That is, unless I could somehow pull a wild card from my pocket. *Hold on, a wild card.* I looked out the window and studied the streets.

"Stop the car," I hollered. Eamon hit the brakes as if we were about to hit into a wall. The tires screeched as his arms locked on the steering wheel.

"What?" Eamon yelled, his eyes scanning the road in front of him. "Is she behind us?"

I tried to stretch out my legs as much as I could in the backseat, arching my back so that I could dig into my pocket. My fingers wrestled around until they felt the hard corner of laminated stock paper. I pried out the business card that the stranger at the train station had given me some time ago. It read, *The Prologue, Rare Books and Magic.* Underneath the title was an address, store hours and phone number.

"Eamon, I need you to get me here," I said while reading the address to him. Eamon nodded before beginning to type the numbers into his phone. Uncle looked over my shoulder, his bushy brow raising like a coiled cobra. "There's someone I need to talk to."

"Should we call ahead of time?" Eamon asked. "No," I objected. "I'll need to talk to them in person." "Why?" questioned Eamon.

"Because I don't know if I can trust them," I answered.

"I'm sick of talking to people we can't trust," Eamon complained.

"All these fairies are driving me bonkers."

"This someone is not a fairy," I reassured.

"Is this someone a bad person?" Eamon asked.

"They're arrogant as hell," I said as I leaned my head between the front seats. "But I don't think this someone is bad."

"And who," Uncle cut in, "*is this someone?*"

"The Ultimate Protector of Chicago." I answered. And with that, we turned onto Belmont Avenue towards The Prologue.

And so the dreamer awakes, the shadow goes by, when one tells a tale, the tale is a lie. But listen to the words fair maiden, listen proud youth— for the tale is a lie, what it tells is the truth.

Chapter 27

"So you're telling me," said Ned as he slurped from the straw of a red slushy, "that there's an entire army of fairies in Chicago?"

We'd arrived at *The Prologue* just before closing time. The dark beauty who'd been with Ned at Union Station, Chelsea, let us in, but only after forcing us to swear on an original *David Bowie: Suffragette City* vinyl that we'd behave. She warned us that the two tiny mustached dogs roaming the bookstore would tear us apart if we tried to test her. I thought she might be joking, but judging from her tone, she wasn't. After collecting Ned, Chelsea asked us to explain the nature of our visit.

Uncle, who'd come in without any disguise, perused the nearby bookshelves located by the register, while Eamon and I had a seat on one of the store's reading benches. Ned had rubbed me the wrong way at Union Station, but I convinced myself that I'd need to swallow my pride if I wanted the *Defender of Chicago's* help. I opened the conversation by confessing that I'd been too weak to stop my evil Grandmother, Queen Aveline, from kidnapping my wife and unborn child. I added that I was also partially to blame for her and her immortal army of sidhe crossing the Green Rift in order take over Earth. That seemed to grab Ned and Chelsea's attention. From there the questions began.

"Yes, there's an entire fairy army in Chicago" I answered through a sigh. "And they're supposed to be meeting with some sort of Earthly contacts tonight to continue their conquest."

"Ha," Ned laughed. "Babe, could you imagine that? Here you are, some evil *Tall Man* looking dude from that movie *Phantasm*, walking in all grim with your suit and briefcase. Then," Ned held his gut, "as you get in the meeting room, you're greeted by a bunch of flying fairies snorting pixie dust?" I frowned.

"Babe," Chelsea nudged him. "You're being really offensive right now. Fairies aren't like that."

Ned winced. "I am?" Chelsea nodded. Ned turned his attention back to me. "Sorry man, I'm just saying that would be funny. Anyhow, so who are these Earthly contacts your Grandmother is supposed to be meeting?" "I have no idea," I shrugged.

Eamon cleared his throat. "Um, Mr. Ned."

"Mr. Ned is my Father's name," Ned said in a deep voice. "That's, if I had a father. Ned will do."

"Ned," Eamon continued, "you have to understand that Adair's dear old grandmother is not some run of the mill fairy. She's an evil creature with all sorts of unimaginable power."

"What level are we talking here?" Ned asked. He looked to me with a crease in his forehead. "Use comic book terms."

I hummed while trying to think of someone comparable. "Think the disposition of Red Skull, the resourcefulness of Loki, and the wrath of the

Dark Phoenix."

"Eek," Ned recoiled. "That bad huh?"

"Yes Ned," Eamon answered. "And if she's allying with anyone, I'm sure they have to be just as nasty."

"Well," Ned shrugged, "I hate to break it to you, but it's no one from Chicago. I've done away with all the big bad spookies in my city. If any outsiders come, we swoop in like Seal Team 6."

"Yeah," I remarked, "I remember."

Chelsea, who was wearing a white sleeveless shirt that said *Flogging Molly*, spoke up. "I think what my stupid," Ned frowned, "but sweet," Ned smiled, "boyfriend is trying to say is that I have a scrying ritual activated. We'd be notified by my magic if any major spookies enter

Chicago."

"Ms. Chelsea," Eamon spoke up.

Chelsea raised a brow. "Ms. Chelsea is what people who want their asses kicked call me."

Eamon tugged at his shirt collar. "Chelsea," he corrected. Chelsea nodded. "I'm new to the evil fairies and spookies thing, but isn't it safe to say that Chicago is a very big city?"

Chelsea tapped her foot. "Go on."

"And isn't it also safe to assume that there's all sorts of strange and interesting folks that could possibly slip under your mystical radar?"

"Maybe," she said flatly, her face expressionless as she blinked at Eamon.

"Oh, well happy day," Eamon rejoiced. "We're in agreement." Chelsea puffed air out of her nose like a bull. "So then, if you had to squeeze blood out of a stone, who would you say Queen Aveline may be meeting with? Because that may help us get Adair's wife back."

"Hey buddy," Ned cracked his knuckles over the emblem of his t-shirt. The dark shirt hidden under a red flannel read, *I don't suffer from insanity. I enjoy every minute of it.* "if the lady says we've taken care of all the bad guys then we have. Once I kicked the local warlock out of Chicago, most of the other guys scattered."

Chelsea, who was staring at her feet, raised her head. "Babe," she called out as she tapped on her chin. "Didn't Collin have two brothers?"

Ned raised his arms and sighed. "Sure. and I'm sure he had a few cousins, too."

"No," Chelsea said with a creased brow, "seriously. He had two brothers, remember? There were three sons of Carman."

Uncle turned to face us. "Did you say," he asked with his throaty voice, "*Carman*? As in Carman the Irish Witch?"

"Whoa," Ned cocked his head back. "Buddy, you could really use a throat lozenge."

"Please," Uncle groaned while clasping his clawed fingers across his lapel, "answer the question."

"Yeah," Ned argued, "but Collin said he hated them. There's no way they'd come to Chicago." Ned snapped his fingers, and a flicker of sapphire fire sparked. "Shoot, what were their names again." "Dub and Dother," answered Chelsea.

"Oh yeah," Ned pointed at Chelsea. "How could I forget such household names like Dub and Dother?"

Ned turned to Chelsea who was studying Uncle. Her eyes darted up and down. I watched as Uncle raised his chin so that Chelsea could get a view of his profile.

"Oh my gods and elements," Chelsea exclaimed. "Ned, I think this is

Puck."

Justin Alcala

"Great, where are the Blackhawks when you need them?" Ned snickered. He looked to me for a laugh. *I didn't.* His smile faded.

"No," Chelsea said while hurrying to a bookshelf near the back of her store. She plucked out a tome. It was a raggedy green book. Chelsea brought it over, flipping through it. After finding the page she was looking for, Chelsea pressed down on the paper and showed it to us as if we were children in reading circle. There was a sketch drawn in heavy black ink. The depiction showed a man in frock coat with frills riding the shoulders of a chubby king with an ornate crown and cape. The rider's hair was parted like Uncle's, and his eyes were wide like a madman's. An inscription above read, *Puck, also known as Robin Goodfellow, is a character in William Shakespeare's play A Midsummer Night's Dream that was based on the ancient figure in Celtic and English mythology.*

Eamon narrowed his eyes to focus on the picture while Ned looked back and forth between the tome and Uncle. It was strange to see someone so familiar on the pages of a Firbolg book. The irony was, while I was obsessing over human comics and graphic novels, mortals were writing about Uncle. I wondered how many other sidhe were in that book.

Uncle looked at me and raised his eyebrows. "I told you I was famous."

"Hey team," I said as calmly as possible, though I was getting impatient, "I hate to be 'that guy,' but we need to stay on track here." I looked

to Chelsea. "What do you think we're up against?"

Chelsea pinched the tip of her nose and hummed. "Hmm. Let's say it's one of Collin's brothers that your Grandmother is meeting. *If* it is," she looked at me with a frown, "and that's a big if, then we need to figure out which one. I can do some research, but from what I know off the top of my head, Carman had three children with three guys. They were all evil in their own way, but then again, so was she."

"My dear," Uncle interrupted, "you're mucking the story up. May I?" Chelsea squinted at Uncle while putting down the green book on a nearby bookshelf.

"You're lucky I'm a big fan of *The Bard*," she said as she crossed her arms.

"Much obliged," Uncle thanked. "Carman the Witch was the foulest and mightiest witch in Ireland. She ruled for centuries, using magical herbs and mosses to prolong her life. Unfortunately, not even her magic could stop death, and as Carman entered her later years, she decided that she wanted offspring before she died. And so the hag bathed in the waters of a Lough Gur to make her appear youthful. Afterwards, she seduced three of the most ruthless and foul men in existence. One was from Hell, another from The Lands of Change, and still a third from the Afterlife. Each child was engrained with gifts from their father and as they became older, they were taught the essence of magic from their mother. While Carman was put to an end by her enemies shortly after, it's said that her sons carried on her misdeeds in different countries, as they were banished by Saint Patrick."

"Cool story," said Ned as he picked in his ear with his pinky finger. "What does it mean?"

"It means," I shouted while grabbing at my temple hairs, "that we're wasting a lot of time. Listen, my wife and child are in the hands of a murderous tyrant. Eamon, Uncle," I growled while standing up, "I'm sorry I've wasted our time. These people aren't going to help us. Let's go."

"Whoa," Ned interjected. "Take it easy Agent Orange."

"Ned," I bit back, "who are you anyhow? Why do you think you're qualified to protect Chicago? I certainly know it's not because of your brains."

"Calm yourself young fairy," Eamon pleaded as he pulled on my jacket sleeve.

"I can fight my own battles grandpa," said Ned as he stepped forward. "Listen pal," added while looking in my eyes. "Long ago, I would have fried you like Colonel Sander's original recipe, but you're lucky. I'm trying to be a good guy now."

"Ha," I hooted while shaking my head. "Let me guess. I don't want to see you when you're angry, do I?"

"That's true," he said matter-of-factly, "but that's not where I'm going." Ned took a deep breath, pushing down an invisible force towards the floor with his open hands. "Center yourself Ned, "he mumbled. Ned looked up at me. "What I'm trying to say is that I get why you're upset. If Chelsea were ever taken from me again, I'd be an atomic bomb. But I've been through this before. Charging in without a plan is always bad news. Don't get me wrong, sometimes you need to break the *Angry-Glass* in case of emergency, but you reserve that for desperate times. You're not there yet."

"I'm not?" I objected. "Sure feels like it to me."

"You're not," Ned objected, "because I'm here. We'll take your case." "Damn it Ned," Chelsea jumped in, "This is not X-Files. Stop calling it a case."

Ned gave a half smile, "Not now Scully." Ned continued over Chelsea's growls. "Listen Beaker, here's the plan. Chelsea there is the best researcher in Chi-town. She's going to see if our hunch is legitimate. Give her a day. Meanwhile, I've been working on a second case for another client. I think it coincides with yours."

"Stop calling them cases," Chelsea barked. Uncle gave a grimy laugh.

Ned moved in towards me and put his hand on my shoulder. "Once my colleagues return from night class, we'll all get in the Ned-Mobile and search for a guy who knows everything about Chicago's underground. Have you ever heard of John Dillinger?"

I hadn't, so I looked to Eamon. Eamon pretended to shoot an invisible machine gun. "He was a famous American gangster. I enjoyed that movie of his with Johnny Depp, but there were a few too many testosterone heavy scenes. I think a good film maker—"

I cut off Eamon, trying to speak instead of yell. "And how is he going to help us find my wife?"

"Dillinger is M.I.A. right now," Ned objected. "But if I can find him, I guarantee he'll know who is dealing with a Fairy Queen. Then from

there, we go all X-Men on them and thwart their evil plans"

I dug deep down inside. I'd mucked things up enough but wasn't exactly sure that getting Ned and Chelsea to help was the answer. They were as obnoxious as when I'd first met them. *Well, at least Ned was.* What would Father do? I sat on the question for a second. He'd swallow his pride and take a chance. He'd commit. He'd risk it all to do the right thing.

"All right Ned," I extended my hand, "I'm putting my trust in you."

"I swear to you Gingerbread Man," Ned held up his hand, "we're going to save your wife and kid." We shook.

Uncle leered closer to the group. "Perhaps," he suggested, "we should write up a contract to be safe?"

Eamon's eyes widened. "Don't do it Ned." Uncle sneered.

Chelsea and Ned stared at each other. I shook my head to Uncle.

"No," I argued, "that won't be necessary."

"Yeah, I agree," Ned answered. "Especially with me."

"Oh happy day," Eamon rejoiced. "And why is that we should trust you again Ned?"

"Listen," Ned responded, leaning on Eamon's shoulder. Eamon winced in pain. "If you can't trust an angel, who can you trust?" And with that, we began planning our next move.

DEFINITELY NOT THE END

Epilogue

A candy blue scooter puttered beneath the streetlights of Broadway Avenue. Several potholes threatened to remove its wobbling sidecar at any moment. The driver, a curvy figure in a leather race suit, hid her face behind the tinted visor of a helmet. Clinging onto her from the back of the bike seat was a scruffy man with dark wind-blown hair, riding goggles, and an unlit cigarette dangling from his mouth. He wore blue jeans, sneakers, and a black Tom Waits t-shirt. A half smirk slithered up his face as his hands crept up from the driver's waste to her breasts.

Hunkered in the sidecar was a second passenger. His face was eerily similar to the scruffy man in the Tom Waits t-shirt, though his slicked hair, clean shave, and business suit set him apart. His mirrored sunglasses were unable to conceal a prominent scowl. He reached out and slapped the scruffy man's arms. The scruffy man stuck his tongue out before lowering his hands back down to the driver's waste.

"How long until we get there?" asked the scruffy man. The driver ignored him, focusing on the road. The businessman in the sidecar looked at a passing green street sign.

"Wait, slow down," commanded the businessman. The buzz of the scooter quieted. Before long the bike was at a crawl. "That was Lawrence Avenue, so it should be to the left. Ah look," his voice went an octane higher as he pointed to a green sign with glowing letters. "There it is."

The gleam of the dated sign bit into the night air. It read, *Green Mill Cocktail Lounge*. The jazz club shared its building with several other storefronts, including a Mexican restaurant, pub and coliseum like theatre. The scooter dragged close to the curb and parked in front. The scruffy man peeled off his goggles as his twin crawled out of the sidecar. They peaked as the driver bent over to remove her helmet.

She had lilac hair that endlessly poured out from her helmet like a magician's handkerchief. Her flowing locks and tightly woven temple braid cascaded down her back, stopping above her hips. She had large innocent eyes that fanned long lashes, while drinking in the streets. A red glow from an intersection's stoplight shined on her apricot skin kissed with soft freckles.

"He's not here," she said disappointedly while looking at the scruffy man. "Azazel, where is he damn it?"

Azazel dug in his jeans and pulled out a steel lighter. He lit the now bent cigarette in his mouth and stepped onto the sidewalk. "All in due time sweetheart," he said as he offered her a puff. The purple haired beauty snarled as she slapped the cigarette out of Azazel's hand before grabbing his manhood.

"Don't toy with me," she said with a squeeze. Azazel howled. "Armen," she called out, keeping her gorgeous eyes locked on Azazel, "what are we doing here?"

Armen the businessman, who was feeding quarters into a machine posted near the curb, pressed several beeping buttons before removing a ticket. He walked over to the scooter and placed the piece of paper on the windshield of the bike.

"What are you doing?" asked Azazel as if he'd been sucking helium.

"This isn't hell," Armen said flatly. "This is Chicago. We'll get towed if we don't pay the parking fee."

"I mean," Azazel cringed, "why aren't you answering the nice lady?"

Armen's eyes followed the woman's hand as they crushed any hopes for Azazel future children. "Sasha, play nice. We promised revenge, but you have to help us first." Sasha's eyes slid towards Armen. "First we need to meet up with our new business partners. They've asked us to join them for a drink."

"Why do we need business partners?" probed Sasha. "We find Nedonius, torture and kill him."

"Simple but effective," Azazel said with a gasp.

"Be-cause Sa-sha," Armen annunciated every hard letter, "As I told you when we were still in hell, Nedonius is merely an avenue to find our true objective. Gethin."

Sasha let go of Azazel and pushed him away. Azazel broke into a storm of coughs and short breaths.

Justin Alcala

"That's *your* objective," Sasha said while flinging her hair so that it effortlessly, yet perfectly fell down her shoulders. "There was no mention of this meeting before."

"Don't try backing out now," Armen insisted as he walked to the lounge entrance. "You can't get home without me. And your disguise will fade soon. So, unless you know how to open a portal to hell, this *is* your objective." Sasha clenched her fists. Her eyes danced back and forth between Azazel and Armen. "Now," Armen added while opening the club's door, "shall we?"

Sasha's soft frown stiffened into a hard smile. It was sweet but loaded. She strolled towards the entrance, her arms swaying in a frighteningly carefree manner. "Okay, Armen," she said sweetly as she crossed the threshold. "Have it your way."

Armen looked at Azazel, who was limping towards the club's door. He focused his thoughts and forced them into Azazel's head. *I don't trust her, Brother,"* he psychically projected. *This may have been a bad idea.*

"Yeah," Azazel said out loud, still pink in the face. "But she's got a really great ass." Armen shook his head and followed his brother inside.

It was a school night, and the Green Mill's patrons were the usuals with a smattering of late shift workers. The jazz club didn't have any live music tonight, instead settling for *Dusty Springfield's* soft voice covering *Spooky* over the speakers. Sasha made her way to the bar. Several sets of eyes followed her as a chubby bartender in overdone makeup greeted her near the tap. Sasha leaned over the bar top and whispered in the server's ear. It made the bartender smile. The bartender walked over to a special shelf and dug through dusty bottles. Sasha waited patiently while swaying her hips to the saxophone-tambourine duet. A pack of CTA workers at the table behind her paused mid-conversation to take in the scenery. Sasha smiled at them as she continued to move back and forth.

Armen dug his hands in his pocket and made his way to Sasha. He leaned on the bar as the bartender handed Sasha an amethyst cocktail. Armen shook his head as Sasha dug out a sword shaped toothpick from the drink and sucked on a cherry impaled over its tip.

"You do know," Armen sighed as he looked up at the ceiling, "that we're supposed to be incognito. There's a reason you're in disguise."

"Relax," Sasha assured, "I'm helping you find your contact." "You're what?" Armen asked as he scanned the room.

Sure enough, as he glanced at the club's patrons, he noticed that everyone in one way or another had been drawn to Sasha's entrance. Everyone except for a couple who ducked in a crescent moon booth near the center of the building. They huddled together over a flickering candle, motionless and mute. Armen examined them.

A Latina woman with dark tightly pulled back hair rested her painted fingernails on the mouth of a full pint of beer. She had a birthmark in the shape of Idaho covering one eye and a red business suit with boxy shoulders. Her counterpart was tall, even when sitting. They wore a full nun's habit, black with a white cotton cap secured by a wimple. Though what showed from the nun's lower face was androgynous, Armen narrowed his eyes and made out an Adam's Apple along the nun's neck.

Armen didn't believe in *thank yous,* and so he didn't give Sasha one. He waived to his brother as he approached the woman with Idaho on her face and the nun. Azazel, who'd been nursing his sore parts near the door, picked up on the cue and followed. Midway to the booth, he grabbed an unguarded drink from a table and continued along. Sasha took her drink down in one hard gulp. She took a deep and then followed the twins.

"Mind if we have a seat?" asked Armen as he drew near.

The pair didn't say a word. Instead they slid over in their pleather seats, making room. Armen let Azazel slide in first before sitting directly across from the strangers. He combed his fingers through his hair before looking up. The nun was wearing welder's goggles over his long bow nose. Meanwhile, the woman was watching the beer foam form an island on the surface of her drink. Sasha brought up the rear, slipping onto the end of the booth's seat and folding her hands in her lap. The candle's twinkle glimmered across her face so that her eyes sparkled.

Azazel sipped on his stolen drink with a clown's smile. "A nun huh? That reminds me of a joke," he barfed out. Armen closed his eyes and sighed.

No Azazel, Armen projected in his twin's head.

"What do you call a nun who walks in her sleep?" Azazel continued. No one said anything. "A roaming Catholic!" Azazel waited for a reaction.

Armen cut through the silence by clearing his throat. "So, rumor has it that you might be able to help us with our little problem. Any truth to that?"

The woman with the state of Idaho on her face folded her hands. "Yes," she said in a stern voice.

Armen stared between the nun and woman. "Feel free to tell me how," he presented. The pair didn't say anything. "Oh, whenever you're comfortable," he added dryly.

The nun turned his head to his partner and nodded. "Do you know what the Trilogy is?" the woman with the state of Idaho on her face asked.

"Like the Father, the Son and the Holy Ghost?" Azazel blurted before taking to his drink. "Or the original Star Wars movies?" "No," stated the woman with Idaho on her face.

Sasha raised her faultless brow. "Do you mean the three parts of existence?" she directed to the woman with Idaho on her face. There was a deadpan stare between the two.

"Very good," confirmed the woman with Idaho on her face as she folded her fingers together. The nun gave a languid turn of his head to Sasha and bowed his head. "The Trilogy is the three components that make up the Circle of Actuality," the woman with Idaho on her face continued. "It's simple. There's Life, Death, and the Afterlife. With them, reality continues. Without them, we cease to exist." "I'm with you so far," Armen said.

"Me, too," Azazel added, not to be outdone.

Shut it, Armen projected in Azazel's head. Azazel pretended to ignore him.

"What if I told you," the woman with Idaho on her face said, "that we have a flawless plan that will conquer all three, thus putting us in charge of the Circle of Actuality?"

Mystery drink spat out of Azazel's mouth. Sasha looked away, shaking her head ashamed. Armen put his palms on the table, pretending to still have credibility after his brother's blunder.

"I'd say that you're mad," Armen put bluntly. The nun grunted, a light smile tracing the curves of his mouth.

"What if I told you," the woman with Idaho on her face continued, "that we've already conquered the domain of *Life* and are inches from taking the other two? Would you think we were still mad then?" "I'd ask you to prove it," Armen asserted.

Without hesitation, the woman with Idaho on her face dug into a purse near her lap and removed a switchblade. While Sasha was unmoved, Armen flinched, and Azazel shielded his drink as the woman with Idaho on her face raised the knife in the air and stabbed hard. The switchblade plunged into the nun's chest. The nun's lips pressed together, and his face turned flush. The woman with Idaho on her face began carving down.

"Stop you fools," Armen forewarned. "Someone will see."

"You can rest assure that they won't," the woman with Idaho on her face insisted as she twisted the knife hard. "This booth is enchanted from mortal eyes." With a quick tug, she pulled the blade out. Along the nun's chest was a tear in the black polyester nun's outfit, but the skin had no wound. "My associate here shares his bloodline with an entire race that we have at our disposal. Imagine an army of immortals like my friend invading Earth? As I said, we've conquered the domain of Life." "Huh," is all Armen could get out.

"That's a great trick lady," Azazel challenged, "but that's all it is."

"Please," the woman with Idaho on her face insisted, handing Azazel the knife. "Inspect the weapon. Give it a try yourself if you must."

"What I mean is that we can do the same thing," Azazel bragged, stretching his hands behind his head. "Shoot us, stab us, throw us in the bottom of Lake Michigan. It don't matter. We're otherworldly."

"Yes, that's true," the woman with Idaho on her face replied. "But can you get every one of your kind together to take over Earth?" "Can you?" Sasha interjected.

"My employer," the woman with Idaho on her face said, "has taken great measures to organize some of the most powerful beings in existence to put us in charge of the Circle of Actuality. They're all on board."

Justin Alcala

"Who," Armen protested, "is *they*."

"I won't mention names until we have a deal," said the woman with Idaho on her face, "but I'll give a few details as to legitimize our operations. We have two out of the three sons of Carman."

"Who?" Azazel asked, his mouth gaping in confusion.

"The offspring of an ancient powerful witch," Sasha said casually.

"Precisely," the woman with Idaho on her face confirmed. "The third son, who was unwilling to cooperate, is no longer in the picture." Azazel swallowed a mouthful of his mystery drink with a heavy and nervous gulp. "In addition," the woman with Idaho on her face added, "son number two has infiltrated Death's domain and is currently working on the recipe for conquering it. Once he does, we'll have control of the lives and deaths of every person on Earth. Then, all we'll need is someone to help us with the Afterlife." "Go on," said Armen.

"Yes," Azazel piggybacked, leaning in while furrowing his brow. "Go on."

Stop that, Armen barked in Azazel's head. Azazel snickered, but didn't look away.

"All we need now," the woman with Idaho on her face replied, "is someone who can intercept the souls escaping Earth to the Afterlife. As you may know, Satan has laid the groundwork for a hell with his portal over Chicago."

"How did you know that?" Armen demanded.

"If we can reroute souls to this portal," the woman with Idaho on her face continued, "and hold all mortal spirits we slay to hell, we will have existence as a hostage. Then, we can give God our demands."

"And what are your demands?" Sasha questioned with her best poker face.

"Step down of course," the woman with Idaho on her face replied. "We'll create our own pantheon of gods and run Earth ourselves." Armen, Azazel and Sasha exchanged glances. "Might I add that anyone who was a major part of our plans will be rewarded generously." "I'm in," Azazel blurted.

Stop talking you asshole, Armen growled in Azazel's head. "And what, pray tell," Armen said aloud, "does this have to do with us finding Gethin?"

"Yes. Gethin," the woman with Idaho on her face said slowly. She crossed her legs and cracked her neck before speaking. "We understand that Gethin knows how to activate the portals. It's in our best interest to find him as well."

Armen puckered his lips and tilted his head. "And then?"

"If we help you recover Gethin for Satan," the woman with Idaho on her face said, "you may get a pat on the back, if that. Am I correct?"

"In our case," said Azazel, "we might be lucky if our lives are spared."

Azazel, Armen hollered in his brother's head. Azazel squinted.

"Sure," said the woman with Idaho on her head. "Now think if you not only bring Gethin home, but you also broker a deal that dethrones God and makes Satan one of the newest rulers of Earth? I'm sure he'll be in your debt."

"That's all well and good, but I have a counter offer," Armen volleyed. The woman with Idaho on her face took her beer to her face and swished it around, sniffing the surface. She placed it back down without sipping.

"Please," the woman with Idaho on her face presented. "Whenever you're comfortable."

"Screw Satan," Armen denounced. "Let's cut out the middleman. Instead, make my brother and I gods of the new pantheon."

The woman with Idaho on her face looked to the nun. The nun's lips curled upward.

"Deal," said the woman with Idaho on her face. "And what about your friend?" she asked while nudging her nose in Sasha's direction.

"I want revenge," Sasha hissed. "And the money Ned owes me."

"Sounds simple enough," the woman with Idaho on her face responded. "Then it looks like we've struck a bargain?"

The group went quiet for a moment. It was a standoff. "We have," Azazel answered before Armen could. The woman with Idaho on her face looked to Armen.

"My big mouthed brother is correct," said Armen while narrowing his eyes at Azazel. "We're in."

"Wonderful," said the woman with Idaho on her face. She dug down in a large purse resting on the seat beside her and pulled out a large manila envelope. "We've rented out a few rooms at the Peninsula. The best of course."

"Naturally," said Azazel as he slurped ice chunks out of his empty glass.

"Your keys are inside," said the woman with Idaho on her face as she pushed the envelope onto the other side of the table. "Along with everything you'll need to know."

"And what is it," asked Armen, "that you know about Gethin?"

"My employer is quite the talented scryer," said the woman with Idaho on her face nonchalantly. "He has a few leads as to where Gethin and his lover are hiding. It's all in the packet."

Armen dragged the packet into his lap. It was thick and heavy. "Fair enough, but I'm curious. Does your packet say anything about how?

Carmen's second son plans on conquering Death?"

The nun's lips parted wide, revealing a row of teeth lined like dominos. It formed into a smile that took up his entire lower face. Seeing this, the woman with Idaho over her eye gave a crooked grin of her own.

"The packet does not," said the woman with Idaho on her face. "But rest assured the plan is flawless." "Flawless?" Armen doubted.

"Oh yes." said the woman with Idaho on her face. "You see, Death has been planning on taking some time off. It's been centuries since his last vacation. We've just been waiting patiently for him to choose his substitute."

About the Author

Justin Alcala is a novelist and nerdologist. He's the author of the novels Consumed, The Devil in the Wide City, and Dim Fairytales. His short stories have been featured in magazines including the upcoming horror story, *It Dances Now* (Crimson Street Magazine) and *The Offering* (Rogue Planet Press). When he's not burning out his retinas in front of a computer, Justin is a passionate tabletop gamer. He's also a blogger, folklore enthusiast and time traveler. He is an avid quester of anything righteous, from fighting dragons to acquiring magical breakfast eggs from the impregnable grocery fortress.

Most of Justin's tales and characters take place in The Plenty Dreadful universe, a deranged supernatural version of the modern world. When writing, Justin enjoys immersing himself in the subject matter, from in-depth research to overseas travel. Much to the dismay of his family, he often locks himself away in his office-dungeon while playing themed videos and music over, and over, and over again. Justin currently resides with his dark queen, Mallory, their malevolent daughter, Lily, and their hellcat, Misery. Where his mind might be though is anyone's guess.

www.ingramcontent.com/pod-product-compliance
Lightning Source LLC
Chambersburg PA
CBHW021220260626
47172CB00002B/518